"You don't have to be strong for everyone. You don't even have to be strong for yourself all the time," John said. **"We're a crew together, we help each other. Support each other."**

"And what happens when we reach Cimarron Springs?" Moira asked.

"What do you mean?"

"What happens when I become dependent on you and then you're not there anymore?"

"Well, it'll be different, that's for sure. Town life is a quite a bit different from trail life."

"It's not only that." She'd promised herself she'd remain aloft from the girls. The more time they spent together, the more difficult keeping her promise became. "Once we're back in town, everyone will go their separate ways."

"You can write letters."

"That'll never happen. Out of sight is out of mind for people. Once this is over, we'll never even think of each other again."

"Do you really think that?"

"Don't you?" She avoided his dark gaze. Lately she worried she'd miss the cowboy most of all.

Books by Sherri Shackelford

Love Inspired Historical

Winning the Widow's Heart
The Marshal's Ready-Made Family
The Cattleman Meets His Match

SHERRI SHACKELFORD

A wife and mother of three, Sherri Shackelford says her hobbies include collecting mismatched socks, discovering new ways to avoid cleaning and standing in the middle of the room while thinking, "Why did I just come in here?" A reformed pessimist and recent hopeful romantic, Sherri has a passion for writing. Her books are fun and fast paced, with plenty of heart and soul. She enjoys hearing from readers at sherrimshackelford@yahoo.com, or visit her website at www.sherrishackelford.com.

The Cattleman
Meets His Match

SHERRI SHACKELFORD

HARLEQUIN® LOVE INSPIRED® HISTORICAL

Recycling programs
for this product may
not exist in your area.

LOVE INSPIRED BOOKS

ISBN-13: 978-0-373-28275-3

THE CATTLEMAN MEETS HIS MATCH

Copyright © 2014 by Sherri Shackelford

All rights reserved. Except for use in any review, the reproduction
or utilization of this work in whole or in part in any form by any
electronic, mechanical or other means, now known or hereinafter
invented, including xerography, photocopying and recording, or in
any information storage or retrieval system, is forbidden without
the written permission of the editorial office, Love Inspired Books,
233 Broadway, New York, NY 10279 U.S.A.

This is a work of fiction. Names, characters, places and incidents are
either the product of the author's imagination or are used fictitiously, and
any resemblance to actual persons, living or dead, business establishments,
events or locales is entirely coincidental.

This edition published by arrangement with Love Inspired Books.

® and TM are trademarks of Love Inspired Books, used under license.
Trademarks indicated with ® are registered in the United States Patent
and Trademark Office, the Canadian Intellectual Property Office and in
other countries.

www.Harlequin.com

Printed in U.S.A.

For which of you, intending to build a tower,
sitteth not down first, and counteth the cost,
whether he have sufficient to finish it?
—*Luke* 14:28

To Kristie Ryan, for knowing me better than anyone and liking me anyway.

To my mom, Bonnie, because I didn't acknowledge her in my last dedication. And she mentioned the oversight—a couple of times. Love you, Mom!

Chapter One

Fool's End, Indian Territory
September 1881

If John Elder hadn't been so furious with his mutinous crew of cattle hands, he might have noticed the woman dangling above his head sooner.

Except nothing had gone right since his arrival in the bustling cow town of Fool's End. Night had long since fallen by the time he'd discovered his four missing cowhands. Drunk. In a brothel. He'd fired them on the spot.

As John had circled behind the row of connected buildings, mud from a chilly autumn rain sucked at his boots and slowed his pace. Walking the alley at night wasn't the wisest choice, but he didn't have much time. He'd discovered the men's horses—*his horses*—at the livery earlier. He was taking back his property before his crew sobered up.

He kept the same rules as his father and his grandfather before him—no gambling, drinking or sporting women until the job was finished.

Moonlight glinted off broken bottles and the stench of sour mash whiskey burned his nostrils. Propped open with a dented brass spittoon, the saloon's rear door released a dense cloud of cigar smoke. John skirted the hazy shaft of light with a grunt. He'd wasted half the day. For nothing.

A scuffle sounded behind him and he pivoted with his fists raised. Only inky darkness met his searching gaze. John dropped his arms. A man couldn't be too careful in this corrupt town.

The space behind the buildings wasn't as much an alley as an afterthought of the hastily constructed cow town. Dreamers and schemers had built Fool's End from one hundred people to five hundred practically overnight. The pains of rapid expansion had ravaged the city's grid work. Hope and despair fought a never-ending battle in the red soil, leaving behind an odd carnage. Buffalo hunters, cattle hands and fortune seekers had sprouted opportunity and corruption in equal measures.

A raucous piano ditty spilled from the nearest open saloon door and John's head throbbed in time with the grating tune. If any one of his six older brothers could see him now, he'd never live it down. Halfway from Paris, Texas, to his final destination of Cimarron Springs, Kansas, and he was spitting distance from failure. Again.

Sure, there'd been times in the past when his optimism had outpaced his good sense. But not this time.

John snorted at the irony. He shouldn't have let his temper get the better of him. Firing the men left him with only a cantankerous chuck wagon cook named Pops who was older than dirt and just as talkative, and eight hundred head of longhorn cattle he couldn't drive to Cimarron Springs alone. A small herd by most standards, but too large for two men alone.

It was imperative he reach the Kansas border or forfeit his dreams of starting his own cattle ranch. Fearful of Texas fever, a disease spread by longhorns to other livestock, the state was steadily moving the quarantine line farther west. He'd gambled the line would hold. Farmers and ranchers were filling the state, and their vote was bound to sway the legislature. Which gave John two weeks to cross into Kansas before the vote to close the borders took place.

Time enough for finding a new crew. But not much time.

The faint scuffing grew louder. Pausing, he glanced left and right, then lifted his chin and caught the first blow on his upturned cheek.

"Out of my way," a feminine voice called down.

The heel of her sturdy boot knocked him sideways. Staggering upright, John clutched his battered shoulder. A slender form dangled from a knotted bed sheet above his head.

His jaw dropped.

The girl craned her neck toward the ground, her face an alabaster oval against the darkness. A blur of pale petticoats covered by a dark skirt met his astonished gaze.

Her gaze snapped upward and her red hair shimmered in the moonlight like a wild, exotic halo. "Let out more rope. I'm still six feet from the ground," she hissed.

Her voice was mature. John craned his neck. The harder he looked, the more he realized this was a woman, not a girl. Her body twisted and his heart lurched.

He thrust out his arms and her flailing leg grazed his right hand. "Ouch."

Scooting aside, he reached with his left hand and she smacked that one too. "Take it easy!"

Retreating a safe distance, he assessed the situation. Either this was a dangerous prank or the woman was involved in something nefarious. *He didn't care.* He wasn't getting involved. No way. No how. Right now he had more problems than time.

"We haven't any more slack," a thin voice replied from the upper window. "That's all the sheets."

A dark-haired girl, no more than twelve years old, thrust her head into the shaft of light from the second-story window.

A blonde of the same age appeared at her right and stretched over the sill, her brilliant pale hair curtaining her face. "Maybe we should pull Moira up. This was a bad idea."

John rolled his bruised shoulder. "That's an understatement."

Their casual assessment of the situation confirmed his first instinct. This *was* some sort of childish prank. And the woman suspended above him was old enough to know better.

The girls chattered away, their heads bent together, complaining about the lack of decent bed sheets while completely ignoring both him and the dangling woman.

John shook his head. Of all the irrational sights he'd seen in this cow town over the past two days, this topped the list.

While yet another young lady joined the overlapping discussion, the woman above his head struggled for purchase on the rough clapboard walls. Her feet slipped up and down against the chipped paint as though she was running in midair.

John heaved a sigh. He had a singular way of sizing up a situation and predicting the outcome. Even his brothers grudgingly admired his innate ability.

He reached up and patted the woman's foot. "Let go and I'll catch you."

"Everything is quite under control," she replied primly.

"Lady, I don't know what kind of stunt you're pulling, but I see four girls in that window, and not a one of them realizes your arms are shaking and you're about to break an ankle. Or worse."

"This is none of your concern," she announced, her voice strained. "The plan is sound. I simply miscalculated the sheet length. I think it was the knots. Yes. That's it. The knots took up more slack than I expected."

"Either way, you're in a pickle."

The females in the window giggled.

"Be quiet up there," the woman ordered, a sense of urgency lacing her words. "If they catch us—"

She lost her grip and John dove forward. He grasped her around the waist and staggered, his feet held immobile in the mire. Keeping a tight hold on the squirming woman, he teetered backward and sat down. Hard. Icy water oozed through his canvas pants and chilled his backside.

The woman scrambled in his loose hold and her elbow cracked his ribs. John flinched. So much for playing the gentleman. She didn't appear at all grateful he'd taken the brunt of the fall—and soaked himself in the process. As she squirmed, her toe dug into his bent ankle.

He yelped and circled her waist with one arm. "Take it easy."

The woman whipped around, battling against his protective grasp. Her eyes widened. "Let go of me this instant or I'll scream. *Please.*"

Sensing her terror, John obliged. With her arms braced against his chest, his sudden release propelled her backward. She sprang from his embrace and landed flat on her back, sprawled in the oily puddle.

A chorus of titters sounded from above.

The blonde girl swung her leg over the sill in a flurry of white petticoats. "I'm going next."

John scrambled upright, slipping and sliding in the muck. "No. Wait."

While his gaze swung between the prone woman and

the knotted rope, the second girl crawled out the window. She shimmied down the length until her feet swayed just out of reach.

John caught sight of a third girl straddling the ledge and his heartbeat quickened.

"Stop!" he ordered ineffectively.

The blonde dropped into his outstretched arms and he caught her slight weight against his chest.

As he set her on her feet, she tipped back her head and struck his jaw. John saw stars. He was going to be black-and-blue by the time this was over.

"Thanks." The girl sketched a wave and scurried aside. "I'm Sarah. I'll help Moira while you catch the others."

A pair of short boots descended into view, and John rubbed his sore chin.

He slanted a glance at the woman he'd rescued first. "Lady, please tell me someone up there has some sense."

"Don't count on it." She avoided his searching gaze and stretched her right hand toward Sarah. "And you may call me Miss O'Mara."

John hid a grin as Sarah awkwardly assisted *Miss O'Mara* onto unsteady legs. For a wild moment the two clung to each other like a couple of drunken sailors on a pitched deck. The moment the woman regained her footing, they sprang apart.

Miss O'Mara shook the mud from her back, then tugged her dark skirts lower. They were too short, showing a good bit of her worn boots and sliver of ankle. Together with her innocent face, it was easy to mistake her for an adolescent at first glance. On closer inspection, it was obvious she was in her late teens or early twenties.

"You'd better stand firm," the woman ordered, swiping the back of her hand over her mud-splattered face. "That's Darcy and she's the heaviest."

Distracted by the enticing smudge on Miss O'Mara's

cheek, John didn't see the third escapee release her hold. His inattention cost him. A sharp elbow hammered his head and a boot scraped along his cheek. Blindly lifting his arms, he groaned beneath the girl's weight and managed to set her aside before another, much smaller, pair of boots descended into his vision.

A curly-haired child hugged the knotted sheets, her ankles crossed.

John reached out. "Let go. I've got you."

The youngster shook her head, her dark curls almost black against the moonlight.

Miss O'Mara stomped forward, her fisted hands planted on her slim hips. "Hazel, we haven't much time. Let go this instant."

The girl frantically shook her head. John rolled his eyes. Logic and orders weren't going to convince Hazel of safety.

Stepping back a pace, he caught the little girl's frightened gaze. "Almost there, Hazel. I'll catch you."

The frightened child sniffled. "Promise?"

"Promise."

John swiped his index finger in an *x* across his chest. The childish display of fealty captured Hazel's attention.

After a moment's hesitation, she tumbled free and he easily caught her slight form. The instant he set her safely on the ground, she giggled. "That was fun. Can I do it again?"

"No!" Moira and John shouted in unison.

The last girl descended the rope and waved him aside. "Don't need your help, mister."

Unlike the previous girls, she released her legs and worked her hands down the length until she was only a few feet above the ground. John crossed his arms and stepped back as she easily dropped the abbreviated distance.

Straightening from her crouch, the girl dusted her

hands together. "Thanks for helping with Hazel. I'm Antonella. But everyone calls me Tony."

The girl pumped his hand once and stomped off.

John searched the empty window. A red velvet curtain flapped gently in the breeze. "Is that all of you?"

Miss O'Mara gathered her charges. "That's four. Darcy, Sarah, Tony and Hazel."

Scratching his head, John studied the motley gathering. "What are your ages, girls?"

Darcy boldly elbowed forward. "I'm fifteen next month."

"Thirteen," Sarah replied.

"Twelve and a half," Tony chimed in.

The littlest girl, Hazel, glanced up. "I'm ten."

John caught Miss O'Mara's gaze and lifted an eyebrow. She pursed her lips. "My age is none of your concern."

Over twenty, he surmised immediately. Over twenty was about the age when a single woman ceased advertising her age. Little did she know. He'd give anything to be in his early twenties once more, when he'd still felt invincible.

Hazel tugged on his pant leg. "Are we safe now?"

The hairs on the back of John's neck stirred. Each building had a distinctive look from the front, but facing the alley, they blended together into one indistinguishable row. He counted the doors from the corner and his chest tightened.

"Hey," a slurred voice called from the open window. "Get back here."

The girls shrieked and spun away.

Summoned by the commotion, a bearded man stuck his head out the saloon door and spit into the mud. "What's goin' on?"

A clamor sounded from the far end of the alley.

Miss O'Mara ushered the girls deeper into the darkness without even a backward glance. John split his attention between the growing cacophony of voices and the escapees.

Indecision kept his feet immobile. The girls hadn't asked for his help. He could leave without an ounce of guilt. Considering they were obviously up to mischief, he'd already done more than most men would have.

"Hey, mister." The drunken man smacked his palms against the sill. "Stop them girls. They stole my money."

Of course. John mentally slapped his forehead. He should have known. He'd nearly been taken by a similar bunch in Buffalo Gap. Hastily stuffing his hands into his pockets, he breathed a sigh of relief. His fingers closed around the cool metal of his money clip. At least they'd rewarded his assistance by leaving him with the contents of his pockets intact.

Desperate children forced into desperate measures.

But what punishment did they deserve? John clenched his jaw. It wasn't for him to decide.

A flash of yellow caught his attention. Half immersed in the mire, a rag doll lay forgotten. He pinched its yellow yarn braid between two fingers and held it aloft in the moonlight.

Above him, the shouting man worked his way down the rope. The sheets held firm and a grudging admiration for Miss O'Mara filtered through John's annoyance. She tied knots like a trail boss.

"Well, mister," the man demanded, his breath a fog of alcohol fumes. "Where'd them little thieves go?"

What now? If his brothers were here, they'd shove John aside like a pesky obstacle. They'd take charge and assume he didn't have anything to offer. Like a herd of stampeding cattle, they'd wrestle all of the decisions—right or wrong—out of his hands. When his brothers were around, he never had to bother with taking responsibility.

John squinted into the darkened alley.

The inebriated man shoved him. "You deaf? I asked you a question."

John clenched his jaw. The sooner he put Miss O'Mara out of his thoughts, the sooner he could continue his journey. Heaven knew he hadn't even proved himself worthy of caring for a herd of cattle. A motley group of pickpocket orphans and a beautiful woman with fiery red hair were problems well beyond his limited resources.

Miss O'Mara and her charges were knee-deep in calamity and sinking fast. Moira required someone with the time, focus and connections to unravel her difficulties. Someone with the resources to steer her charges toward a respectable path. A hero. She'd gotten him instead. Maybe she'd have better luck down the road.

The drunken man took off in the direction Miss O'Mara and her charges had escaped. John snatched the man's arm and pointed the opposite way. "I'd check down there."

Moira heard the cowboy's betrayal and her heart lodged in her throat. She tugged on Hazel's arm and quickened her pace. With each pounding step her lungs burned and her vision blurred. What did speed matter when they were running blind? They'd be caught again for certain.

A hand tugged on her sleeve and tears of defeat sprang in her eyes. She yanked away. She wasn't giving up. Not yet. The fingers kept a brutal grip.

"Miss O'Mara," the cowboy spoke near her ear. "Let me carry Hazel. We'll make better time."

"No. You betrayed us."

Moira stumbled and the cowboy steadied her with a hand cupping her elbow.

"I didn't. Look around if you don't believe me."

At his calm reassurance, she slowed and glanced behind them. The alley was empty. No one pursued them.

While her exhausted brain grappled with the realization, the cowboy knelt. With childish faith, Hazel clambered onto his back. The little girl wrapped her legs around his waist and buried her face in his neck, effectively forcing Moira to follow. They ran another two blocks, her hand clasped in his solid grasp, before he halted.

The cowboy jerked his head toward a closed door. "In there."

Frightened and weak with hunger, Moira instinctively reacted to the innate authority in his tone. She tore open the door and guided the others inside.

The pungent aroma of animals assailed her senses. Her eyes gradually adjusted to the dim light and she noted Dutch doors lining either side of a cavernous center corridor. The cowboy had led them into the livery.

Horses stamped and snorted at the disturbance. The girls whispered together and Moira quickly shushed them. Their footsteps sounded like a stampede and their raspy, labored breathing chafed her taut nerves. She crept across the hay-strewn floor behind the cowboy, her index finger pressed against her lips for silence.

The cowboy gently lowered Hazel and propped an empty wooden saddle rack before the exit. Walking the aisle, he peered into each stall in turn, pausing before the third. He swung his arm in an arc, motioning them forward.

While the girls scurried inside the empty stall and huddled in the far corner, Moira bent and clutched the stitch in her side. In an effort to calm her rapid breathing, she dragged a deep breath into her tight lungs. The stall wasn't much of a hiding place, but at least they weren't out in the open anymore.

The cowboy returned a moment later with an enormous hay bale and tossed it onto the ground. He came back twice more in quick succession. Understanding his intent,

Moira yanked on the bale wire, grimacing as it dug into her palms. Each bundle must weigh a hundred pounds, yet the cowboy showed no signs of strain.

He returned again with a stack of burlap feed sacks draped over his arm. "Cover yourselves with these and don't make a sound. If he searches the building, don't move, don't talk, don't even breathe."

"Wait," Moira called in a soft voice. "Why are you doing this?"

He hesitated and she sensed a war raging within him.

During their escape from the brothel, she'd noted his lean, muscular build and caught a glimpse of his square jaw. In the milky light of the stable, she made out the dark hair curling from beneath his hat and the raspy-looking whiskers darkening his jaw. He had an aristocratic face with deep-set eyes, a patrician nose, and lips that qualified as works of art.

He was, without a doubt, the most handsome man she'd ever laid eyes on. If only she had her sketch pad. He'd make a superb subject. Like a hero in a *penny awful* rescuing the damsel in distress, he had the sort of face that inspired romantic dreams.

Moira mentally shook the wayward thoughts from her head. Dreaming of a happily ever after was like building a house on a shifting sandbar. She'd seen too many people caught by the enticing trap, starting with her own mother. Over the years she'd guarded her heart well, and she wasn't about to weaken her resolve for a chiseled jaw.

A muscle worked in John's cheek. "Keep your head down. I may have to cause a distraction. Whatever you hear, stay out of sight unless I tell you to run."

His voice was rough and uneven and the look in his eyes did nothing to reassure her. Moira had effectively trapped them in a corner.

She swallowed around the lump in her throat. She'd entrusted their lives to a stranger, albeit a handsome stranger. "What's your name?"

"John. John Elder."

Oddly comforted by the harmless name, she nodded. At least he hadn't replied with something like Deadly Dan or Killer Miller.

Searching for an innocuous rejoinder, she blurted, "I'm Moira."

He lifted the corner of his mouth in a half grin that sent her heart tripping. "Nice to meet you, *Miss* O'Mara."

Her cheeks burned beneath his reference to her earlier insistence on his use of her formal name. She might have been a touch rude, but there weren't exactly rules of etiquette for a brothel escape.

She cleared her throat. "You never answered my question. Why are you helping us?"

He stared into the distance. "Because it suits me for now."

"What happens when it doesn't suit you?"

"I guess we'll find out when that happens."

Her stomach dipped. For a moment she'd thought he was different. That he was actually helping them out of the kindness of his heart, out of Christian charity. Turned out he was like everyone else. He obviously had an ulterior motive. Maybe they were an amusement, maybe he was bored, maybe he'd flipped an imaginary coin and their predicament had come up tails. His motivation didn't really matter.

Whatever the reason, he'd cease helping once they ceased serving whatever purpose he'd assigned them. People only cared when they needed something.

With a last appeal for silence, John stepped into the corridor and slid the door closed behind him.

Finally grasping the gravity of the situation, the girls remained unnaturally quiet. Moira flopped into position.

Blood thumped rhythmically in her ears. She rubbed her damp hands against her thighs, then tugged her too-short skirts over her ankles. The dress was a castoff from the foster family she and her brother, Tommy, had lived with before Tommy ran away. Mrs. Gifford had recycled the expensive lace at the hem for her own purpose and left Moira with her ankles showing.

The cowboy probably thought… Moira fisted her hands. Why waste her energy worrying about what Mr. Elder thought of her clothing when they were still in peril? She'd heard Fool's End was dangerous, but every one-horse town she'd passed through had been dangerous.

She should have heeded the warnings this time.

Normally she'd never go out after dark, but she'd waited two hours for Mr. Grey, only to be told that he didn't know anything about her brother Tommy.

Tears pricked behind her eyes. Another dead end, another disappointment. After four years, she was certain this time she'd finally catch up with him. A maid from the Gifford house who remembered her fondly had discovered the charred bits of a telegram in the fireplace of Mr. Gifford's study. Piecing together what few words she could read, Moira had made out the names "Mr. Grey" and "Fool's End." The sender's name had been clear as well: Mr. Thomas O'Mara.

A name and a location weren't much to go on, but it was all she had. Tommy must have forgiven her for the trouble she'd caused if he'd contacted her. She'd stolen Mr. Gifford's watch, and in her cowardice, she'd let her brother take the blame. He'd run away that same evening and she hadn't seen him since. There was no doubt in her mind the telegram had been for her. She doubted Mr. Gifford burned his own correspondence.

She'd considered posting a letter to Mr. Grey but then quickly dismissed the thought. Letters were impersonal and mail service unreliable. Instead, she'd set off almost immediately. Yet her arrival today had been too late. Tommy was nowhere to be found.

Mr. Grey had denied knowing anything about Tommy or the telegram, but something in his denial didn't sit right with her. On her way back to the hotel, not two blocks from her destination, some drunken fool had nabbed and locked her in that second-story room with four other girls.

Children.

She hadn't seen a one of them before that moment. Yet they'd formed an instant bond against a mutual enemy. Moira shuddered at the implication. She might be naive, but she knew a brothel when she saw one. If they were discovered, there'd be no escaping unscathed the next time.

Keeping her expression neutral, she passed each of the girls a sack. The less they picked up on her terror, the better. Being afraid didn't change anything anyway. It only made the waiting more excruciating.

Together they huddled silently in the deepest recess of the darkened stall, barely concealed behind the stack of hay bales. Hazel crawled onto her lap and Moira started. The frightened little girl had clung to her since her kidnapping. Had that been only a few hours ago? It seemed like an eternity. Hazel burrowed deeper. Unused to such open displays of affection, Moira awkwardly patted the child's back.

Tony took Hazel's cue and clustered on Moira's left side, Sarah on the other.

Darcy sat a distance apart, wrapping her arms around her bent legs and resting her chin on her knees. "This is stupid," she announced in a harsh whisper. "You should have waited until I thought of a better plan."

Moira pursed her lips. At fifteen, Darcy was the oldest of the girls—and the most sullen. The only words she'd uttered in the past two hours had been complaints or criticisms.

Darcy snarled another gripe beneath her breath.

Since they were all terrified and half-crazy with hunger, Moira bit back an angry retort. "We're here now and we'll have to make the best of it."

Darcy scowled but kept blessedly quiet.

For the next several minutes they waited in tense silence. As time ticked away, the air beneath the burlap sacks grew thick and hot. Sarah shifted and coughed. Footsteps sounded from the corridor and Moira hugged Hazel tighter.

"Can I help you, sir?" an unfamiliar voice spoke.

"I'm looking for a gang of thieves."

Moira immediately recognized the second man as her kidnapper. His raspy voice was etched on her soul.

"Five of them," the kidnapper continued. "A bunch of girls. One of them picked the wrong pocket this time. Stole Mr. Grey's gold watch."

"Why didn't he nab the little thief right then?" the first man spoke, his voice tinted with an accent that might have been Norwegian or Swedish.

"Because he didn't notice his watch was missing right off."

"Then how does he know who done took his watch?" The Norwegian sounded dazed.

"Because we got three reports of the same kind of thing." The kidnapper's voice raised an octave. "An orphan girl comes in begging for change or food, and the next thing people know, their watches and money go missing."

"Well, I'm plum confused by the whole thing. Is it one girl you're after or five?" The Norwegian sputtered. "Did all five of them pick Mr. Grey's pocket? What'd she look like? Wait a second. What did *they* look like?"

"Well, let me see here. Mr. Grey seen a girl with red

hair just before—" The kidnapper huffed. "Never mind. It ain't your business. Have you seen them or not?"

Moira's blood simmered. *Why that low-down, no good, drunken...*

Another thought jerked her upright. *A watch.* Four years ago a pocket watch had set off a chain of events that had changed her life forever. It was somehow fitting a time-piece had been at the center of this evening's troubles.

Would John Elder protect them if he thought they were thieves? Who else would help them if that vile man spread lies to cover his foul deeds?

"I ain't seen nobody," the Norwegian replied.

A scuff sounded, as though someone had opened a door.

"Now you'll have to leave," the Norwegian ordered. "That's a paying customer and you're not."

"Hey," the kidnapper snapped. "Ain't you the fellow from the alley?"

"Yep, that's me."

Moira started. John Elder was the "customer" who had come through the door. He must have escaped through the back and circled around front.

"The name is John," her rescuer answered, sounding bored and a touch annoyed. "And I already told you where to find the girls."

"Except I didn't find them, did I?" The kidnapper cackled. "Maybe you're saving them for yourself."

Moira's heart hammered so loudly and she feared they'd hear its drumbeat thumping through the slats in the stall door. She'd misjudged her reluctant rescuer once already tonight. Or had she?

"Look yourself," John replied, his annoyance apparent. "They're your problem, not mine."

The horse in the neighboring stall whinnied and bumped against the wall. Moira stuffed her fist against her mouth. Itchy hay poked through her clothing and she resisted the urge to scratch. A moment later the footsteps paused before their stall. The door scraped open. She held her breath and prayed.

An eternity passed before the door slid closed once more. Moira heaved a sigh of relief, then offered a silent prayer and a couple of promises concerning future atonement for good measure. Another few seconds and they'd be safe.

Sarah stifled a sneeze. The sound was faint and muffled, but it might as well have been a shotgun blast. The door scraped open once more.

"Hey," John called. "What did you just say to me?"

"Back off," the kidnapper snapped. "I didn't say nothing."

"I think you did."

Boots scuffed in the dirt and Moira winced at the sound of flesh hitting flesh. She whipped the bag from her head and sat erect, swiping her tangled and static hair from her eyes. From her vantage point, she watched as the cowboy spun the kidnapper around. John was obviously diverting the man's attention.

Setting Hazel aside, Moira leaped to her feet. She'd best spring into action before John Elder decided that rescuing a bunch of orphans no longer *suited* him. She snatched a pitchfork from the corner and charged, jabbing her kidnapper in the backside. Yelping, the man sprang upright, his hands clutching his back pockets.

The kidnapper whipped around with a snarl and her stomach clenched. Roaring in fury, he hurtled across the distance. Moira quickly sidestepped, then stumbled.

A glint of light reflected from a star on the kidnapper's lapel. Moira blanched.

Had her past finally caught up with her?

Chapter Two

Fear spiraled through Moira's stomach and shot to her knees, weakening her stance. She'd gone and done it now.

The cowboy was easily two paces behind the kidnapper. Feinting right, she swept the handle around and batted her attacker's legs. The man staggered and his arms windmilled. His left hand smashed against a hanging lantern. Glass shattered and sparks showered over the hay-strewn floor. Like a wild animal set loose, brilliant orange flames spread across the dry kindling. Astonished by the sudden destructive force, she staggered back a step.

In light of this new threat, Moira tossed aside the pitchfork and stomped on the rapidly spreading danger.

"Get back!" John hollered.

The kidnapper's face twisted into a contorted mask of rage.

He pointed at Moira through the growing wall of smoke separating them. "It's fitting you'll die in fire, you little hoyden."

With another shouted curse he pivoted toward the exit. Midstride, his right foot caught the curved tongs of Moira's discarded pitchfork. The handle sprang upright and ricocheted off his forehead. The kidnapper's expression morphed into a comical mask of astonishment before going slack. He stumbled back a step, jerked and collapsed. A soft cloud of hay dust billowed around his motionless body.

Moira stifled a shocked peal of laughter.

The cowboy gaped. "You are a menace."

Her sudden burst of hysterics dissipated as quickly as it had appeared. Flames licked across the floor, belching black smoke in their wake.

Moira waved her hand before her face. "Stop bickering and help me put out the fire. I'll get, I'll..."

She stumbled over her words and her feet as she dashed back into the stall.

She lifted the sacks, revealing four flushed faces. "Fire! Everybody up. Help me beat out the flames."

The girls scrambled from their hiding place and dutifully rushed past, each of them snatching a sack in turn.

Using his coat, the cowboy had already doused two of the smaller fires. "Wet those sacks first!" he shouted.

Without needing instruction, Moira and Tony doused their sacks and joined him. Hazel tugged a heavy bucket of water from a nearby stall. Sarah met her halfway and together they hoisted it into the air and dumped the contents onto a pile of glowing embers. The water hissed and steamed over the scorched ground. Darcy flitted around the edges, snapping her damp sack and adding more fuel than help.

The horses whinnied and kicked at their stalls. Tony opened the enclosure nearest the fire, then covered the horse's eyes with a scrap of cloth.

A panicked shout announced the arrival of yet another man. He was old and grizzled, his back bent into a *c* and his arms no more than long, thin twigs jutting from his spare body. Judging by his muttered grumblings, Moira figured he was the Norwegian she'd heard earlier—the livery owner.

He joined their efforts, stomping on the dying embers in a frantic jig.

Between the seven of them, they had the flames under control in short order. As the smoke dissipated, Moira kicked at the dusty floor, scraping away the top layer of ashes. The room went silent for a tense few minutes as they searched for hidden embers.

Once they determined the fire was well and truly extinguished, their forced camaraderie ceased.

The irate old man flailed his puny arms. "What in the world? You nearly burned down my barn. I ought to call the sheriff." He stilled and scratched the prickly gray patchwork of whiskers covering his chin. "Except Sunday is poker night. Maybe the new deputy is around. Haven't met that feller yet."

John dug into his pocket and pulled out a wad of bills. "This is feed and board for my horses." He added several more bills to the fat pile. "This is for the damage."

The wizened man accepted the money with one gnarled hand and rubbed the shiny bald spot on the back of his head with the other. "Suit yourself."

Moira wasn't certain the exact amount the cowboy had paid, but it was enough to send the livery owner away whistling a merry tune.

Gathering her scattered nerves, she folded her burlap sack into a neat square. Her eyes watered and her lungs burned from the grit she'd inhaled.

John paced back and forth before her, his face red. After three passes, he halted and opened his mouth. No words came. Moira tilted her head.

"Are you crying?" he demanded at last.

"No. It's from the smoke."

"Good." The cowboy worked his hands in the air before her as though he was strangling some invisible apparition. "I gave you very specific instructions. What did you think you were doing?"

"Assisting you, of course. And you might have thanked me."

"I had everything under control. You, on the other hand, nearly burned down the barn. And us in the process."

"That's a bit of an exaggeration, don't you think?"

"If you had followed my *very* simple instructions, none of this would have happened. Give me some credit. I happen to know what I'm doing." The cowboy thrust his hands into his flap pockets and his expression turned incredulous. He lifted his jacket hem, revealing where his fingers poked through a charred hole. "You've ruined my best coat."

Moira stifled a grin at this outrage. He didn't appear in the mood to appreciate the absurdity of the situation. "You were the one who used it to beat out an open flame."

"I didn't want to *die*."

Moira's eyes widened. She'd never heard anyone enunciate that clearly with their teeth still clenched together.

And why on earth was he angry? She planted her hands on her hips. Judging by the mottled red creeping up his neck, he wasn't merely angry, he was furious. His searing glare would have melted a less hearty soul.

Moira straightened her spine. "You were hardly at risk of death."

"You don't know that. Your crazy stunt set this place ablaze."

"I beg to differ. My *crazy stunt* saved our hides. Not to mention I used this perfectly useful burlap sack and not my *best jacket*. You might have done the same."

"You could have trusted me. I haven't proven myself unworthy *yet*. You might have at least waited."

She cast him an annoyed glance. "What are you blathering on about now?"

"You are the most—"

"I haven't time to debate with you." Moira rubbed her eyes in tight circles with the heels of her hands. She instinctively knew their plight no longer suited John Elder's interest. He'd be gone in a flash for certain.

Moira smoothed her hair and adjusted her collar. For a moment she'd thought the kidnapper was sporting a silver star. The glimpse she'd seen must have been a trick of the light. Besides, St. Louis was a lifetime ago. If the Giffords hadn't looked for her after she'd left four years ago, they certainly weren't looking for her now.

Dismissing the cowboy, her reluctant rescuer, she faced the girls.

Her stomach roiled. *What now?*

She hadn't thought much past their immediate escape. Judging by their dazed expressions, neither had the others. Darcy had abandoned her indifferent sneer and Hazel's lower lip trembled. Tears brimmed in Hazel's wide brown eyes. Even Tony had lost her swagger.

"It's safe now," Moira announced and flapped her hands dismissively. "I believe our kidnapper will be indisposed for an extended period of time. You may all go home."

"I'm sorry I sneezed and gave away our hiding place." Sarah wrapped her arms around her slight body. "I can't go home."

"Of course you can," Moira urged. "Mr. Elder will walk you safely home, won't he?"

She lifted a meaningful eyebrow in his direction. Let him wiggle out of that one.

Sarah shook her head. "We haven't any place to go."

Moira caught sight of the safety pin, the number long-since faded, attached to the girl's pinafore. Nausea rose in the back of her throat. "You were on the orphan train?"

"I have an uncle." Tony cut in, her expression defiant. "He gave me a letter and everything. He said he'd come for me."

Darcy braced her legs apart and planted her hands on her hips. "Then where is he now? You can claim whatever you want, but you're no better off than the rest of us."

"The woman on the train took my letter." Tony lifted her chin. "She stole it while I was asleep. So I ran away. Folks don't want children. They want workers. We're free labor, plain and simple." Tony jabbed her thumb at her chest. "I'm worth more. I was doing fine on my own until I was caught." Her face blanched. "Until that man. Until tonight when we were…you know. I got sloppy, but it won't happen again."

"Don't worry." Moira patted her hand. "It's all over now."

The hollow platitudes stuck in the back of her throat. They were children. Alone. They'd never be safe. Her head spun with the implications of the impossible situation. Life for discarded children was ruthless and devoid of fairy-tale endings. At best they'd be neglected, at worst they'd be exploited. Driven into impossible choices.

The air sizzled with emotion and the girls crowded around her, speaking over each other, demanding her attention. She backed away from the onslaught and they crowded her against the stall door.

"I have a sister," Sarah announced with a nod. "She's older than me. She said she'd take care of me, but her husband didn't want me. They put me on the train anyway."

Moira swayed on her feet. The past came rushing back. She pictured her mother standing on the platform, her ever-present handkerchief pressed against her mouth as she coughed. Moira had held her brother's hand clasped in her own.

"I'll take care of you, Tommy."

She knew better than anyone did the perils of survival. She'd been tested herself. Tested, and failed.

"Miss O'Mara," John Elder's voice interrupted her memories. "What's going on here? Aren't you together?" He circled his arms and touched his fingertips together. "Aren't you a gang of little pickpockets?"

Her body stiffened in shock. "You'd believe a drunken kidnapper over a bunch of innocent children?"

She hadn't stolen anything in the four years since she'd left the Giffords'. Not even when she'd been near starving. He didn't know anything about her. He was making a blind guess, that's all.

A horse stuck its head from the stall door and nuzzled her ear. Moira absently scratched its muzzle.

Hazel tugged on her skirts. "What's a pickpocket?"

Guilt skittered across the cowboy's face. "I'm sorry," he spoke. "I'm not certain what's going on here. It's not that I don't have sympathy for your predicament, but I've got a herd of cattle." He motioned over his shoulder. "I can't leave them for much longer."

Moira ran her hand through her sweat-dampened hair. What was she going to do? She couldn't hide them all. "I'm renting a room at the hotel. It's the size of a water closet."

She was tired and hungry and bruised. The entire trip had been a waste of time and she was penniless. Stuck in this corrupt town unless she could find a respectable job. As much as she wanted to help, there wasn't much she could do. She could barely take care of herself.

The four girls cowered before her like penned animals who'd escaped their enclosure. They were wide-eyed and curious, frightened and hesitant. And lost. That was the thing about growing up in a caged environment, a person could always feel around the edges and find where the ground dropped off. Even being homeless was as much of a cage as anything else. When the basic needs of food and shelter consumed every waking moment, survival was a jail all its own. No time for dreams or hopes or plans of the future. The moment they'd found one another, the rules had altered. They were a team.

Moira vividly recalled her first year alone after leaving the Giffords—the fear, the uncertainty, the uneasy exhilaration of holding her own fate in her hands, unencumbered by the push and pull of others. A similar feeling was blossoming in the girls.

Having stretched beyond their solitary struggles, they showed the first trembling signs of hope. They'd discovered kindred spirits, and they were holding on tight, lashing together their brittle fellowship like a flimsy raft against troubled waters. Moira hadn't the heart to tell them they were better off alone. Sooner or later, everyone wound up alone.

Sarah hung her head. "No one picked me at the last stop," she spoke quietly. "I couldn't stand it anymore. It's like at recess when nobody picks you for a team. When the chaperones came for us at the hotel, I hid. I did what I had to do. I know I've done things wrong and I've prayed for forgiveness. After you helped us, I felt like my prayers were answered."

The room swayed and Moira's vision clouded. She knew the feeling of being passed around like a secondhand coat nobody wanted anymore. Though she feared the answer, she asked anyway, "Where have you been staying since then?"

"We all just sort of found each other and stuck together. There's an abandoned building near the edge of town." Sarah ducked her head. "That's where that man found us."

Darcy's expression remained defiant. "You all knew it couldn't last. You knew they'd catch us sooner or later.

I was on my own for four years without getting caught." She noticed Moira's curious glance and her countenance faltered. "I was on my own for four years," she repeated.

Though Moira didn't want to hear any more, didn't want to know any more, she'd set her questions into motion and there was no going back.

She knelt before Hazel, the youngest. The little girl wore a faded blue calico dress, the grayed rickrack trim ripped and drooping below her hem. "Do you have a home?" Moira asked gently.

The littlest girl shook her head. "A family picked me, but I was bad and they took me back." Hazel sniffled. "I left the chicken coop open by accident and the dog got in. All the chickens died. Mrs. Vicky didn't want me any more after that. Then tonight I only wanted an apple… I would have worked for it. I would have."

Sarah rested a hand on her shoulder. "You don't have to say any more."

Moira gritted her teeth. They were just children and they'd been discarded like so much rubbish. She was sick of it. Sick of people thinking children didn't have thoughts or feelings. "How did you wind up in Indian Territory?"

"Because this is the end of the line," Darcy said.

There wasn't much between the Indian Territories and California. Moira supposed No Man's Land was as good a place as any to dump the unwanted children.

Ten years ago she'd been a rider on the orphan train. She and her brother, Tommy. She hadn't kept the promise she'd made to her mother. She hadn't taken care of Tommy.

Sometimes she felt as though she was being punished for her failure. She hadn't felt peace since that fateful day when she'd slipped Mr. Gifford's watch into her pocket. She'd known it was wrong. She'd known it was stealing. She couldn't help herself. She often wondered what kind of person she'd become. She wondered if there was any going back. If she'd slipped once, how much temptation did she need before she slipped again?

Mr. Gifford had blamed Tommy for the missing watch and she'd been too terrified to admit the truth. Mr. Gifford had promised retribution, but Tommy hadn't waited around for the punishment. By the following morning, he was gone. And he hadn't even said goodbye.

Once she found him, once she confessed what she'd done, this pain would end. She'd waited another year at the Giffords' even though staying had been near torture. She'd waited hoping Tommy would return so she could explain the truth and finally take the blame. Except he'd never come back.

After she'd left the Giffords', she'd remained in St. Louis, hoping against hope she'd glimpse him. It was crazy, but it was all she had. She'd kept in touch with anyone she thought she could trust, but most of the servants were too scared for their jobs to return the favor. Then she'd received the charred bits of the telegram from the maid with Tommy's name. Her prayers had finally been answered.

The girls stared at her, their faces expectant. Moira knew better than anyone what fate awaited the orphan girls, but there was nothing she could do. The system was too far broken for one lone person to fix. She glanced at the cowboy. He looked away. Mr. Elder wanted a crew, not a bunch of waifs.

Moira shook her head in denial. They didn't know her. They didn't know how she'd failed Tommy. How she'd fail them if they put their faith in her. They'd turn on her for certain if they knew how she'd betrayed her own brother.

Shame robbed the breath from her lungs. "I'm sorry, but I can't help you. Any of you."

* * *

The defeat in Moira's voice knocked John down a peg. For the past twenty minutes he'd been patting himself on the back, lauding his clever handling of the situation. While the rescue hadn't been particularly elegant, he'd accomplished his goal. He'd saved the girls from the dubious justice of a drunken vigilante and disabled the man in the process. What had his false pride netted him? He hadn't solved anything. He'd mined a heap of new problems instead.

One night, John told himself. He'd lost a whole day already, what was one more?

His brothers' words rang in his ears. *You'll never make it without our help.*

All his life they'd treated him as though he wasn't capable. Every bit of clothing he'd had growing up had been a hand-me-down. If he had an idea, they had a thousand reasons why it wouldn't work. If he wanted to try something new at the ranch, he had to ask permission like a child. At thirty-three years old, they still treated him as though he was a kid. Truth be told, he was the odd man out in his family. He'd always been more relaxed, more easygoing than the rest of his siblings.

His brothers attacked their responsibilities, no matter how minor, with all-consuming zeal and they expected him to do the same. John figured there were times when letting go was just as difficult as fighting. Yet he'd never once seen a monument erected in honor of a calculated retreat.

He and his brother Robert had fought the worst. Their last argument had divided the family, and John had realized it was time to set out on his own. If he stayed, one of them was bound to say something they couldn't take back. The only way they were going to get along was if one of them backed down. He'd demanded his share of the herd and declared his intention to take over the homestead his older brother Jack had abandoned when he'd married.

You'll never make it without our help.

Robert's words rang in his ears. John pulled out his watch and checked the time. Eleven o'clock. Too late for anything but sleeping. He'd quit tomorrow, when things were less complicated.

Hazel tugged on his pant leg. "I'm tired. Can we come home with you?"

"I don't have a home. Not here anyway." Weary resignation softened his voice. When had his simple goal become this complicated? "I'm driving a herd of cattle to Cimarron Springs, Kansas."

He felt another tug on his pant leg.

Hazel's liquid brown eyes stared up at him. "Do you have any food at your camp?"

John's throat tightened. His whole life he'd been surrounded by the suffocating pressure of family. But he'd never gone to bed hungry.

And he'd never been homeless. "When was the last time any of you ate?"

Hazel shrugged.

John studied each of the girls in turn, their personalities already forming in his mind. Sarah kept her face downcast, as though asking for help was an imposition. Tony met his questioning gaze straight on, challenging. Darcy remained hesitant, uncertain, caught between rebellion and desperation.

Moira's eyes haunted him most of all. A curious shade of pale blue-green, the color of the tinted glass of a mason jar, translucent and ethereal. *Hopeless.* The foreign emotion resonated in his heart. You couldn't mourn for something you'd never had. What had Moira hoped for, and lost? She hadn't hoped for someone like him, that much was certain. She'd made her disdain of him apparent. Yet the desolate look in her eyes was hauntingly familiar. He'd seen that look once before.

Years ago, Robert had lost his wife during a bank robbery gone sour. He'd never forget the agony his brother had suffered. The pain of loss his niece and nephew had worn from that moment on. The death of their mother had bent them like saplings in the wind. They'd survived the tragedy, but they were irrevocably changed.

Robert had changed, too. He'd been married and widowed young. A man who'd grown old before his time beneath the weight of tragedy. Four years separated the brothers in age, though it might as well have been forty. He couldn't bridge the chasm between them—because knowing why Robert had changed and getting along with him were different things. After their last fight over how to run the family ranch, John had known he could no longer stay without tearing the rest of the family apart.

He rubbed his forehead. He had enough food back at camp to feed four hungry crewmen. Certainly enough for a few scrawny females.

He was well and truly trapped by his own conscience.

One night, he repeated. What was the harm in sheltering the girls for one night? Yet the past two months had taken its toll on his endurance. Even the most basic problems had multiplied, popping up like wild mushrooms after a spring rain.

Impatient with his indecision, Hazel took his hand. "Why are you taking your cattle for a walk?"

"It's not a walk," John patiently explained. "It's called a drive. I'm driving them to Cimarron Springs."

"How come?"

"Because I was tired of trying to prove myself," John grumbled beneath his breath.

Hazel's innocent questions struck too close to the heart of the matter. He didn't have any strength left to pretend he didn't care. Feigned complacency took energy, and he was plum out of flippant answers. Everyone in a family had a role, and John's role had been determined before he'd toddled off the porch and cut his chin. A scar he still bore. A preconceived legacy he couldn't shake.

He was the one who dove in headfirst without heeding the dangers. He was the most impulsive of his family, the most easygoing, too, as far as he could tell. Which meant his brothers rarely took his ideas seriously. When he'd declared his intent to purchase his brother Jack's plot of land in Cimarron Springs and drive his share of the herd north before Kansas closed its borders against longhorns, Robert had scoffed.

You'll lose your shirt.

John hadn't lost yet.

He *did* have an idea how to stop the girls' incessant questions. "You can stay with me tonight." A body couldn't talk while eating. "I'm coming back to town tomorrow. We'll find help during the day. There's nothing else we can do this late."

The relief on their faces disgraced him. "Can any of you ride?"

Tony and Darcy nodded.

Moira shrugged. "Some."

He'd earlier judged Miss O'Mara's age as early twenties. Old enough for courting and pretty enough for dozens of marriage proposals. John pictured the girls back home with their giggles and coy smiles. Moira could easily pass for one of those girls. She had a sweet face, pale and round, with a natural dusting of pink on her cheeks. Her lips were full and rose colored, perfect for kissing. But despite the natural innocence nature had bestowed on her face, her eyes held a jarring, world-weary cynicism.

John plucked the hat he'd lost during the fight from the ground and dusted the brim. He slanted a glance at the prone man who lay where Moira's discarded pitchfork had rendered him senseless. Their pursuer would come to soon enough, and he'd be spitting mad.

They didn't have much time. "I'll take you back to my camp. We'll figure out the rest in the morning."

Moira moved protectively before the girls. "Is there anyone at camp besides you?"

"Yes," John answered truthfully.

She pursed her full lips and he glanced away from the distraction.

Moira tsked. "Then the answer is no. I'll take care of the girls myself."

The return of her elusive temper buoyed his spirits. That was more like it. "I've got a cook. His name is Pops and I'm pretty sure he's as old as dirt. And ornery. But he makes good grub." John laughed drily. "Too bad you weren't a bunch of boys. I'd hire you on as my new crew and save myself another trip into town."

His joke fell on deaf ears. A myriad of emotions flitted across Moira's expressive face. Doubt, hope, fear. She wanted to trust him, she didn't have much other choice, but he sensed her lack of faith. Not for the first time he wondered about Miss O'Mara's background. What was her story? She was at once an innocent girl and a jaded woman, and he couldn't help but wonder what forces had shaped her.

"I've got five horses I need delivered back to camp," John continued. "You'd be helping me out."

Hazel appeared crestfallen. "If I can't ride, does that mean I can't go?"

His heart heavy, John knelt before the little girl. "Of course you can go. You can ride with me."

He marveled at their expressive personalities. Darcy was petulant and defiant—he'd keep an eye on that one. Sarah was meek, with a thread of steel behind her shy demeanor. Tony pressed her independence, but she wasn't as brave as she appeared. Nothing prevented Tony from leaving. She'd stayed instead. And Hazel. What kind of heartless person discarded a little girl because of a simple mistake?

John faced Moira, the unspoken leader. Her eyes drooped at the corners and he realized she'd reached the end of her rope.

He knew that feeling well enough. "Trust me."

Her eyes sparked with emotion. "For tonight," she replied, her voice a telling mixture of exhaustion and determination. "Just for tonight."

The kidnapper stirred and groaned. John crossed the distance and looped his arms beneath the prone man's shoulders. Heels dragging tracks through the dirt floor, he dragged the dead weight into an empty stall. A glint of silver on the man's coat caught his attention. John flipped the lapel aside and groaned. The silver star knocked the wind from his lungs. The words stamped into the metal flickered in the lamplight: Deputy Sheriff.

John staggered back a few feet and braced his hands on the slatted walls. *Hang it all.* He'd gone and decked a lawman. A burst of anger flared in his chest. None of this nonsense would have happened if the fool deputy had declared himself a lawman right out. The drunken man had never once identified himself. Pacing the narrow enclosure, John considered his options. He didn't know what any of this meant, but he knew well enough this situation had gone from bad to worse.

His stomach grumbled. Time enough tomorrow for facing the consequences. As hungry as he was, the girls must be ravenous. Sorting out the details when they were all exhausted and near starved would only make matters worse.

He briefly considered waking the deputy before he caught another whiff of the alcohol. Moira and her charges were too vulnerable for a man who was bound to wake up mean. Keeping his gaze averted, John slid shut the stall door and dropped the T-bar into place.

He motioned toward Moira. "Let's get this show on the road."

With no other choice but to move forward, John gathered his five horses and had them saddled and ready in short order. Growing wearier by the moment, the girls groggily followed his orders, stifling yawns behind patched-elbow sleeves. Their eyes blinked slower and slower.

While the horses stamped and snorted, he quickly emptied his men's saddlebags into a burlap sack. When that task was completed, he cinched a rope around the top and placed the belongings with the livery owner for safekeeping.

The elderly man jerked upright from his half doze and accepted the parcel. "Your men ain't gonna be too happy when they come back and find their mounts gone."

John braced his knuckles against the doorframe. "They can keep their gear and the pay they earned this far. The horses are mine. They're well aware of that."

"You don't have to convince me." The livery owner kicked back in his chair and closed his eyes.

John set his jaw. He'd been second-guessed his whole life by his own family, he wasn't paying a bunch of two-bit cowhands for the privilege.

As the girls clustered in the moonlit corral, John took stock of their attire. Each of the younger girls wore warm coats buttoned to their throats. Not Moira. She wore only her thin cotton dress with its too-short hem—a dress more suited for a sultry summer evening than a crisp fall night. How had she wound up crawling out the window of a brothel? Why had the deputy stashed the girls in such an unlikely place? Snippets of girls' conversation rattled around his brain.

I was doing fine on my own until I was caught...

I got sloppy...

I only wanted an apple...

He pinched the bridge of his nose. He was too weary for the answer. Too cowardly to face what his questions might uncover. Tomorrow would come soon enough. He'd get his answers then. None of them appeared injured, at least not physically, which meant any questions he had could wait. A good night's sleep would make the reckoning that much easier.

Moira blinked at his lengthy silence.

John tilted his head and considered Miss O'Mara. The more time he spent with her, the more he realized she wasn't like the girls back at home at all. She didn't fill the silence with chatter. She hadn't asked for anything. Not food or help or even money. Certainly money would solve their most pressing problems. The fact remained, she hadn't asked and he wouldn't offer. He'd accepted responsibility only for their safety, at least for this evening. A guarantee he planned on keeping.

A light mist gathered on Moira's eyelashes, sparkling like tears in the moonlight. A delicate shiver fluttered down her arms. He realized she'd been holding herself rigidly, hiding her discomfort.

Feeling like a first-rate heel for letting her suffer in the chill night air, John shrugged out of his jacket and tossed it to her. "Take this."

She caught the material against her chest with a shake of her head. "I mustn't," she protested, but he couldn't help but note how she clutched the material, her knuckles whitening. "Thank you."

"I've got a slicker in my saddlebags." Her obvious gratitude roughened his voice. "That'll be good enough."

She should have been chastising him, not thanking him. His mother had taught him better. No matter the surroundings or the circumstances, he'd been raised a gentleman.

Moira glanced up shyly, staring at him through the delicate fringe of her eyelashes. She fingered the charred hole in his pocket and a mischievous grin lit her face. "Are you certain you trust me with your best coat?"

Heartened by her teasing, he replied, "Just don't set it on fire. Again."

For a moment her guard slipped. She smiled at him, a wide grin that plumped her cheeks and lit her eyes. His heart sputtered, an irregular beat as though it was searching for a new rhythm. Miss O'Mara was beautiful, though not from the perfection of her features. Her lips were too full, her nose too pert for classic beauty—yet her smile was captivating and her eyes tipped and exotic. Her brilliant red hair shimmered in the moonlight, a ruckus of curls tumbling over her shoulders, torn free from its moorings by the night's activities. She was perfect in her imperfection, and his addled brain grappled with his unexpected fascination.

Worrying that he'd give himself away at any moment, John tore his gaze away and cleared his throat. "We should, uh, the night's not getting any younger and neither am I."

Her expression faltered at his abrupt dismissal. As she turned he reached out his arm, then let it drop. It was better she didn't see him as her rescuer. A misty haze of desolation surrounded her, unsettling his judgment. She'd seen more of the world than was meant for one so young. More of the darkness.

John shook his thoughts back to the task at hand.

Having studied the girls while they saddled the horses, he had a fair idea of their experience. All of his mounts were trained and relatively well mannered. He'd broken them himself. He'd always kept his own horses on the ranch, all of them raised from foals and trained by his own hand. A gentle touch resulted in the best mounts, a theory mocked by many of the ranch hands. He ignored their jeers because his results spoke for themselves. His horses were sought out from Illinois to Nevada. Through his brother Jack's contacts, he'd even provided trained mounts for the Texas Rangers.

As with all animals, each of them had a personality, and he matched the girls accordingly.

"Mount up," he ordered, watching them from the corner of his eye.

Tony, the most experienced of the group, effectively scurried into the saddle. John swung up behind Hazel and found the other three standing uncertainly beside their horses.

"Mount up," he ordered again.

Sarah shifted and spread her hands. "Um. I don't think I can."

John paused and assessed the problem. The stirrup hit at her shoulder. Between the height of the saddle and her confining skirts, she was stuck. Why hadn't he noticed before? *Because I don't usually ride out of a livery at midnight with a bunch of girls, that's why,* he reminded himself. Men, he understood. He'd been raised on a ranch full of men. Women, not so much.

"I'll help." John swung off his mount. He touched Hazel's leg and met her questioning brown eyes. "Wait here and don't wiggle too much."

The little girl patted the horse's neck. "What's her name?"

"*His* name is Bullhead."

"How come?"

"Because he's bullheaded."

"I don't like that," Hazel scowled. "I'll call him Prince

instead. I like that better." She leaned forward and one of the horse's ears swiveled in her direction. "You like that better, too, don't you?"

The horse nickered, as though in approval. Hazel grinned triumphantly. "See? He likes his new name much better, don't you, Prince?"

Another nicker. John rolled his eyes. "Whatever strikes your fancy."

Not like the name was going to stick. She could call the horse Pretty Britches for all he cared. By tomorrow evening, he'd have Bullhead back.

A half smile at Hazel's antics plastered on his face, he gave Darcy and Sarah a leg up, then paused before Moira. She'd reluctantly donned his coat, and the sleeves hung well below her fingertips. Her scent teased his senses and he searched for the elusive source. It was floral, and familiar, inspiring a sense of peace and well-being. He pictured a summer's day, white moths fluttering above a field of bluebells, a gentle breeze whispering through the grass.

Peonies. That's what had struck a chord. She smelled like peonies.

He lifted her hand and turned back the cuff, then repeated his action on the other side.

Keeping her eyes narrowed, she remained stubbornly quiet during his ministrations. John recalled what he'd stuffed in his pocket earlier. He reached out and Moira started. He stilled immediately, then moved more slowly, approaching her as he might a frightened animal—gradually, gently. She was as skittish as a newborn calf. Cautiously reaching into the pocket of his coat, he lifted his hand and revealed the rag doll he'd found earlier.

Moira's face lit up. "That's Hazel's doll! Where did you find it?"

"In the mud beneath the window."

She took the doll from him, cradling the soft material in her cupped hands. She glanced in the direction of Hazel and Bullhead—newly christened as Prince. The little girl murmured softly, petting its neck. Fascinated with the horse, she certainly wasn't missing her lost doll.

Moira thoughtfully stroked the braided yarn, absently fingering the hand-sewn stitches. Her fingers moved reverently, lovingly, as though the fabric was silk instead of muslin.

Her rapt interest gave him pause. "Did you have a doll like that growing up?"

He didn't know what had inspired his question, this wasn't exactly the time or place for casual conversation.

She shook her head, her face melancholy. "No. I never had anything as fine as this."

John choked off a laugh, certain she was fooling around. When her expression remained somber, he cleared his throat. "You should keep it safe. Until we're back at camp."

"She needs a bit of washing, that's all. A little scrubbing and she'll be good as new."

"Of course." He floundered. "She'll be as bright as a brass button."

Lost in a world he didn't understand, Moira carefully wrapped the doll in a faded red handkerchief and gingerly replaced the bundle in the pocket of his jacket. For a moment the ground tilted on its axis and the world turned topsy-turvy. With Moira, the feelings sputtering in his chest were foreign, tossing him out of his element. This wide-eyed sprite carried a mixed bag of reactions. One minute she was chastising him, the next moment she was teary-eyed over a battered rag doll.

John shook his head. He'd never understand women. Not if he lived to be one hundred and ten years old.

"You ready?" he asked.

She nodded, then swiveled her head left and right, uncertain. She'd said she was a rider. She'd lied. Near as he could tell, she wasn't sure which side to mount on—a basic skill of horsemanship. In deference to her novice ability, he grasped her around the waist and easily lifted her, surprised by her diminutive weight.

She was slight and delicate, vulnerable and threatening all at the same time. As she sheepishly attempted to cover her ankles, he averted his gaze. The self-conscious action sparked a burst of sorrow in his chest. Someone as proud and brave as Moira deserved a wardrobe full of new dresses that dusted the ground, like a well-heeled lady.

Quelling his wayward emotions, he turned away. To his enormous relief, the livery owner scuffled into the corral, splintering the tense moment.

The older man gestured toward the stables. "What am I supposed to do with that fellow in the stall?"

"Let him out when he wakes up," John called over his shoulder. "You don't know anything."

"True enough," the man replied. "True enough."

Moira adjusted her feet in the stirrups and stared down at John. She must have discovered the starch in her spine while his back had been turned. She sat up straighter, her face a stern mask of disapproval. "You better not double-cross us, mister."

The obvious rebuke in her voice triggered a long-forgotten memory. Years ago at a family wedding he'd joked with Ruth Ann, his on-again, off-again sweetheart, about getting married. She'd looked him straight in the eye, her disappointment in him painfully clear. *"You're too easygoing. I need someone who can take care of me."*

Ruth Ann had married his best friend instead. They had five kids and a pecan farm not far from the Elder ranch.

John had set out to prove himself, and so far he'd come up short. He couldn't even take care of a herd of cows, let alone this vulnerable woman with her sorrow-ful, wounded eyes.

"I won't double-cross you," he replied evenly.

Moira's fears weren't unwarranted, just misdirected. He wasn't a hero. There was no one riding to the rescue and the sooner he separated from this bunch the better. Before they found out they'd placed their fragile hopes on the wrong man.

There was something else going on here, and he wasn't the man to sort it out.

Chapter Three

A short time later Moira swung off her horse and pain lanced up her legs. She winced, hobbling a short distance. She'd ridden a handful of times before and understood the rudimentary skills, but she wasn't nearly as confident as she'd let on.

She'd thought she'd fooled John Elder. The sympathy in his perceptive eyes had exposed her mistake. He'd known she was a fraud, and he'd been too polite to voice his observation. She'd paid the price for her bravado. With each step, her untried muscles screamed in protest. She unwittingly sank deeper into John Elder's coat and inhaled its comforting scent.

Over the years she'd come to associate two smells with men—cloying, headache-inducing cologne and the pungent scent of exertion. John's coat smelled different, a combination of animal, man and smoldering wood. The unfamiliar mixture was strange and soothing. Despite the cool night, warmth spread through her limbs.

Shadows dotted the horizon, silhouetted against the moonlight. Restless cattle lowed at their arrival and Moira shivered. The glow of a fire marked the center of the camp. A wagon and three oatmeal-colored canvas tents were pitched in an arc around the cheery flames. The orderly sight was reassuring.

When she'd turned eighteen, she'd left the Giffords with little more than the clothes on her back. The gentleman who'd delivered their milk took pity on her and talked his brother-in-law into giving her a job. The brother-in-law owned a hotel and she cooked and cleaned for her room and board. She'd even kept in touch with the delivery boy from the grocer, and he'd promised to tell her if Tommy returned to the Giffords.

She'd never have considered it possible, but she'd traveled the West in style up until now. Moving from train depot to train depot, staying among people, clinging to the last vestiges of civilization, keeping her adventures urbane. Everything beyond the trampled town streets was wild and untapped.

While she drank in her new surroundings, John gathered the girls into a tight circle and spoke, "These cattle aren't easily spooked, but they're not used to your voices or your scents. They don't know you're a bunch of harmless girls. No loud noises or sudden moves. Stay within fifteen feet of the fire at all times. Once an animal that size stampedes, there's no stopping."

Hazel fiddled with the drooping rickrack on her hem. "Can we pet them?"

"Not now," the cowboy replied without a hint of impatience. "Maybe in the morning. It's for your own good. I'm keeping you safe."

Safe. Moira hugged her arms around her chest. They weren't safe. They'd simply turned down the flame. That didn't mean they were any better off than they were before. Well, except the odds were better and the doors weren't locked. They could run if they chose.

John whistled softly and a blur of white and brown padded into view. Moira took an involuntary step backward.

A large gold-and-white collie appeared. The dog took its place at John's heel and tilted its head. The cowboy absently patted the animal's ears.

The four girls immediately rushed forward.

"He's so cute!"

"What kind of dog is he?"

"Can he sleep with us tonight?"

John held up his hands. "Easy there. This is a working dog. He's not real friendly."

Moira craned her neck for a better view. The "working" dog had rolled onto its back. Its pink tongue lolled out the side of its snout while four paws gently sawed the air.

Darcy snickered. "He looks pretty friendly to me."

Though the dog appeared harmless, Moira kept her distance. She'd been bitten once and the experience had left her wary. Dogs were unpredictable and temperamental. Best not to get too close.

Hazel rubbed her hand along the puff of fur of the dog's belly. "What's her name?"

"*His* name is Dog."

"He's far too handsome for such a plain name," Sarah declared, rubbing one furry ear between her thumb and forefinger. "I think we should call him Champion."

"Or Spot," Hazel added.

Darcy shook her head. "That's stupid. Why would we call him Spot? He doesn't have a single spot on him."

The cowboy pressed two fingers against his temple. "He doesn't need a name. He's already got a name."

"Dog is a silly name," Hazel grumbled. "Just like Bullhead is a silly name. You're not very good at naming pets."

John smothered a grin with one hand. "I've been accused of a lot of shortcomings, but I have to say that's a new one."

"Then we'll give him a better name." Hazel backed away several paces. "Come here, Champion."

The dog trotted over.

Though the cowboy's face remained impassive, Moira noted the rise and fall of his chest as he heaved an exasperated breath.

She grudgingly admired John's even temper. Weak with hunger, her mood swung between rage and despair at a moment's notice. Right now she'd give anything for a soft bed and a slice of pie. *Apple pie.* A thick cut of crispy crust. She pictured cinnamon-flecked filling oozing between the tines of her fork. Her mouth watered and she swayed on her feet.

"What's all this?" another voice called.

Moira snapped to attention. A squat man emerged from the farthest tent. As round as he was tall, his bowed legs were exactly half of his size. A shock of gray hair topped his perfectly round head and his plump face was smooth and cleanly shaven. He adjusted his belt and crossed his arms over his chest.

The cowboy tossed a log onto the fire, sending a shower of sparks drifting skyward. "I've brought you some mouths to feed."

"What happened to the fellows?"

"Gone."

The abrupt answer piqued Moira's curiosity.

"Good riddance, I say," the older man replied. "Not a decent one in the lot."

John grunted and motioned between the squat man and the girls. "This is Pops. Pops, this is Darcy, Tony, Sarah, and little Hazel. They'll be staying with us tonight. And they could all use some grub."

John motioned Moira forward. "And this is Miss O'Mara, she's in charge of the girls."

"Well, not exactly, I wouldn't say—" Moira stuttered over her scattered explanation.

She was the outsider.

No one ever put her in charge of anything, let alone *anyone*. Her vagabond life from orphan to foundling had shaped her into an expert at dealing with rejection. She spent her time hovering on the fringes, unnoticed. She came and went before anyone had a chance to know her.

Folks didn't trust loners. Which at times she found annoying, especially considering the people who'd betrayed her trust most egregiously were the ones she'd known best of all.

Pops extended his hand. "Pleased to meet you, Miss."

Moira offered a quick shake and a weak smile.

"You look fit to eat your shoe leather," the old man continued. "Let me fetch something that'll stick to your ribs."

"I'll help," Sarah offered quickly.

Moira blinked. As the most shy of the bunch, she hadn't expected Sarah to step forward.

The next twenty minutes passed in a blur. Moira and the girls ate quickly, devouring the simple stew with gusto. Their chattering gradually quieted and their shoulders drooped. Pops and John rustled up a stack of blankets and Moira arranged them inside the tent nearest the warming fire. Once all four girls had pulled the covers over their shoulders, she sat back on her heels.

The dog wove his way through the tent, sniffing each girl in turn before returning outside and lying before the closed tent flaps and resting its snout on outstretched paws.

With her hunger sated for the first time in days, Moira transformed from bone-weary exhaustion into a bundle of nerves. Not tired, but not quite awake either. She was anxious and uncertain. The evening had been a chaotic ride fraught with danger. There'd been a time when she would have lit a precious candle and read until her restlessness passed, but she hadn't either a book or a candle.

Emerging from the tent, she gingerly stepped over

Champion before arching her back. John crouched before the fire, arranging the logs with the whittled point of a stick.

Moira glanced around. "Where's Pops?"

"Asleep." John relaxed against his cinched bedroll and stretched out his legs, crossing his ankles and lacing his hands behind his head. His hat sat low on his forehead, shadowing his eyes as the firelight danced over the planes of his face. "I've never seen Pops that agreeable. It's worth having you girls around to enjoy his rare good temper."

Moira scoffed. "You're pulling my leg." The grandfatherly man was as gentle as a spring lamb.

"Don't let him fool you. He's meaner than a sack full of rattlesnakes."

She shrugged out of John's coat and approached the cowboy. "Thanks for letting me borrow this."

"Keep it."

Too tired for arguing, Moira put it back on. Stretching her arms through the sleeves once more, she inhaled his reassuring scent. She sat cross-legged before the cheery blaze, her hands folded in her lap. Cocooned by darkness, she was content with the silence between them, comforted by the lowing cattle and the crackling fire. Gradually the tension in her sore muscles eased.

The flames danced in the breeze, orange and yellow with an occasional flash of blue at the base. A fire not contained by brick and mortar was foreign. More beautiful and compelling.

John glanced across the distance, shadows flickering across his face. "The girls okay?"

Moira nodded.

"Did anything happen back there?" He tipped back his hat, revealing his clear and sympathetic eyes. "Anything more?"

Moira knew what he was asking, and she answered as

best she could. "I don't think so. We were all taken this evening and locked in together."

A sigh of relief lowered his shoulders. "Thank God."

He visibly relaxed, and she realized he'd been carrying the tension since he'd counted the windows. He hadn't known she was watching, but she'd observed his studied concentration, seen his face change when he'd recognized the brothel.

"Amen to that," she replied quietly.

The question had cost him, that much was clear, and Moira admired his courage. It was easier ignoring the evil in life, easier looking away than facing wicked truths. Most folks would rather skirt a puddle than fix the drain.

She replayed the events of the night in her head. What did she know about John Elder—other than he smelled like an autumn breeze and looked like he should be advertising frock coats on a sketched fashion plate. Not that looks and scent counted for much. She knew he was driving his cattle north because *he was trying to prove himself.* He didn't appear the sort of man who'd let someone else hold him back.

Unable to curtail her curiosity, she braced her hands against her bent knees. "Where is the rest of your crew?"

"They went bad on me. Or maybe I went bad on them. It's hard telling sometimes."

"Surely you can't drive the cattle alone?" Moira frowned. She didn't know much about cattle drives, but she didn't figure he could accomplish the task single-handedly. "What will you do now?"

"Go back into town. Start over." He shook his head in disgust. "I'll figure it out. I always do." John cracked a slender branch over his bent knee. "I guess I'll find a short crew. It's seventy-five miles to Fort Preble, and double that to Cimarron Springs. That's ten days with good weather. Only ten more days." He grunted.

"Where'd you start from?"

"Paris."

Moira bit off a laugh. "Paris? What's wrong with American cows?"

"Paris, Texas." A half grin slid across his face. "My family owns a cattle ranch there."

Her cheeks heated. She was obviously too exhausted for witty banter. "Are you driving the cattle to Cimarron Springs to sell?"

"Nope." The cowboy paused for a long moment and Moira let the silence hang between them. Finally he replied, "Starting over," he spoke so quietly she almost didn't hear him. "It's a small herd, but it'll grow. Times are changing. The big cattle drives are drying up. In ten years' time, you will hardly see one."

Moira knew a lot about starting over. A man with roots and family shouldn't feel the need. "What about your kin?"

He stared at her as though she'd grown a second head. "It's a long story."

Moira nodded her understanding. "They treated you unkindly."

"Not, uh, not really. Not mean exactly."

"It must be really dreadful. I didn't mean to pry."

"It wasn't really bad, we just, uh, we just didn't get along, that's all. There's no deep dark secret." The cowboy plucked another handful of kindling from a pile at his elbow and tossed sticks onto the crackling flames. "What about you? Where's your family?"

Thrown off guard by the abrupt turn of the tables, Moira considered her answer carefully. She didn't share details about her past with strangers. She didn't want pity or judgment.

Yet something in the night air and the cowboy's affable, forthright eyes compelled her confidence. "I'm searching for my brother. We were separated as teenagers. Last month I received a telegram. Well, part of one. It's a long story. Anyway, I gathered what information I could and came straight out, hoping he hadn't gone far. Except I got here too late. He's already gone." She recalled the cowboy's previous comment. "What did you mean earlier? If we were boys, you'd take us on as your crew?"

A chuckle drifted across the campfire. "It was a story my father used to tell. Back in forty-nine you couldn't find any able-bodied men for work. They'd all been lured away by the gold rush. A local rancher, desperate for hands, hired him and ten other boys. They drove twelve-hundred head of cattle almost four hundred miles. None of them but the rancher and the cook was over the age of fifteen."

"That's amazing!"

"Yeah, but I'm not sure how much I believe." John scoffed. "The story got bigger each time he told it."

Moira braced her hands behind her and leaned back. For the first time in years, she'd lost her direction. She'd run up against dead ends before. For some inexplicable reason, this time felt different, more final…more devastating.

"Too bad about your brother," John said. "I have six of 'em and I'm the youngest. Never lost a one though. They were always around. Too much so."

Moira's eyes widened. "What a blessing, having all that family."

The cowboy kept his eyes heavenward. "I don't know if I'd put it that way."

She followed his gaze, astonished by the sheer number of stars blanketing the night sky. She couldn't recall the last time she'd stared at the moon. If she was out after dark, she kept her defenses up, watching for strangers and pickpockets, not staring at the twinkling stars. "What about your parents?"

"Both dead. My pa died first and I guess my ma

couldn't imagine living without him. She died a short while later."

"I'm sorry to hear that," Moira murmured. "I guess you're an orphan, too."

"I never thought about it that way." A wrinkle deepened on his forehead. "Except I'm the youngest, and I sometimes feel like I have six fathers. My reasons for leaving seem small now, after talking with you, but I had to set out on my own. When our folks were alive, they had a way of making sure we all had a voice. Now it's as if we're all fighting to be heard, only no one is listening. It got to the point where we'd argue over something just for the sake of a good brawl. I figured if I didn't leave soon, all that fighting would turn into hate. And hate is a hard thing to come back from. I know my folks wouldn't have wanted that for us."

Moira plucked a handful of prairie grass and held it in her fisted hand. "I wouldn't know."

Her own father had run off the year Tommy had been born. Her mother had once been young and beautiful, but time and illness had stolen the bloom from her cheeks. The more she needed and the less she gave, the less her husband came home at night. Once she'd lost her usefulness, he'd run. He'd run from his wife and his children. His responsibilities. He hadn't run far enough. He'd been killed in a factory accident three months later.

Moira had been in charge of herself for as long as she could remember. Her mother had worked herself sick, and Moira had cared for her little brother. When her mother could no longer even care for herself, a woman from the Missouri State Charitable Trust and Foundling Society had arrived.

Never outlive your usefulness, her mother had said.

Moira had felt her mother's death somewhere along the way, although she'd never received proper notice. One day she'd finally accepted that no one was coming for her. The realization had hardened her heart and made her more determined than ever to prove her worth.

Shortly after the Charitable Trust had found them, she and Tommy had been taken in by the Giffords. Mrs. Gifford had fancied herself a society lady, except Mr. Gifford had never made enough money to keep her in the style she figured she deserved. Moira had initially been humbled, awed by their fine house and brocaded furniture. She'd soon learned it was all superficial luxury.

From the beginning, the Giffords had treated them like hirelings. To her foster family, she was a servant. Mrs. Gifford took great pride in parading her *charity* before her friends. The truth was far less charitable. The Giffords had put them to work. The siblings rolled cigars for ten hours a day, sometimes more. Pacing and frowning, Mr. Gifford had timed them with his ever-present pocket watch. More cigars meant more income for the Giffords.

Making Moira work from sunup to sundown for nothing more than a roof over her head and a castoff dress each spring didn't place Mrs. Gifford in the annals of sainthood, though she acted as if it did. After Tommy ran away, Moira had marked off the days until her eighteenth birthday and left that morning.

Mr. and Mrs. Gifford had figured she'd be back in a week, begging for help. She'd never doubted her decision. Tommy hadn't returned and neither would she.

The cowboy stretched and yawned. "When did you see Tommy last?"

"Five years ago. He was fifteen and I was almost seventeen. He ran away. I, uh, I thought he'd come back. I'd given up ever seeing him again until I received the telegram. It was the sign I'd been searching for all along."

She'd find him and make things right. She'd apologize for taking the watch, for getting him in trouble. No one had loved her, truly loved her since that fateful day when she'd hidden Mr. Gifford's infuriating pocket watch behind a tin of crackers in the pantry and let Tommy take the blame.

She was supposed to take care of him, and she'd failed. She'd failed in the worst way possible. The cowboy dug his heels into the soft earth. "That's a long time to look for someone."

"Not very long when you love the person."

"Point taken."

"We'll be a family again."

The cowboy resumed his stargazing. "You're what, twenty-one, twenty-two? He's almost twenty? That's a long time apart. People change. Maybe you should think about starting a family of your own."

Moira shook her head. "Not until I find Tommy."

"Well, he's probably looking for you, too. I'm sure it'll all work out."

The cowboy's casual words buoyed her fragile hope. Would her brother accept her? He'd never returned to the Giffords. He must have known it was her fault. She'd have told the truth, except she'd been too much of a coward. By the time she'd screwed up her courage, Tommy was gone. She'd waited for him at the Giffords then stayed on working at the hotel in St. Louis, hoping to catch a glimpse of him.

If he'd been looking, surely he'd have found her. Yet this past month she'd finally been given proof, courtesy of the Gifford's maid, that he'd tried to contact her. His concession had to mean something. "Everything will be better when we're together as a family again."

He'd forgive her. If she found him, if she explained, he'd forgive her. Then she could finally be whole again. They could finally be a family again. She'd have a purpose once more.

John stood and dusted his pant legs. "It's late. You should get some sleep." He held out his hand. "You did real well tonight. You tie knots like a trail boss. Those girls are lucky to have you."

As she took his proffered hand, her heart stalled beneath his unexpected compliment. "Why are you doing this? Why are you helping us?"

No one ever did anything without an ulterior motive.

"Didn't have much other choice," he answered easily.

Moira kept her own counsel. He'd want payment for his help. She only hoped the price wasn't too steep.

Either way, she hadn't the energy to sort out his motives. She'd find Tommy, she'd settle for nothing less. Lord knew she'd pave a street to his doorstep brick by brick with her bare hands if only she knew the way. There was an empty space inside her, and she wouldn't be whole again until they were family once more. This was merely a detour in her journey. She wouldn't be distracted by the handsome cowboy and his deceptively kind eyes. Not now. Not ever.

She'd never open up her heart to the disappointment her mother had faced. She wouldn't spend her life proving her worth just to be abandoned in the end. Sooner or later everybody left. The first year at the hotel she'd tried to make friends, but no one ever stayed long. One by one all the people who'd been important to her were plucked away. She'd learned her lesson well—she was better off alone.

Moira glanced around and realized John was heading for the horses and not the tents. "Where are you going?"

"Keeping watch. Checking the remuda."

Champion scrambled upright. John pointed a finger. "Stay. Keep watch over the camp."

The animal immediately lay down and rested its head on its paws.

Moira followed the cowboy's shuffling steps and her

earlier animosity softened. His shoulders had slumped since she'd first seen him striding through the darkened alley. He must be exhausted. If he didn't find a crew tomorrow, what then?

Thoughtful, she gazed into the darkness. Those cattle sure didn't care if she was a boy or a girl. Why should anyone else? If a dozen boys could drive twelve hundred head of cattle, couldn't a few girls drive this bunch? If they were useful, maybe that would be enough payment.

Moira shook off the crazy thought. She'd find another way.

Alone.

The less time she spent in the company of John Elder, the better. She'd only known him a short while and already her resolve was weakening. His shoulders were strong, and it had been a long time since she'd had someone to lean on. She was exhausted, that was all. After a good night's rest she'd be stronger. And after tomorrow, she'd never see him again. She was used to being on her own. Life was easier that way. Lonelier, perhaps, but she'd rather be solitary than grow fond of someone who would only be in her life a short time.

As the lavender fingers of dawn branched out from the east, John braced his hands against the saddle horn and locked his elbows. A faint haze on the horizon showed the first signs of the morning sun. He'd kept watch all night, dozing off and on, and was so exhausted he could hardly think straight.

Outside of Texas, the terrain had leveled. John had never considered himself a sentimental man, yet the changing landscape left him melancholy.

His longhorns would thrive on the rich buffalo grass of the plains. Cities like Wichita were growing while Dodge City faded. Kansas was shutting out the Texas cattle, but folks still needed to be fed. If an army marched on its stomach, then nations flourished on a full belly.

Pops poured a cup of coffee and John reached for the steaming brew. Pops had been around the Elder family for as long as John could remember. He should be retired now, kicking back and relaxing. Instead he'd chosen a grueling cattle drive. Some men just weren't made for retirement.

John's horse sidestepped and he carefully balanced the hot liquid over the ground.

The older man poured another. "What's the story on them girls?"

"Hard to say," John replied. "Looks like the deputy sheriff was rounding them up. Searching for pickpockets. Put 'em up in a sportin' house while he sorted out the details."

Pops scoffed. "Why'd he take them to a sportin' house?"

John sipped his coffee and winced against the heat. "Didn't ask."

"What do you think?"

"I think something doesn't feel right."

They'd dropped out of the sky onto his head. Literally. Then Moira had inadvertently knocked the sheriff's deputy senseless. *It's fitting you'll die in fire,* the deputy had said. That threat felt personal. Had they encountered each other before? Had Moira had a previous brush with the law?

The girls were still sleeping which gave John time for thinking. Too much time. The law in town was rounding up pickpockets. And not just any pickpockets. They were specifically looking for young girls.

While Moira was definitely a woman, she could be mistaken for an adolescent with her girlish skirts, petite stature and fresh-faced smile. The gang he'd encountered in Buffalo Gap had worked as a team. One member distracted a fellow while another lifted his belongings.

Was one of his unlikely charges in possession of Mr. Grey's watch? John's thoughts immediately lit on Darcy. Of all the girls, she had the hardest edge. While John was tempted to speculate, he shook off any supposition. All he could do was place them in someone else's safekeeping.

Pops stood and stretched his fisted hands toward the sky. "What are you going to do?"

"I'll go into town this morning. See if I can get the lay of the land while I'm posting a notice for a new crew." *See if I'm a wanted man.* John didn't suppose assaulting the sheriff's deputy was a crime without punishment.

In the crisp light of dawn he couldn't easily dismiss the way Moira had looked at him last evening. As though he'd already disappointed her. Ruth Ann had looked at him that way once, when he'd playfully asked her to marry him and she'd declared him unfit. At least he'd given Ruth Ann a reason. What reason did Moira have for doubting him? Though her opinion shouldn't matter, it did. He didn't like her looking at him as if she'd sized him up and was waiting for him to show weakness. To fail.

John shook his head. It was better this way. He didn't need the distraction. And Miss Moira O'Mara was definitely a distraction.

"I'll watch the girls while you're gone," Pops spoke, interrupting John's reverie.

"Suit yourself." His head pounding, John gulped the last of his cooled coffee. "Be sure and hide the valuables."

There was a good chance he'd brought a gaggle of half-size pickpockets into camp. They couldn't get away with much, but better safe than sorry.

Pops didn't appear concerned at the prospect. "I'll take my chances."

"What would the boys do?" John asked, knowing Pops would understand the question better than anyone.

The older man considered his answer as he hooked the

handle of his Dutch oven with an iron rod and hoisted it over the flames. "I don't suppose it matters what your brothers would do. They're not here, are they?"

"The one time I wouldn't mind a little help, and they're not around."

Pops grinned. "Never say God doesn't have a sense of humor."

John stifled a sigh. If Moira was guilty of a crime, then she'd have to answer to a higher power than him. No matter what the outcome, he needed some distance between them. He had an uneasy sensation the feelings stirring in his chest wouldn't change based on the outcome of her guilt or innocence. According to Ruth Ann, he wasn't the sort of man people pinned their hopes on.

John's horse sidestepped and he glanced up. Two riders appeared on the horizon. Judging by the dirt clods they kicked up in their wake, the men were coming fast. The one on the right was lanky and tall. Familiar. John groaned. Even from a distance he recognized the deputy sheriff.

He tightened his fist around the reins. "Pops, why don't you round up the girls. We've got trouble."

"What kind of trouble?"

John nodded toward the approaching riders. "The law has caught up with us. Looks like I don't need to go into town after all."

Pops threw up his arms. "What in the name of Sam Hill happened last night?" He eyed John, his speculation manifest in his watery gray eyes. "I'm guessing there's more to the story than what you told me."

"I might have assaulted the sheriff's deputy."

"Might have or *did?*"

"I hit him." John shot his cook a quelling glance. He'd hoped to avoid admitting that particular transgression. "It's a long story and I don't have time to tell it right now.

I'll meet our company. Let the girls know we have visitors."

Pops shook his head. "I'll round 'em up. But you're on your own after that. I've got a stew to finish."

John glanced behind him at the quiet tent. One thing was for certain, he sure hoped Miss O'Mara unraveled knots as well as she tied them.

Chapter Four

Moira stumbled into the early morning light and held the tent flap aside for the other girls. She stretched and yawned, then pressed her hands into the small of her back and arched.

Tony rubbed her eyes, blinked and blinked again.

Following her gaze, Moira bolted upright. The kidnapper and another man stood before them.

"Well, well, well. If it isn't the orphan bunch," the kidnapper said with a smirk.

"Stay away from us or I'll fetch the sheriff," Moira said.

The second man rubbed the back of his neck. "That would be me."

Nausea rose in the back of her throat. Both men wore stars on their lapels. Though one was tarnished and dull; the other twinkled in the morning sunlight.

"Some of you have met already," the second man continued. "Perhaps more formal introductions are in order. My name is Sheriff Taylor. This is my deputy, Wendell Ervin."

Moira glared at the deputy sheriff. One shirttail hung loose from his sagging, brown trousers while greasy stains from a long-forgotten meal interrupted the black-and-gray satin stripes lining his vest like jailhouse bars. He'd removed his hat revealing a crown of thinning, sandy-colored hair pressed into place by layers of dirt and grime. A goose-egg bruise stood out between his shaggy eyebrows and purple half moons flared from the inside corners of his eyes.

He leered at her, showing a yellowed nightmare of a gap-toothed smile. Suppressing a delicate shudder, Moira leaned away. His close proximity revealed the bloodshot whites of his faded blue eyes. He pointed a crooked finger at her. "You'll be spending the rest of your life in jail."

She might have felt a modicum of satisfaction from his self-inflicted injury if she wasn't terrified of his threat. Moira figured the situation could only degrade from there.

While the deputy swaggered and postulated, it was clear he wasn't in charge. The man who'd introduced himself as the sheriff managed to overshadow his deputy with nothing more than a dismissive glare. Unlike Wendell, there wasn't a speck of dirt marring the sheriff's impeccable black suit. A crisp white shirt with a starched collar glowed between the dark folds of his lapels and his silver star sparkled.

Moira had a sudden absurd image of the sheriff blowing a hot breath against the metal and polishing the tin against his tidy black sleeve before riding into camp.

Her four charges stomped and huffed, rubbing their hands against chill shoulders. Despite the deputy's blustering threat, their expressions were dull and uncomprehending. The girls blinked and yawned, wrinkled and blurry-eyed from sleep.

The sheriff smoothed his neat, dark coat into place and focused his attention on John. "Your name?"

"John Elder," the cowboy replied, his voice a low growl.

He kept his face averted from Moira. Come to think of it, John hadn't met her eyes once this morning. As though sensing her perusal, he turned, revealing his stark profile and the hard set of his jaw. There was nothing reassuring about his demeanor and her chest throbbed with something weighty and ragged.

The sheriff dusted his hat brim. "I knew an Elder once. From Texas. You a relation?"

"Probably."

Her kidnapper stepped forward and hitched his thumbs into his belt loops. Moira took an involuntary step back. He might be a deputy sheriff, but he wasn't getting any closer. He took another step and she matched her withdrawal. They repeated the odd dance twice more. John and the sheriff watched the display with curious detachment, waiting to see how the impasse would play out. Moira glared at their lack of interference. She'd back her way right into Kansas at this rate, but she didn't care.

Champion growled.

The sound spurred John into action. With only a slight tension in his jaw, he ambled over and edged his sizeable form between Moira and the deputy sheriff until the two men stood nose to nose. Moira leaned away for a better view and sucked in a breath. The deputy, Wendell, narrowed his eyes and scraped his hand through his hair, leaving gummed furrows in the strands.

Another menacing growl sounded from Champion.

Wendell's gaze flickered toward the animal and his mask of indifference slipped. He ran one finger around his collar and skittered away.

At the deputy's hasty retreat, John held out a hand toward the dog. "Down, boy."

Sensing he'd lost ground in the exchange, Wendell's thunderous expression darkened. He drew himself upright, straightening the curve in his spine. "That's the man who jumped me last night. I'm gonna arrest him."

"Arrest Mr. Elder? I think not." With the cowboy safely

lodged between her and the deputy, Moira's courage returned full-steam. "You, sir, snatched me and four innocent girls off the street and tossed us into a brothel. Mr. Elder was rescuing *us*. From *you*."

The sheriff dusted his coat sleeve with the back of his hand. "Looks like I came into this poker game without all the cards." He tilted back his head and stared down his tapered nose. "You left out the best parts of your story, Wendell."

His deputy touched the bruise between his eyes. "Where was I supposed to put them? The jail was full of men. That wouldn't have been safe now, would it? I did the next best thing. It was Sunday, after all. That's the slowest night for business."

"You'd know, wouldn't you? And I suppose you took the opportunity to imbibe?"

With a thumb and forefinger, Wendell rubbed the inside corners of his bloodshot eyes "I did not imbibe. I had one drink. But I was definitely not imbibed."

The sheriff's expression fluctuated between resignation and disgust. "Never mind. I think we have a misunderstanding. One thing is for certain. Wendell is my deputy and you all broke the law."

A burst of chatter erupted from the girls. They peeled away from Moira, forming a tight circle. Huddled together, they spoke in frantic whispers. Snippets of the exchange drifted beyond the boundaries of their bent heads.

"What if they—"

"Don't even say it."

"Nobody's coming for you."

Hazel clutched her recently returned rag doll against her chest. "Are we going to jail?"

Moira scooted closer and draped her arm around Hazel's shoulder. She offered her most encouraging smile.

"Don't worry. This is all a misunderstanding. Mr. Elder will sort out the whole thing."

The chatter fell silent.

A muscle ticked along John Elder's jaw. "*I'm* sorting this out, am I?"

He obviously hadn't slept much. Lines of fatigue feathered from his eyes and the edges of his mouth. His clothing was rumpled, his boots dusty. The added layer of grime lent him a patina of danger that had her heart thumping uncomfortably in her chest.

Moira shivered. "*We* shall sort out this misunderstanding."

John shrugged his shoulders and moved defensively before the frightened bunch of girls. "If Wendell is your deputy, what was he doing kidnapping young girls?"

"Yes," Moira added. "Please explain yourself."

John held her in place, his touch on her shoulder firm and somehow comforting. "Let the man speak, Moira. We need to hear what he has to say."

"Exactly, Mr. Elder." Sheriff Taylor offered a twitch of his lips that might have been a smile. "We have a very special band of pickpockets targeting Fool's End these days." He slid his considering gaze over each girl in turn. "They've become an inconvenience for me, and I don't like to be inconvenienced. One particular young girl swiped Mr. Grey's watch. He's one of our finest and most upstanding citizens. He's none too pleased."

The sheriff grimaced on the words *finest* and *most upstanding.*

A collective gasp erupted from the group. Tony stomped her foot. "It ain't one of us."

Moira fought John's protective grasp. "What proof do you have?" she demanded.

The sheriff lifted one shoulder in a negligent shrug.

"I have enough circumstantial proof to make a case." He frowned at Moira. "You look familiar. Have we met?"

She instantly reversed her direction, leaning away from John. "We most certainly have not met."

The cowboy's grip tightened on Moira's sleeve and she shook off his fingers. He released her but held her gaze for a charged instant, his expression intense.

Wendell grunted. "This has gone beyond a bunch of pickpockets. That man attacked me. He assaulted an officer of the law. He's got to be punished."

The sheriff flipped back his jacket and rested his fingers on his slim hips. "Something's been gnawing at me all morning. I've seen a lot of fights in my time, but I don't ever recall an injury quite like that egg on your forehead. How exactly did that happen?"

"Well, uh." Wendell stuttered. "It don't matter. He should be in jail. That's all." The deputy sputtered into silence like a petulant child.

John splayed his arms. "We still haven't solved the first problem. You have no proof that any of these girls is a thief." He tossed a bitter glare toward the deputy. "And your law enforcement is shoddy at best."

Wendell reared back. "You gave me the orders yourself. Round up any of them girls that looked to be homeless. Mr. Grey even found me special last evening when I was leaving the saloon—I mean the post office. He was especially interested in a particular redhead. Musta had a good reason, I figure."

The deputy spat in the dirt at Moira's feet.

Champion barked and John lunged. The sheriff caught Wendell by the scruff of his coat and yanked him back.

Moira's stomach lurched. "I was minding my own business. And I'm not homeless or a young girl. I'm certainly not a pickpocket. What gives you the right to accost me simply because of the color of my hair?"

"Whoa, whoa, whoa." Wendell shook out of the sheriff's hold and swung his head from side to side. "Easy there."

Momentarily distracted, Moira stared in fascination at his enormous head. Not a single hair moved out of its pressed mold. Grease made a powerful pomade.

"I didn't *accost* you," the deputy jerked Moira's thoughts back to the task at hand. "I just put you in that place for safekeeping. Nothin' else happened. So don't be blabbering about people getting accosted and whatnot. That ain't right. I'm a deputy sheriff and all. I got an image to uphold."

Moira rolled her eyes. "You've exhausted your supply of big words, Wendell. I said accost, not rap—"

"Enough." John interrupted. "Do you have any proof that this particular *woman,*" he emphasized the word and cast a meaningful look in Moira's direction. "Had anything to do with stealing Mr. Grey's watch?"

Wendell had the decency to look sheepish. "It was getting dark. I had my orders. A red-haired woman who dresses like a girl. That's what I was told to look for. No women I know wear their skirt above their ankles outside the saloon."

Moira flushed and kept her gaze pinned on a shrub tree in the distance. It was somehow fitting she'd be falsely accused of stealing a watch after letting Tommy take the blame for the same crime all those years ago.

Wendell postured. "Everything fit. I spotted you right off. I was doing my job and I did good. One of them girls is a thief and a liar. Maybe all of them."

The sheriff waved Wendell's ramblings to a halt. "It seems we have more than one misunderstanding. My deputy may have been a touch overzealous in his approach to law enforcement, but his intentions were sound. If a crime has been committed, he has the right to round up suspects. In this case, he assumed, quite logically, that the suspects were young girls without adult supervision. I believe each of you meets the criteria?"

The girls scuffed the ground and avoided his searching gaze.

"My point precisely. With the noted exception of Miss O'Mara, Wendell had every right to think you might have been the pickpockets he was seeking." His paused. "Then again, Miss O'Mara was the only one with an accurate description."

John rubbed his forehead. "I'd like to know what your witnesses were *imbibing* if these are your suspects." He pointed at Hazel. "A nine-year-old with curly black hair." He indicated Sarah. "A blonde with pale blue eyes. A redhead. What's next? A trained bear with a yellow bow in its fur?"

Hazel giggled.

"Your conditions are far too broad and your temporary jail was a travesty," John said. "As far as I knew, these girls had been kidnapped. I was protecting them. If your drunken deputy had identified himself, things might have turned out different."

The sheriff flashed a toothy smile. "An honorable cowboy. What an oddity around these parts. And you bring up a good question. Why didn't you identify yourself, Wendell?"

"I forgot, that's all. I only been doing this job for a week." The deputy snorted. "Let's haul them all back into town and search 'em. We'll have this sorted out soon enough once we shake 'em and see what falls out."

Sarah drew in a sharp breath and Tony placed a secure arm around her shoulder. "You ain't taking us nowhere," Tony challenged.

The sheriff rubbed his chin. "As Wendell has so ably

demonstrated, I don't have the facilities to house you while we sort which of you has sticky fingers."

"Then let's search the lot of them right here." Wendell declared, looking unaccountably proud of his inspired suggestion. "Search them right now."

"No!" Darcy shouted. "You have no right."

Agitated by the raised voices, Champion barked and bounced from side to side on his front paws. In a flash the scene spiraled out of control. The girls erupted into a noisy argument, shouting and gesturing. Darcy shoved Tony. Sarah grasped Tony's arm against retaliation. Sheriff Taylor paced around the fringes, his orders for calm lost in the fray. Wendell flapped his arms like a chicken that forgot it couldn't fly.

After a moment, the sheriff let out a shrill whistle. Champion sat back on his haunches and whimpered, then let out a defiant bark.

John remained motionless in the fray. "Enough. This is getting us nowhere. If you people don't stop whistling and waving your arms around, we're going to have a stampede on our hands."

His quiet announcement flummoxed the group and everyone fell silent.

Wendell recovered first. "I'm taking this one back to town no matter what." He snatched Moira's arm. "She's the ringleader. She's the one you want. You cut off the snake's head and the body will die."

Moira stumbled and fell hard on her knees. Pain shot up her legs. Wendell yanked her upright.

John charged. The sheriff threw his left shoulder into the cowboy, knocking him off balance. Using his momentary advantage, Sheriff Taylor whipped out his gun and aimed the barrel at John's chest. Moira blanched.

The sheriff shook a scruff of hair from his eyes. "Wendell, I'll be taking charge of the woman before you get us all killed." He gently extracted Moira from the deputy's hold while keeping a wary eye on John. "You've made your point. I'd suggest you not rile Mr. Elder any further."

Sick and tired of being manhandled, Moira rubbed her bruised shoulder.

"Him?" Wendell slapped his chest. "What about me? I'm the abused party. Why isn't anyone worried about getting me riled up?"

"Because you have a singular way of escalating even the most benign situations into shambles." The sheriff holstered his gun and raked his hair back into one place before repositioning his hat.

"But," Wendell sputtered. "It's her. We got to take her."

John caught Moira's gaze. "Why her?" the cowboy asked. "You seem awfully fired up about Miss O'Mara. Is there something more you're not telling us?"

Moira wondered the same thing. Why single her out? The cowboy looked more confused than accusing, and for that she was grateful. He hadn't immediately taken Wendell's side. That had to mean something.

"Look what she done to me!" Wendell pointed at his face.

Moira blanched. His injury explained a lot. He'd gone and knocked himself out before a group of witnesses. His pride had been hurt as much as his head.

The sheriff tucked his chin to his chest and rocked back on his heels. "Explain your injury or I leave right now."

"She hit me with a pitchfork."

"I did not," Moira declared. "Well, not in the face...I mean, there was a pitchfork involved."

She let her voice trail off. The long version of the explanation didn't exactly help her cause. She *had* whacked him. Just not in the face. "I hit him in the backside with the pitchfork." She caught the deputy's warning glare. "He did the rest himself. And that's the truth."

"You gotta do better than that." The sheriff hoisted a dark eyebrow in question. "Why don't you tell me the whole story, Miss O'Mara?"

Hazel giggled. The other girls snickered.

"Well..." She cleared her throat. Humiliating the deputy didn't feel like the best way to advance her case. "You must understand that I was under the impression I had been kidnapped. Your deputy never identified himself as a lawman. It was quite understandable that I had the wrong impression."

"Yes, yes. I got that part."

"He chased us into the livery." She cast a sidelong glance at Wendell.

The deputy glowered.

The sheriff heaved a breath. "The scene of the crime, as it were."

"Events progressed from there." Moira studied her laced fingers. "There was a brief altercation. Then a small fire. Well, um, I dropped a pitchfork and he, um, stepped on the tongs. Knocked himself out cold."

The sheriff threw back his head and laughed. Gathering himself, he swiped at his forehead with a turkey-red bandanna. He then straightened his lapels and buttoned his jacket. "As much as I'd like to pursue this line of explanation further, it's a waste of time. All we're doing is talking in circles, and I have more important work. Last night there was a shoot-out over a land claim. One of the fellows was gut-shot and it doesn't look good. If that fellow dies, I'll have a murder on my hands. Do you have any idea how much paperwork comes with a murder?"

The sheriff ran his thumb and forefinger down the crease of his lapel. "Pages. I've gone through a whole box of pencils this month alone. Not to mention I don't have any love for Mr. Grey or his two-dollar watch." He paused. "Why don't we strike a bargain? As long as you and the girls stay out of town, there's not much I can do. You show your face, even once, and I'll be forced to take action."

Moira opened her mouth and John silenced her with a quick slice of his hand. "What if Mr. Grey doesn't agree?"

"I'll handle Mr. Grey. I'll even let you in on a little something." He lowered his voice. "I'm only the interim sheriff here. I'm just biding my time until the permanent man arrives. Which means I don't have to play nice with Mr. Grey. So do we have a deal?"

"Yes!" Moira shouted immediately. Right then, anything was better than putting herself at the mercy of Wendell Ervin.

"No." The cowboy spoke low.

Her knees buckled.

"It's important I go back into town." John paced before the girls who watched his back-and-forth movements like spectators at a quick draw. "I've got no crew and eight-hundred-head of range cattle. What am I supposed to do with a bunch of girls out in the middle of nowhere?"

"You got food?" Sheriff Taylor asked.

"Yep."

"Shelter?"

"Yep."

The sheriff shrugged. "Seems like you're doing fine to me."

"Fine? How is that fine? These girls have nothing but the clothes on their backs." John threw up his arms. "Well, I guess if you don't count a couple hundred head of cattle and an absent crew, then, yes, everything is just dandy. Couldn't be brighter if there were two suns in the sky."

"You had a crew coming into town. Not my fault you lost them on the way out."

The cowboy made a strangled sound in his throat. John clutched his head and muttered beneath his breath,

"I should have walked the long way home last night. I was tired and angry and not thinking straight. I tried to take the easy way out, but there are no shortcuts in life. I know better. I shouldn't have let my temper get the best of me. Yep, that was my first mistake. My second mistake was looking up. Always keep your head down, my brother Jack told me. But did I listen? No. All the years he lectured me, who knew he'd be right someday?"

Tony's eyes widened. "Oh my, he's gone and lost his mind, hasn't he?"

"Yep." Sarah nodded. "The same thing happened to my Great-Aunt Sylvia. One day she was frying pork chops, the next thing she was babbling like she'd lost her wits."

Darcy frowned. "Did she ever get 'em back? You know, her wits."

Sarah scratched her temple. "Not that I know of. And my ma was terrified of pork chops after that. She'd get all white and shaky over frying bacon even."

The girls nodded and elbowed each other, each recalling stories they'd heard of people losing their minds at the drop of a hat. While John muttered, the sheriff and his deputy spoke in low, agitated tones.

The cowboy had gone half-loco, the deputy was an imbecile and the sheriff was the worst of the lot. The head of law enforcement in that corrupt cow town was abandoning them. By refusing to declare their innocence, he'd effectively declared their guilt—because he didn't want to whittle down another pencil over a person's life. A sharp pain throbbed behind her eyes.

She'd lost patience with the lot of them.

Moira crossed her arms over her chest. "We'll take care of ourselves."

The sheriff jerked around and snapped his fingers. "It's the voice. It's right there on the edge of my memory."

Moira stiffened and tugged at her hair. "I suppose your

watch is missing, too? Well I didn't take that either. And the gentlemen of Fool's End should keep better track of their valuables instead of accusing anyone who happens to be walking down the street at sunset."

"It's not that." The sheriff circled around her, one hand on his chin, his gaze appraising.

Once again Moira caught John's intent gaze and her heart froze. She didn't like the way the cowboy kept looking at her. Studying her as though he expected stolen coins and jewelry to shower from her person.

She met his accusing glare with one of her own. "You'd like that, wouldn't you?"

John reared back.

"You'd like for me to be some sort of pickpocket. Then you could run away and pat yourself on the back at the same time."

The wrinkle between the cowboy's eyes deepened. "That doesn't even make sense."

"Uh-oh." Tony slapped her leather hat over her dark hair and adjusted the rawhide strap beneath her chin. "We've lost another one. Now they've both gone loco."

The girls each nodded in unison.

The sheriff squinted.

Moira squirmed.

"What's your name again?"

"Moira." She drew herself upright. She was tired of cowering from all these oafish men. "My name is Miss Moira O'Mara. You may call me Miss O'Mara."

"Aha!" The sheriff clapped his hands. "That's the connection. I had a run-in with a fellow by that name not long ago. He spoke like he was all high-and-mighty, too. Like you did just now. *Call me Mr. O'Mara.*" The sheriff rubbed his jaw with a thumb and forefinger. "His first name was Ted. Or Thomas, something like that."

"Tommy! Tommy O'Mara?" Her spirits soared. "That's my brother."

Chapter Five

Moira's animosity toward the sheriff evaporated immediately. He was doing his job, that was all. No hard feelings need come between them.

"Tommy O'Mara," the sheriff repeated, his voice thoughtful. "Sounds right. Red hair. Not real tall. You two look alike. Heard rumors he ran afoul of Mr. Grey."

A trickle of horror filtered through her stomach. "Tommy? Is he all right? What happened? Is he still living in Fool's End? Mr. Grey said he hadn't ever met him. But I had a feeling he was lying. Did something happen to Tommy?"

"Easy there, little lady." The sheriff flashed a charming grin.

Moira remained stoic.

When the sheriff realized his dime-store charisma was wasted on her, his smile faded. "Nah. Talk around town was that Mr. Grey's daughter had taken a shine to your brother."

A girl? Tommy was only...nineteen, well, almost twenty. But that was young. The sheriff must be mistaken.

He smoothed his sleeve. "Keeping a couple of lovebirds out of trouble isn't part of my job."

Moira clutched the sheriff's forearm. "Do you know where he is?"

The sheriff glanced at his rumpled sleeve, only recently straightened. Moira released her hold and sprang backward. She mustn't antagonize the man any further. Not if she hoped for more information about her brother. Other than the telegram, the sheriff was the first person she'd met who knew Tommy by name.

"Can't say that I know what happened to him after he lit out." The sheriff brushed out the wrinkle on his elbow. "If I find something, I'll send word. Where can I reach you?"

"Let me follow you back into town." Moira clasped her hands together. "I'm not who you're looking for."

"Can't do that." The sheriff's expression turned sympathetic. "Where's your next stop, Mr. Elder?"

The cowboy ceased his pacing. "I *had* planned on going across the border up through Cimarron Springs," his voice dripped with sarcasm. "I'm not real sure anymore. At this rate, I may have to circle back to Texas."

"You're not quitting now, you're going north. Everyone gets funneled through Cimarron Springs at some point. If I remember something, I'll drop you a line. Ask for Jo Cain at the telegraph office. I've gone through her before. She's reliable." The sheriff mounted his horse, his silver spurs jingling. "Don't forget our deal. I'm dead serious. It's not safe for those girls in town." He cast a meaningful glance toward his deputy. "I can't protect them next time."

Moira's earlier generosity faded like morning dew. Events were moving too quickly. "You can't just leave us here. What makes you think we'll be traveling together? And what about my personal belongings? My bag. I was staying at the hotel."

The sheriff shook his head. "That's not part of the deal. If any of you return, I'll have you arrested and brought before Mr. Grey. If he identifies you as the pickpocket, you'll be in jail by this afternoon."

"That's not fair! I didn't do anything."

"Then you're welcome to come with us. Take your chances. It's quite a gamble, considering what *each* of you has to lose."

His subtle rebuke wasn't lost on her. She'd been momentarily distracted by the news of Tommy. She wasn't alone; she had the girls to consider. They could all wind up behind bars.

Moira studied the two lawmen. Her choices were thinning out by the moment. She sure didn't trust Wendell and she didn't have much faith in the sheriff either. Neither man was interested in justice or sorting out right from wrong. One wanted revenge for his humiliation and the other wanted an easy fix and an early lunch.

She turned and caught the cowboy's attention. Her courage faltered. They were a burden to him. An unfair burden considering all he'd done for them up to this point. If the sheriff left them, they were stuck in the middle of Indian Territory with no resources.

Worse than the middle of nowhere, they were stuck in No Man's Land.

"None of this is my fault." She hadn't done anything after all. "You can't steal my belongings."

"I'm not a man you want to threaten." The sheriff's voice hardened. "And that sounds an awful lot like a threat."

Her heart died in her chest. She'd mistaken the sheriff's easy charm for an easy nature. He was setting her straight.

The sheriff watched her capitulation and set his easy grin back in place. This time Moira wasn't fooled.

He pulled a silver dollar from his pocket and balanced the coin on the tip of his thumb. "Never say I'm not a generous man."

The sheriff flipped his coin into the air. It arced and caught the early morning light, glinting through its downward spiral.

An easy catch. Moira refused the insult. She wouldn't grovel in the dirt for his money. That's what he wanted, after all. He wanted to show her who had the power between them.

The coin landed with a thud. She'd considered begging for his help, the cowboy didn't deserve any more trouble, but that changed her mind. She'd rather set out on her own than endure the sheriff's disdain.

The sheriff winked. "I've got your Irish up now, don't I?" He leaned forward. "Mr. Grey didn't like your brother stirring up trouble. He's not going to like you either."

The whole undercurrent in the conversation instantly crystallized and Moira groaned. No wonder they'd snatched her! Mr. Grey didn't want her because he thought she'd stolen from him. He had a bone to pick with her brother and she'd waltzed into his offices and flaunted her name and her family connection. Then, on her way back to the boardinghouse, she'd been abducted. She didn't believe it was a coincidence. She'd left Mr. Grey all the information they needed to find her. The deputy said as much when he outlined Mr. Grey's instructions. Her capture hadn't been an accident.

If Mr. Grey wanted revenge for the trouble Tommy had caused, she was an easy target. If that awful man had been lying, if he knew where her brother had gone... Moira fought the play of emotions simmering in her chest. Tommy would come for her if he thought she was in trouble. Wouldn't he?

While the men talked, Moira tugged her lower lip between her teeth. *No.* She couldn't do it. As much as she wanted to find Tommy, she couldn't risk laying a trap for him. She'd betrayed him once already. Besides, there was no guarantee Mr. Grey had more information.

"I'll stay here," she grudgingly replied.

Atop his mount, the sheriff loomed over them, showing his strength. He leaned one elbow on his saddle horn, his voice no more than a whisper, "Too bad really. I think you and I could have gotten along real fine."

Moving so quickly that Moira had no warning, John Elder shoved Moira behind him, shielding her from the sheriff's view. "I don't like your tone."

The sheriff tipped his hat with a grin, appearing as though he'd just won some grand prize. "Good luck to you," he said. "I have a feeling our paths will cross again."

John gripped the reins of the sheriff's horse. "This is not a deal. We don't have a deal. We have a disaster. You can't just leave me out here with a bunch of girls. I don't have the resources. I've got a herd of cattle and no crew."

"Not my problem either. Maybe next time you won't fire your crew until you have another one in place." The sheriff chuckled. "I bet you won't make that mistake again."

John Elder's shoulders stiffened and fear shot through her heart. Though she couldn't see his face, she felt the tension radiating from his body. His throat worked and she sensed the battle within him once more. Just like the previous night when he'd ushered them into the empty stall. He was fighting something, an enemy only he could see. After a moment he appeared to make a decision.

She didn't know how she sensed that, but she did. Even in such a short time she'd become attuned to his changing moods. The cowboy sucked in a deep breath, his chest rising and falling with the effort. His shoulders dropped a notch, his stance widened.

The sheriff stared at the girls, his expression thoughtful. "There's a drummer from the mercantile in town. He's usually heading south this time of year, but I can send him your way. Those girls will need to be outfitted proper."

"What if he can't find us?"

The sheriff scoffed. "If you were moving any slower, you'd be going backward. There can't be many all-girl cattle drives this side of Fort Preble. I'll point the drummer toward the fly swarm and let him take his chances. His name is Swede and I'll give him an idea of what you'll need. He's good people."

"I don't like it. We're defenseless out here. You must at least see that. We're in Indian Territory."

"I'm aware of your situation, Mr. Elder. Have a little faith in my judgment. The Indians are too beat down to cause you much trouble. Stay on the trail. They won't come near the army forts."

Moira held up her hand. "Send my bag with him."

"I dunno," the sheriff picked at a spot of lint on his lapel. "That's not part of the deal."

John snorted, then motioned the sheriff farther away from the group of girls. "I need a word. Alone."

The sheriff furrowed his brow and dutifully reined his horse aside. The two bent their heads together in a hushed conversation.

Moira tensed. What on earth was he up to now?

Tony touched her shoulder. "What are they talking about? Can you hear anything?"

"Nope," Moira answered. She sidled closer. She didn't like this. She didn't like this one bit.

What was John Elder saying that he didn't want the girls hearing?

Hazel halted her progress by hugging her leg. "Are we going to jail? I stole some apples from the grocer. I was real hungry. I know I shouldn't have done it."

"Don't worry." The men immediately forgotten, Moira

ran her hands over Hazel's soft curls. "Everything is going to be all right. You'll see."

Darcy snorted.

Tony stuck out her chest. "You got something you want to say? Then say it."

"Why don't I tell them why you're here?" Darcy challenged. "How about that?"

A flush of red crept up Tony's neck.

Moira shushed them. "It's not your fault. It's nobody's fault. We've been blamed for something we didn't do. We're being punished for crimes we didn't commit. It's unfair and it's unjust and we're stuck. He's got all the power and we've got nothing. Fighting among ourselves only makes it worse."

The cowboy pivoted from his conversation, keeping his head down. From the set of his jaw, Moira figured the discussion hadn't gone too well.

Wendell crowded his horse closer. The deputy leered, a half grin on his face. Moira met his challenge. He fisted his hands around the reins, tugging on the bit and sending his horse sidestepping. "I'll say it again, Taylor. You're making a mistake, letting them go. I got nothing to do with this." The deputy dug his heels into his horse's sides and galloped off in a kick of dust.

John adjusted his hat low on his forehead.

The sheriff swiveled in the saddle and followed his deputy's hasty retreat. "You assaulted my deputy. While I'd like to give you a medal for that, I can't. You did ask me for a favor and I'm not completely heartless. I'll see what I can do."

John remained impassive.

"I saw the crew you fired." The sheriff watched for a reaction from the cowboy. "My elderly mother has more gumption than that bunch. Besides, looks to me like you've got plenty of help."

"What's that supposed to mean?"

"Figure it out." The sheriff tipped his hat.

At his exit, they all remained in confused silence, uncertain what to do next. John whirled and kicked the loose pile of kindling near the campfire, scattering the twigs.

Moira sucked in a breath and faced the girls. They cast worried glances between her and the cowboy. She pulled her lower lip between her teeth.

Tony lifted her head. "What are we going to do now?"

"I don't know."

"Well..." Darcy began. "Maybe we should ask the cowboy."

"He doesn't appear to be in a talkative mood," Moira stalled.

Tony punched one fisted hand into the opposite palm. "I'll get him talking. I'll talk some sense right into him."

"No, no," Moira quickly admonished. "I'll...I'll handle this. He's a touch upset. I think a more delicate approach might be in order."

As much as she dreaded the realization, John Elder held their fate in his hands. None of the girls had anything more than their shabby clothing and few coins in their pockets. She glanced at the silver dollar resting in the dirt and got a sour taste in her mouth.

"Suit yourself." Tony shrugged. "But if you need a *less delicate touch,* you let me know."

"I'll do that." Moira squared her shoulders and approached their dubious rescuer. He *did* need something from them, he just didn't know it yet. He didn't deserve to be saddled with a bunch of orphans, but when did anyone get what they deserved?

He didn't look up. Not a good sign. "What now, Mr. Elder?"

A grunt answered her question. Moira cleared her throat. Despite all that was happening, she kept thinking about the cattle. The rest of them had choices. The animals were entirely at the mercy of others. "What are you going to do with the cattle?"

"Nothing I can do." He stared into the distance, his expression resigned. "Leave 'em here, I guess. Once word gets out there's range cattle for the taking, they'll be gone soon enough."

"You'd just leave them?" The action struck her as callous. "For anyone?"

"What else am I going to do? I can't protect you girls and drive the herd at the same time."

Moira searched the desolate horizon. She wasn't spontaneous. She was careful. Deliberate. She folded her clothing in neat squares, she layered her hairbrush and mirror in the folds to avoid breaking them. She arrived at the train station two hours prior to departure. Acting on impulse wasn't her strong suit. Even her spur-of-the-moment trip out west had been meticulously planned—hastily planned, but carefully planned.

How did she make him see their value? She tipped her head to the sky. "That didn't go so bad, did it? Considering we assaulted and confined a deputy sheriff. I mean, after all, none of us is in jail."

Even without looking, she could tell her question had thrown the cowboy off guard. Good. That's what she wanted. If he was off guard she had a better chance.

He grunted. "At least in jail a fellow gets three squares."

"Don't you have any faith in a higher plan? In God's powers?"

"I'd have a lot more faith if He sent me a crew," John mumbled.

Moira stepped closer, crowding his space, forcing him to tip his head back and look at her.

She had one chance to convince him of the impossible. "He did."

Chapter Six

"Whatever idea you've got, it won't work," John spoke.

Moira retreated and he almost mourned her easy capitulation. He needed a fight he could win. Anything to make him feel as though he had a modicum of control over *something*.

John rubbed his face and stared at the ground. For the first time in his life, he was plum out of ideas. Always before he'd found a way, invented a solution, defied the problem. Not this time. This time he was stuck in the middle of nowhere with eight-hundred-head of cattle, four orphans and a woman whose doleful eyes had him wishing he could save the world.

No one could blame him for being out of ideas. No one, not even his brothers could fault him for giving up this time.

Champion lay at his feet and he absently scratched behind one raised ear. As much as it pained him to admit it, the dog seemed to like the name.

Moira had an idea. John guffawed. It wouldn't work. He didn't even know what she was thinking, but he already knew her plan was doomed. He knew because he'd considered everything and all his ideas ended in calamity.

A sound caught his attention and a pair of familiar, scuffed boots came into view. He lifted his head and met Moira's steady gaze. The eyes that had haunted his dreams the previous night. They weren't forlorn anymore. They were determined and that didn't bode well for either of them. Tension tightened around his shoulder muscles.

She knotted her arms over her chest. "You said you were crossing the border into Kansas and traveling on to Cimarron Springs. How far is that?"

"It's about seventy-five miles to Fort Preble. That's the closest thing to civilization between here and Kansas. And there's nothing in between Fort Preble and Cimarron Springs except for a couple of cow towns that aren't safe for women and children."

"How many miles can the cattle travel per day?"

"About fifteen."

Moira did a quick mental calculation. "That's only five days to Fort Preble. You can find another crew there."

"In terms of math, yes, it's five days." He bit off a curse. "Except math is just numbers. Out here it's wind and weather and rugged trail. You can't put that in an equation."

"We'll drive your cattle as far as Fort Preble."

"Who is 'we'?"

"The girls and I."

John barked out a laugh. "Thanks for the joke, but I'm not in the mood just yet."

"The way I see it, you don't have any choice."

"Oh, I have choices." He bluffed. "Lots of choices."

She tilted her head. "Name one."

"I'm still sorting out the details," John grumbled. So much for bluffing Miss Moira O'Mara.

"The older three can ride well enough," she continued. "Tony can rope. We're your best option."

"Do you know how much those cattle weigh?" He

scoffed. "You'd be hurt or killed before you crossed the Snake River. And the Snake River is about twenty yards away. You'd be ground into dust by Fort Preble."

Her chin tilted up a notch and she braced her feet apart, planting her hands on her hips. "You said children drove twelve-hundred-head of cattle twice the distance. Why can't we?"

"Because you're not boys. You're girls."

"What's the difference?"

John stood and mirrored her implacable stance. He didn't relish the task, but she needed a lesson. Conjuring his most intimidating glare, he lowered his voice into a deep, frightening growl. "The difference between boys and girls is weight and strength."

She drew herself up another notch. "What we lack in size we make up for in brains. I've seen plenty of cow-hands. They're not real smart."

She had him there. "The cows aren't real smart either. That's why you have to be strong."

"You think women aren't strong?" Her lips tightened. "Do you have any idea what we go through each day? Have you ever worn a corset?"

John raised his arms in supplication. "I think we're wandering off the topic."

"Have you ever had your hair curled with a flaming hot iron?"

"Can't say that I have."

"Look at this." She palmed a ringlet from her forehead, revealing a faint raised scar. "That's from a curling iron. And I've barely scratched the surface."

He studied the shimmering halo of brilliant red curls cascading over her shoulders. "You shouldn't be using an iron anyway. Nature has done a fine job already."

"My hair is not the issue," she spoke through gritted teeth. "Please stick to the subject."

John gaped. "Don't get mad at me. You brought it up."

"I was trying to explain the difficulties of being a woman."

"Truce?" he said. He'd never understood the complexities of a woman's beauty regime, and not one word of this conversation left him wanting more information. Which was the exact flaw in her argument.

He had her now. "Women can be strong. But you don't have women, you have girls." *Aha!* She couldn't dispute that. "And I'm not risking the lives of girls."

Let Miss Moira O'Mara argue his logic now.

Her expression turned incredulous. "Then you'll just let the cattle starve here waiting for someone to stumble upon their corpses?"

"Don't change the subject when I'm winning."

"This isn't about winning or losing. This is about honor and integrity."

His ears grew hot and his vision blurred in a haze of red. "Don't you lecture me on honor and integrity. I could have left you in that alley."

"You still wouldn't have a crew."

"I could have gone back into town. I could have gotten my old crew back."

"Would you have taken them back? Really?"

He was many things, but he wasn't a liar. "No." He kept his gaze averted. He recognized the accusation in her voice. This wasn't the first time he'd disappointed someone, and it wouldn't be last. Ruth Ann had accused him of being too easy going to be a good husband. His brothers thought he was too reckless to make a good cattleman.

For once in his life he was being thoughtful and cautious, and he'd found the one person who wanted him to return to his old ways. "I told you. I'll drive the cattle toward richer pasture. Eventually, word will spread that there's free cattle for the taking. The rest will take care of itself."

He'd rather keep Moira safe than win her approval. It was that simple.

"Then you're quitting?" she asked.

His hackles rose. "No. I'm not quitting. I'm walking away from an impossible situation while ensuring the best possible outcome."

"That's just a fancy way of saying you're quitting." Moira smirked.

A low growl lodged in the back of his throat. If John didn't know better, he'd have thought his brothers sent Miss Moira O'Mara to torture him. It was as though he was being lectured by all six of them except the view was better. Yep. She was all half dozen of his brothers rolled into one beautiful, infuriating, redheaded package.

John scrubbed his hands down his face. There was no way he was winning a verbal sparring match. He was outgunned and outflanked. The best choice was a calculated retreat. "I'm not playing word games with you. This conversation is over."

"Fine. Then you're abandoning your cattle to anyone who sees fit to take them."

"Yes. Exactly." He huffed.

Oh no.

John staggered a step and rubbed his chest. He was huffing. Men didn't huff. Only one day with the girls and already they were changing him. This was not a good sign at all. Squaring his shoulders, he refocused his thoughts.

He might have lost his dignity but at least Moira finally understood the bigger picture. "I'm leaving the cattle and taking you girls to Fort Preble. That about sums it up."

"Excellent." She pivoted on her heel and stalked toward the campsite, tossing a last triumphant glare over her shoulder.

John studied her ramrod-stiff back and a cacophony of alarm bells sounded in his head. She hadn't won. Which begged the question: Why was she acting as though she'd won? What kind of trick was that?

Pops, who'd kept himself hidden since the sheriff's arrival, chose that unfortunate moment to reappear. He sipped his coffee and followed her progress. "You should go into town more often. I don't recall a more exciting cattle drive. Nope. I do not. And that's saying something. I've been around a while."

"Don't you have a stew that needs stirring or something?" Feeling like he'd been picked up and dropped by a twister, John struggled for a reply. "What does she think she's doing?"

Before his suspicious gaze, Moira gathered her charges. Keeping her voice low, she talked and gestured. Champion barked and danced around the group. The girls shot him concerned looks every so often but mostly kept their attention focused on Moira. After a moment, a wave of nods rippled over their bent heads.

The roar of alarm bells in John's head grew deafening. They were most decidedly up to mischief. Judging from the determined looks on their deceptively innocent faces, a decision had been made. The last time they'd put together an idea as a group, they'd dropped onto his head and gotten him banned from Fool's End. Well, this time he was prepared. He'd defuse this round of dynamite before they got him blown out of Indian Territory altogether.

Her expression smug, Moira approached him once more. "We've reached a decision."

John crossed his arms over his chest. "About what?"

"You've abandoned your cattle, Mr. Elder. We hereby assume responsibility for the herd."

He leaned closer, turning his face and angling one ear in her direction. "Say again?"

"You heard me."

John reared back. "If you're thinking what I think you're thinking, you'd better think again."

"I'm thinking you've gotten too much sun today. You aren't making a lick of sense. Would you like to sit in the shade for a moment?"

"I'm making perfect sense." He needed sleep, that was all. After a good night's rest, everything would make sense again. "I don't need shade."

"You're also a touch cranky."

He ignored the trap. A denial only sounded petulant.

"If the herd is up for grabs," she said. "We're taking it."

John searched for an ally. "Pops. Help me out."

The older man didn't quite meet his gaze. "She makes a sound case."

Rocking back on his heels, John absorbed the blow of betrayal from his most trusted advisor. "Don't tell me you're on their side?"

"I'm not taking sides," Pops began in a conciliatory tone. "I admire the lady's gumption. And she has a sound point. If you're abandoning the herd, she's got just as much right to the cattle as anybody else."

While John mulled over the dubious logic, Moira stepped forward. Her cheeks were flushed and she appeared taller somehow. "There's another thing. We'd like to trade twenty head of cattle for five horses."

John touched his forehead. She was right about one thing, the sun had obviously baked his brain. He must be hallucinating because she couldn't possibly be suggesting what he thought she was suggesting. "They're my cattle. I can't trade *my* cattle for *my* horses."

"The way I see it, you and Pops can lead twenty head easy enough. You can sell them in Kansas."

She was definitely taller. Had she changed shoes? John checked her boots. Nope. They were the same ratty pair she'd been sporting. "I'll give you that. But why would I make a trade with my own horses?"

"Because I counted ten horses in the remuda." She explained as though the argument made perfect sense. "Without your men, you don't need that many."

Pops bobbed his head in agreement. "That's true."

"Stop!" John shouted then immediately lowered his voice. "Stop helping me."

"I'm not the problem here." Pops lifted both shoulders, sloshing coffee over the side of his mug. "Since Moira and the girls have claimed the herd, the cattle are hers to trade."

"I... You..." How could the lunatic proposal make sense to one person, let alone two? And two people he had previously considered sane, no less. "You've both gone loco. They're my horses and my cattle."

"Not after today," Pops added, warming right up to the idea like a snake to an occupied sleeping bag. "The way I figure, it's a good deal. You won't get that trade in Cimarron Springs, that's for certain."

"I'm dreaming. I must be dreaming."

A sharp pain stabbed his arm. He glanced down as Hazel released her fingers.

"Nope," she said. "You're not dreaming. I pinched you."

John rubbed the spot on his arm. "Not you, too!"

The kid did have strength, he'd give her that. He'd have a bruise come morning.

Moira ignored his outburst and stared him down. "Do we have a deal or not? I'd like the ten horses for rotation, but I figure we can make do with five since we're girls. I figure we're lighter than men are and we'll set an easier pace. The horses will be under less strain."

"You can't possibly be serious." John considered his next words carefully. Since his first, logical reasons weren't working, he decided on another tactic. "What are you going to do with all those cattle if, and that's a big 'if,' you make it as far as Fort Preble?"

"We'll sell them, of course. The fort will have plenty of buyers. We'll split the money and start over. It's not the best solution, but it'll do for now."

For an agonizing moment he followed her logic and found her argument sound.

Then he remembered the whole idea was impossible. "It's true. You've all gone crazy. I'm the only one here making sense." He opened and closed his mouth a few times. "I hear myself talking, but no one is listening. You'll never make it across the Snake River."

"Say," Pops interrupted John's rant. "Can I take my ten head of cattle and add them to the girls? I think I'll hitch a ride with the herd."

John felt like he'd been gut-shot. "Quit fooling around."

"The way I figure it," Pops babbled on. "Six of us make better odds than five. And I know the way. We'll point the cattle north and take our chances. What do we have to lose? The herd has come this far already. They're trail broke by now. Seasoned. All the fight is out of them. Northern Indian Territory into Kansas is the easiest stretch. The terrain is flat, the grass is holding out and there's plenty of water holes."

"I… You… But…" When had he lost control of the situation? John eyed the source of his problems. He'd lost control the moment Miss O'Mara had kicked him in the head. She must have shaken loose his brain. "You still don't see the point. You can't trade cattle that don't belong to you."

"They don't belong to you either."

"Yes. They do."

"Then what are you going to do with them?"

"Well I'm not handing them over to a bunch of girls. Children. Greenhorns no less."

Pops glared. "I'm not a greenhorn and I'm certainly not

a child. I'm experienced. I'll take the cattle. I'll even keep the same deal. You can drive your share, the ten head, all the way if you want. Start over in Cimarron Springs. We'll keep the extra horses."

"I didn't make a deal," John's voice cracked beneath the strain of his disbelief. "There was no deal. That's the whole point."

Moira shook her head. "You're talking in circles again, Mr. Elder. And wasting daylight in the process. I've got a busy day teaching these girls the rudimentary skills and then we've got a stream to cross."

"It's a river."

"It's two feet deep in most places with more sandbars than water. It's not exactly the Missouri."

"There are places that drop off to five or six feet. And you don't even know the rudimentary skills yourself. How are you going to teach them to somebody else?"

"She's got good instincts." Pops tossed his coffee dredges onto the red earth and tugged on his suspenders. "I'll pack up camp." He stuck out an elbow. "Join me, Miss O'Mara?"

Behaving as though John wasn't an active participant in the conversation, Pops and Moira linked elbows and walked away.

The other four girls shifted on their feet and eyed him as though he was a stick of dynamite with a lit fuse. He recognized the emotions flitting across their faces—curiosity, doubt, fear, and worst of all, excitement. They were wary yet fascinated all at the same time.

He clutched his throbbing head. "What just happened?"

Tony chucked him on the shoulder. "You just got outwitted."

John rubbed his shoulder, still bruised from his rescue the previous evening and Hazel's pinch. "I did not get outwitted. You can't reason with crazy. Therefore, you cannot be outwitted by it."

The dark-haired girl scratched her head. "I know you think you're making sense, but I understood Moira a lot better."

John blew out a breath. He'd ceased understanding his own reasoning somewhere around the time he'd traded his own horses for his own cattle and lost his cook in the process. "I can't convince Moira, but you've got some cattle experience, Tony. I could tell by the way you rode yesterday. You know the dangers."

Her expression hardened and raw pain flickered in her dark eyes. "I did grow up on a ranch. My pa was a hand and my ma was a cook in the big house. Then the influenza came. My whole family got sick, but only I survived. The owner said I lived because I was special. He said I was so special, someone would surely pick me from the orphan train. But I knew he was lying, see? Because if I was such a great kid, why didn't they let me stay on the ranch? That was the only home I'd ever known. But I wasn't special. I was just another orphan."

John imagined Tony losing one family member after another and then being displaced from the only home she'd ever known. "You are special. He was a fool for not seeing that."

"I know that. My uncle said he'd come for me once he had money saved. Except the chaperone on the train stole my letter. That was my last chance at having a real family. At least that's what I thought. I have another chance. That's a good feeling and I'm not letting it go."

"This isn't the solution."

"I also know what I've left behind," she continued. "I'm not sure you do."

She turned away, leaving him in uneasy silence. He knew what they had to lose. He knew all too well. They were risking their very lives. That's why he couldn't let this cattle drive go forward.

"Are we going to jail?" Hazel asked. "Darcy says we're going to jail."

"Darcy is wrong." Moira cast a surreptitious glance over her shoulder.

John and Pops were engaged in a heated conversation. Well, more specifically, John was involved in a heated conversation. Pops kept his head down, carefully packing the chuck wagon. He offered the occasional nod, never looking up, never speaking.

Moira pulled a wad of bills from her pocket and let the folded edges unfurl in her hand. The meager offering represented everything she owned in the world. All of her possessions. She'd left everything else behind in a town that didn't even have a proper name as far as she could tell. Who named a town Fool's End, anyway?

Her scarred leather valise remained in her room at the hotel. A change of clothes, a few toiletries, her sketchbook. It hadn't seemed like much at the time. Except it was more than she had now. Nearly twenty-one years old and she had nothing to show for her life. *Nothing.* Hardly any money, no possessions, no sketches, no family.

Her mother's brush and mirror were in that bag. Moira tamped down the flood of sorrow.

Sucking in a fortifying breath, she took the sight of the peacefully grazing cattle. She might not have anything of substance, but she had a plan. And that counted for something.

She tipped back her head and offered up a quick prayer for guidance. She wasn't a leader. She wasn't anything. Yet the girls looked to her as though she was the answer to *their* prayers.

She was just Moira O'Mara. Unfortunately, that *didn't*

count for much. "We're not going to jail, but we can't go back to town."

"Good riddance, I say," Tony declared. "That town was full of nothing but thieves and criminals."

"You'd know," Darcy sneered.

"Hey!"

Sarah brushed the hair from her forehead. "Leaving is fine by me. But what happens after we reach our destination?"

"You heard her," Tony spoke. "We're gonna sell the herd and start over."

Darcy shook her head. "Impossible. We don't know what we're doing."

Sarah shrugged a shoulder. "It's not complicated. Like Moira says, we just have to be smarter than the cattle."

Tony snorted. "Yeah. You think you can manage that, Darcy?"

The older girl lunged and Moira snatched her by the collar. "This will never work if we waste our energy fighting. All we have right now is each other."

"If all we have to count on is each other, then this whole idea is doomed," Darcy grumbled.

"Goodbye, then." Tony sketched a wave. "Those cattle are dollar signs for all of us. We've got nothing but our wits right now. With money I can find my uncle. I'm sure he's looking for me now. We'll start over."

Hazel stuck out her lower lip. "This doesn't feel right. We can't steal Mr. Elder's cows. Not after everything he's done for us already. He found Miss Molly." She displayed her mud-splattered rag doll with its wilted yarn braids. "What's he going to do without his cows?"

Moira clenched her jaw. Mr. Elder had made his choice. Losing his cattle wasn't her fault. She hadn't asked to be kidnapped and she hadn't asked to be rescued. She'd been minding her own business and now she was good and trapped. If Mr. Elder was too pigheaded to do the same, it wasn't her problem. He had a willing and able crew camped out right beneath his nose, and he'd ignored their offer. He'd rather sacrifice his future than trust them, and that was his own downfall.

They were useful. Someday maybe he'd see that.

She leaned in and lowered her voice. The girls huddled closer. "Mr. Elder has made his choice. It's not our responsibility to make that choice more palatable to him."

Hazel frowned. "What's palatable?"

"It means tasty," Tony cut in.

Moira sighed. "Close enough. We don't have to make his decisions tasty for him. He might have helped us out last night, sure. I'm grateful. Things have gotten complicated, though. He's done helping us now. We're on our own."

"I still think it's stealing," Hazel grumbled.

Tony rubbed her chin. "Those cattle are worth a lot of money if we sell them."

Moira's stomach dropped. She hadn't calculated the animals' worth. "How much?"

Tony named a sum that raised a gasp from her rapt audience.

"Are you certain?" Moira's hands trembled.

"Maybe more. We're in army country now. The rancher always liked army folks. Said they had deep pockets."

As she considered the tremendous sum of money, Moira hung her head. How could John Elder walk away from all that? Had he so little faith in their abilities that he wasn't even willing to try?

"I agree with Hazel." Sarah remained somber. "It feels like we're stealing. It's not right."

Moira felt a flush of heat creep up her neck. They didn't deserve that much if they only took the herd as far as Fort Preble. "What if we sell the herd and give the money to

Mr. Elder? We'll only take fair wages." At a sudden loss, she faced Tony. "What is a fair wage?"

"I heard the boys talking plenty of times back on the ranch. Fifty silver pieces for a drive, start to finish."

The girls gasped and Darcy's eyes widened.

"That'd take forever to earn." Sarah spoke, her voice filled with wonder. "I worked in a hotel once. That was two bits a week."

Moira didn't know whether to laugh or cry. "This is more. A lot more." With fifty silver dollars she could hire a Pinkerton detective. Or even two. They'd find Tommy for certain. "We're not stealing. We're helping him out. Like when we rode his horses back from the livery."

Sarah chewed her bottom lip. "I suppose if we give Mr. Elder the money from the cattle, it's all right. You know, if we only kept our fair wages."

"Well, we may not have started this," Moira said. "But we can finish. We'll take our share of the pay and give the rest to Mr. Elder. That way we're all in the clear. He can't fault us for that."

Tony jerked a thumb over one shoulder. "I don't think he wants our help."

John had saddled his horse. He mounted and kept his head low as he kicked his horse into a gentle canter.

"See? He's leaving."

Moira's heart shattered. Without his expertise and guidance, the future loomed before her, bleak and foreboding. She'd known he was a loner. She'd known he didn't want a bunch of orphans around beyond a certain reluctant obligation. Yet somewhere in her heart she'd hoped he was different. She'd hoped he'd stay.

"Mr. Elder isn't part of this anymore. It doesn't matter how many people quit on us as long as we don't quit on each other. Right?"

Something passed between Tony and Darcy. A look

Moira didn't quite understand. Yet the odd exchange stirred the hairs on the back of her neck. The moment quickly passed and their expressions mirrored acknowledgment. Whatever bit of silent communication they'd shared seemed to have set them in accord.

She'd keep an eye on those two. There was an undercurrent there. Moira returned her attention to the other girls. If anyone dissented, the plan was lost. "Are we all in agreement? A show of hands."

Tony's hand shot up first, followed immediately by Darcy, then Sarah, then Hazel. Moira felt the heat of excitement flowing through her limbs. Her blood pumped, invigorated. It felt good. Having a goal. Having a purpose.

She glanced at the kick of dust John Elder had left in his wake and an unexpected ache settled in her heart, shadowing her excitement. She shook off the pall. There was no use wishing things had turned out any different. She refused to beg John Elder for help.

Moira cleared her throat. "Mr. Elder might not believe in us, but that doesn't matter. We believe in each other. We have each other. And that's enough for me."

She shook off the cowboy's rejection. They were doing something good. Something worthwhile. He could run as far as he wanted, but he couldn't run from himself. She'd learned that truth the hard way. Some lessons were like that. He'd find out for himself.

John rode a safe distance away before stopping. Once out of view of the campsite, he dismounted and sat on a squat boulder. Nothing but red soil and the occasional shrub tree met his gaze. He glanced at Champion. The animal circled and whined.

"Don't look at me. It's not my fault." John snorted. "Don't get that judgmental gleam in those brown eyes of yours. I suppose you'd have stayed, too."

Another high-pitched whine met his question.

"Well, of course you'd rather stay with the girls. They've done nothing but coddle you the whole time. And feed you."

Champion nuzzled his hand.

"Yeah. You've gone and let yourself go all right. But we can't save them. We'll follow from a safe distance. Then, when things go horribly wrong, and things are bound to go horribly wrong, we'll be there."

Another whine.

"What's that supposed to mean?" Champion tilted his head to one side. John scoffed. "You don't actually think they can do this, do you? What do a bunch of girls know about driving cattle? About riding the trail, about hardship...."

He kept thinking of Moira's haunted eyes. She wasn't a quitter that was for certain. She could be married with a family of her own instead of searching for a brother she hadn't seen in years.

The thought led him to his own brothers. After Robert had lost his wife, their brother Jack, a Texas Ranger at the time, had set out to find the killer. He'd searched for over a year, never giving up, never slowing. The killer's trail had led him right to a lovely widow and her newborn girl. Even when Jack had known the truth might break her heart, that the widow's late husband had been a killer, he hadn't quit. His perseverance had paid off. He and the widow were married and their family had grown with two more boys.

John hung his head. Moira had questioned his honor. He was trying to save their lives and someday they'd thank him for it. Maybe not soon. But someday.

Champion barked and padded in the direction of the herd, then glanced over one shoulder.

"No. We're not going yet. They have to see how hard this is. We can't help yet."

The dog lifted both ears.

"You won't convince me."

Another bark.

"You do what you want. I'm done with the lot of you."

John pushed himself upright. He glanced around and found Champion sitting in the same spot, staring in the direction of the herd.

"Dog!"

Nothing.

"Champion."

Nothing.

Of all the betrayals he'd felt that day, this one stung the worst.

Chapter Seven

Moira couldn't stop looking over her shoulder, searching the horizon for any sign of John Elder. She missed the way his hat rode low on his forehead. The way his left hand curled on his thigh when he rode. She couldn't help wishing he'd stayed.

It was a foolish wish, and she was foolish for caring. Too bad her traitorous heart wouldn't listen.

The girls had saddled the horses and scouted the river for the lowest crossing. Pops had taken Hazel and crossed the water in the chuck wagon, scouting the next leg of the trail. When they'd discovered the point where the water stayed below the wheels, they marked the spot with a pile of stones.

After gathering the group at camp, Tony sketched out their path in the dirt. Moira stood guard for any sign of dissent or rebellion. To her immense relief, once the girls had declared their allegiance, the planning had fallen into place. Only one piece left her uneasy. While Tony had the most experience, the girls looked toward Moira for the ultimate guidance.

Which left her as the only adult in the group. The person in charge.

Moira ducked her head and tied a scarf around her neck as modest protection against the sun. "It's past noon, we should have left hours ago. We'll have to make the best progress we can today."

Tony stuck out her chin. "The hardest part is crossing the river. Once we're over, the rest will be easy."

Moira linked her hands behind her back and braced her feet apart. She'd gone over everything with Tony and Pops earlier. The instructions were simple, the execution deceptively straightforward. "Let's go over this one more time. Pops has taken the wagon on ahead with Hazel. Tony will be the point man. I'll take the right flank and watch the swing."

She paused and studied their reactions, breathing a sigh of relief when no one questioned her orders. "Once we drive the herd out of the gulley, we'll turn them east toward the creek. Sarah will watch the left flank. That leaves Darcy as the drag man. It's a small herd, and while we'll lose sight of Pops and Hazel, we won't lose sight of each other. Since we might not hear each other over the noise, don't forget the signal. Pops gave us each a red bandanna. If you get into trouble, wave your bandanna. We'll halt and regroup. Does anyone have any questions?"

The girls remained silent, solemn. After a moment, Sarah spoke, "I feel like we should have a name."

"What kind of name?"

"I dunno. For us. Something that says who we are."

Moira laughed. "How about the Calico Cowboys?"

The girls exchanged slow grins.

Sarah adjusted her bonnet. "We're the Calico Cowboys."

"The Calico Cowboys," Darcy repeated. "I like that, too."

Sarah closed her eyes and took a deep breath. "I think we should offer up a prayer."

The girls nodded.

They clasped hands and formed a circle. With Darcy

on her right and Tony on her left, Sarah began, "Dear Lord. Please keep us safe on our travels. Guide our feet and guide our thoughts toward the path of righteousness. Give us peace on our journey. Amen."

"Amen," the girls spoke in unison.

They took their places and scrambled onto their mounts without assistance. Moira led her mount near a large boulder and clambered astride. She'd been getting tips from Tony and she'd chosen the easiest mount, the one John had assigned her last evening. If she mostly let the horse have its way, it seemed to know what to do.

Adjusting her skirts in the saddle, Moira recalled the previous night, how John had clasped her waist, his hands strong and sure. She quickly brushed the memory aside. He was gone now. They were on their own. For everything. Even something as simple as mounting a horse.

With a last glance toward the group, Tony kicked her horse into a gentle canter toward the point. Sarah and Darcy took their positions. Moira heaved a sigh. It was all well and good hearing how things must be done. Listening and doing were two separate things. They had to make this happen with no practice.

Moira swallowed around the lump in her throat. The cattle were enormous. They munched the grass, the horns occasionally clacking each other or a protruding rock.

She sat for a moment, nonplussed. Of all the things they'd planned for and discussed, she'd never once considered the mechanics of stirring the beasts into action.

"He yaw!" Moira shouted. "Go."

The enormous bull nearest her lifted his head for a moment before resuming his unhurried grazing. "Go on, you lazy beast. We've got five miles before sunset."

The animal snorted.

From the flank and the drag, Moira heard the faint echo

of Sarah and Darcy joining her encouraging shouts. The cattle paid them no mind.

Moira chewed her lip. This particular dilemma had never even occurred to her. That they wouldn't even be able to start the herd. She hollered louder. Nothing happened. Well, one or two of the cattle wandered closer. If she didn't know any better, she'd think they were mocking her. One enormous bull shook its horns left and right, jiggling the muscles along its neck. Oh, yes. That animal was most definitely mocking her.

Sucking in a deep breath, she hollered again. And again. Exhausted, she shouted one last time. "Move, you stubborn bea—beasts!" her voice cracked.

Darcy reined her horse closer. "At least the drummer won't have any trouble finding us."

Moira brushed the hair from her forehead, wishing she had a hat. "We'll figure it out. Take the flank again."

As a last-ditch effort, she decided to rein closer. The horse jerked right instead. Moira whipped around and realized someone held the bridle.

John Elder met her astonished gaze. "I don't recommend going any closer. It's not safe."

"I suppose you've come to gloat at us." Moira kept her gaze averted. The humiliation stung. "As you can probably see, we can't even get them started."

The cowboy squinted into the distance. "Most tasks are more difficult than they appear."

"Is that what you came back to say? How encouraging. Thank you so much for the confidence. As you can tell, it's going swimmingly thus far."

He kept his focus on the horizon. "I see that."

Moira remained stubbornly silent. She wouldn't give him the satisfaction of seeing her frustration. "You want us to quit now and save you the trouble."

John placed his gloved hand over hers. "I'm keeping you safe."

She felt the warmth of his fingers. His touch was firm and weighty, comforting. Her body swayed toward his strength. She snatched away her hand. There was no use growing accustomed to something fleeting.

Swallowing hard against her potent feelings, she avoided his gaze. "Are you going to help us or not?"

"The first sign of trouble and I'm putting a stop to this crazy stunt. Is that a deal?"

Her lips parted in surprise. "I—"

"Cover your ears."

Moira was still staring in confusion when he let out an earsplitting whistle. The cattle picked up their heads. The biggest, a dappled red bull who'd been staring her down all morning took a resigned step forward. The old moocher tossed a baleful glare over one enormous shoulder. Moira stuck out her tongue.

Once their leader set off, the others soon followed. First, one ambled forward, then another and another. Soon, like a great rumbling train they formed a line, moving together three to five abreast. The flank swung toward Moira. John nudged his horse toward her and pointed.

"Move ahead. They're used to this. Don't get too close. Stay within ten or twenty feet. That's enough. Give the horse his head, he'll do all the work for you. It's his job. He's been trained by the best."

A wicked grin tipped up the corner of his mouth.

"Trained by the best, you say?" Moira noted his proud nod. "And who would that be? One of your older brothers?"

His expression shuttered and she instantly regretted her teasing. He'd helped them out and she'd rewarded his assistance with an insult. She hadn't meant...what did it matter? He'd taken her prodding the wrong way and she had only herself to blame.

He tipped his hat. "Keep this pace. I'll stick with you for a spell. Once you're started, I'll check on the others."

Moira let slack in the reins. The horse maintained a steady distance from the cattle. Their hooves kicked up dust, rumbling the ground beneath their feet.

"They're moving!" Moira shouted over the thunder of hoofbeats. "Can you see that? They're actually moving. We did that."

He appeared completely oblivious to their remarkable accomplishment.

She reached out and yanked on John's sleeve. "We're doing it, don't you see? We're actually making this happen!"

Their gazes clashed and her breath lodged in her throat. The space between them sparked with emotion. The air crystallized around her, full of promise and renewal. For a moment anything seemed possible. More than that, *everything* seemed possible.

He reached in his saddlebag and pulled out a pair of leather gloves. "Take these."

"Is that your only pair?"

"The only extra."

"Thank you."

Moira reached across the distance and accepted the gloves. John held the halter of her horse as she awkwardly tugged the enormous gloves over her fingers. She'd give them to Tony first thing. She'd have asked John to pass them on, but she had a feeling her request would put him in an awkward situation. He couldn't outfit them all and pointing out the shortfall only exposed their weaknesses.

They'd scrounged up the bandannas that morning and managed hats for everyone save Moira.

She set her chin in a stubborn line. They'd take care of themselves. "And thank you for coming back."

"You won't be thanking me for long. This isn't going to be easy."

"You think it's been easy for those girls up to this point?"

John tossed her a sharp glance. "I don't suppose it has."

"I'm betting they're tougher than they look."

"What about you, Miss Moira O'Mara? Are you up to the challenge?"

Moira thought of the endless hours of rolling cigars. The pungent scent of tobacco that permeated her clothes and hair and leached its way beneath her very fingernails. The pads of her fingers had been perpetually darkened, perpetually calloused. The work was easy. Monotonous. And it gave her too much time for thinking. Too much time for thinking how nice it would be without the infernal tick, tick, tick of Mr. Gifford's watch. He'd fill the presses with the completed cigars at each interval, and if a space remained empty, some punishment was meted out. Sometimes it was no break, sometimes no dinner.

Moira shook off the memories. "I know a thing or two about hard work."

Her answer must have mollified him because he lapsed into the silence. A familiar silence that once again gave her too much time for thinking.

When she'd gone to the Giffords', she'd thought she was stepping into a dream. At first she'd thought their fortunes had improved. But it had all been a distortion. The Giffords were just another false facade. Once the doors closed, the beautiful picture had blackened. They were all pretending, pretending to be something they weren't.

It was exhausting keeping up appearances.

Moira glanced around her. Out here everything was stripped away, elemental. There were no rocks, no trees to cower behind. There was just wind and brush and miles of nothing. She was dirtier than she'd ever been. Her hair needed a good washing and soon she was bound to attract as many flies as the cattle. The primitive conditions liberated her soul. No false fronts here. This was survival, pure and simple.

John's question hung in the air between them. *Are you up to the challenge?* Moira squinted into the distance. Tony waved and Moira sketched a hesitant wave in return. A sudden ache squeezed her heart. Developing a relationship with the girls wasn't wise. Who knew what the future held for any of them? After they sold the cattle, they'd be scattered like spring blossoms in the wind. The closer they grew, the more difficult the parting. She'd use her age as a barrier and hold herself apart.

John's expression turned grim as he watched the play of emotions on her face. "Surviving in the city is still different than making it in the country."

"At least out here you know the enemy."

"How do you mean?"

"It's easier to hide among people. Easier to put up a false front. Out here there's no hiding."

"There's nothing to hide behind, that's for certain." He swept his arm in a wide arc. "What about you? Are you hiding from something?"

"Disappointment, I suppose."

He was far too perceptive for his own good. Moira recalled an advertisement seen in the St. Louis train station. A tableau featuring a handsome, suited father holding open a book while his equally perfect family gathered around him. Those folks only existed in pencil drawings. Back in that old cow town, in the bottom of her leather bag, she kept the picture she'd sketched from the advertisement. She couldn't get the image out of her mind. She wanted that picture. She wanted those relaxed smiles.

When she pictured Tommy, it was like picturing that perfect life. She'd have a dress that touched the floor and didn't show any ankle. A dress she'd pick out herself for once. A dress that no one else had ever worn. A pair of boots that fit right and didn't need papers stuck in the toe.

"Hey," the cowboy interrupted her thoughts. "Forget I said anything. We're all disappointed in something. This wasn't exactly what I was expecting either."

Moira forced an easy grin. "I'm sorry things didn't turn out for you."

She'd been shortsighted. Caught up in her own survival. She hadn't given his predicament much thought and he'd lost as much as the rest of them. More even. More because he had more to lose. Since he had a home, she'd convinced herself he wasn't suffering. A selfish oversight on her part. He deserved compassion and sympathy as much as any one of the girls.

The cowboy rested his wrist on his saddle horn. "Nothing ever turns out the way we picture. Sometimes it's better and sometimes it's worse. Right now I'm going to see it through."

"I guess that's fair."

He halted his horse and caught her mount by the bridle. "I don't regret the past twenty-four hours. No matter what happens, no matter what I said before. I'm glad it was me in that alley. It terrifies me when I think of all the ways that could have gone wrong."

Her head throbbed. She hadn't known it until that moment, but she'd needed to hear his confession. He might resent the situation, but he didn't resent them—the girls and Moira.

"You're good to say so."

"It's true."

He released the bridle and her horse shied away. "If I'd have known how things were going to turn out, I'd have taken a bath before I left yesterday. I'd give anything to feel clean again," she said.

"You're cleaner than Wendell, that's for certain."

Moira gave a ruthless laugh. "His hair was held to his head with dirt and grease. I bet if he gave it a good washing, it'd all fall out."

"He'd probably look better."

Moira jerked her chin toward Tony. "You should check on the others."

"Sure. Keep the flank in line. Remember what I said, let your mount do the work. Signal if you have trouble."

"I will."

"And don't get too close. The horns are lethal."

"I won't."

"And don't—"

"Enough," Moira cried. "We'll be in Canada before you finish this lecture."

Looking sheepish, John tipped his hat once more and kicked his horse into a canter. "I'll be back around."

"I'm sure you will."

She watched his progress, feeling the loss of his company. Sun sparked off the Snake River in the distance and Moira shivered. If she didn't screw up her courage for the next test, the whole drive was doomed.

She'd never found the right moment to admit that crossing the river terrified her.

"Well, Mr. Elder," Tony said, lifting the brim of her leather hat. "Looks like we've reached our first test."

The ground sloped beneath his horse's hooves, driving them inexorably downward toward the riverbed. "That sure didn't take long."

John had circled around the herd, checking on each girl in turn. Despite his worst fears, they handled themselves well. All the while, he kept thinking of Moira's obvious joy when they'd started the herd moving that morning. He'd never seen such elation from such a simple task. They hadn't saved the world. They hadn't done anything really. He'd whistled and the cattle had done what they'd been doing for the past several weeks. Champion nipped at their heels, spurring them into action, just as the animal had been trained. Nothing very special. The cattle responded by habit, following each other nose to tail.

Yet the simple task had lit Moira's face as though he'd given her a new pony on Christmas morning.

She remained at the center of his attention, the enchanting freckles scattered like buckshot over her cheeks and nose.

Near as he could tell, he'd gotten outwitted because he let her. At least that's what he was telling himself. Sparring with Moira left him invigorated, rejuvenated.

He fisted his left hand and braced his knuckles against his thigh. Over the past few weeks he'd forgotten how much he loved riding the trail, how much he relished the freedom and the untamed spaces. Not that he didn't enjoy modern conveniences. He liked staying in town just as much as the next fellow. He was looking forward to having his own house. To building his own ranch.

Once he had his own cowhands, he'd see things were done his way.

Tony snapped her fingers. "Are you listening?"

John started. "What were you saying?"

She indicated a spot along the riverbank. "That's the pile of rocks we left to mark the shallowest passage."

He shook his head, clearing his thoughts. He'd get them all killed if he didn't stay focused. "You already scouted the crossing?"

"Of course."

"I'll take the lead across with you. After the first half of the herd makes it, I'll circle back around and check the flanks. If one of the cattle gets into trouble, don't go near it. They'll thrash about and you risk getting killed."

"Okay."

"Keep an eye out for strays. Even with the rain we had yesterday, the river is shallow. The cattle are accustomed to the routine by now, but one or two of them still might balk. Let me know if you run into trouble. Don't push them, though. Let Champion and me handle that."

"Mr. Elder," Tony said, her cheeks flush with excitement. "If you don't quit talking, we'll still be here come next spring."

John sheepishly tugged on his ear. "I'll lead the way."

"This'll be easier than roping a penned calf."

A half grin lifted the corner of his mouth. He'd expected a lot of things. He'd expected uncertainty and caution. He hadn't expected the overwhelming excitement and enthusiasm. Their eager anticipation of the adventure reminded him of his first cattle drive. How long ago had that been? Seemed like forever since he'd been young.

Tony kicked off beside him and together they splashed into the river. John's horse slipped for the first few steps, then caught its footing. As the chill water gushed into his boots, he hissed in a breath. The nights were cooler up north, and the river's chill temperature brought the tale. He hadn't much time before the first frost.

A splash sounded behind him and he followed the rumbling progress of his finest bull. A great beast of an animal with a mean temper and an insatiable appetite. If John made it as far as Cimarron Springs, this bull was his best asset. As the animal pushed ahead, unhampered by the rushing water, he tamped down his fears.

Behind the bull, the first line of cattle followed without a hitch and John blew out a sigh of relief. Tony had positioned herself opposite him in the river, keeping the funnel of cattle narrow and contained. He pointed to an outcropping of brush trees in the distance. "Head toward that point. Sarah can take up your position. I'll catch up with you once we've gotten the whole herd across."

Tony grinned. "Have we passed your test yet?"

"Not hardly."

"I take that as a challenge."

"I was afraid of that."

He rounded back and took note of Sarah's position on the left flank. She'd reined her horse into the river where the water met the animal's belly. A moment of pride flashed in his chest. She'd positioned herself perfectly, and without any direction from him. She'd done it on intuition.

The right flank had bulged with the cattle wandering out of line. One particularly lazy beast had paused in the middle of river and lapped at the water.

John and his mount fought their way against the tide and urged the beast into motion. Once corrected, the others followed. He kept watch on their progress for a few moments more, then searched for Moira.

She remained on the bank. Champion danced around the legs of her horse, tracking the cattle, nipping at their heels and skirting away from their horns. For the next few minutes he marveled at how well everything was proceeding. The girls were green, but they had good instincts. Tony kept the lead cattle moving northeast and Sarah kept the water crossing manageable.

With only a few dozen cattle on the opposite bank. Darcy, the drag man, appeared near the shore.

John flagged her. "Move ahead and keep the right flank steady."

She offered a distracted nod in return.

He caught Moira's attention. "You and Darcy will be the last ones across. You want me to stay?"

"No. We're fine. You keep up with Tony."

A slight hitch in her voice caught his attention. "Are you certain?"

"We're plenty capable, Mr. Elder. It's not like I'm afraid of a little water."

Chapter Eight

Terrified was more like it.

Moira glanced down and her whole body trembled. Her horse, sensing her unease, remained stock-still. Champion barked and nipped at the heels of the last remaining cattle on the shore.

Moira pressed a hand against her roiling stomach. The cattle were crossing. Tony was a dot in the distance. Sarah and Mr. Elder moved up the line of cattle, letting their numbers increase to four and five abreast once they reached the top of the riverbank.

Darcy lifted her head. "My feet are freezing from this water. It's your turn. I'll meet you on shore."

Without waiting for an answer, Darcy and her mount splashed through the water, emerging from the icy river on the far side.

Her heart pounding, Moira kneed her mount deeper. The animal waded in until the water seeped through the seams of her boots. Moira sucked in a breath at the icy chill. No wonder Darcy had wanted dry land.

Though the reins remained slack in her hands, her mount drove through the current. Moira kept her eyes plastered on the horizon. Rushing water pulled at her boots, sucking her skirts around the horse's belly.

White-hot terror shot through her veins. Her limbs paralyzed and she remained frozen. The horse paused. Moira squeezed her knees and dug her heels into its flanks. "Keep moving."

Her mount moved a few lengths forward and stopped once more.

Moira groaned and glanced around her. John Elder had trained his horses well. Too well. The animal wasn't budging until the last bull climbed out of the water. Unless she wanted to swim the distance, she was stuck.

Champion nipped the final two heads of cattle into the water and splashed in beside them. Keeping its head above water, the dog surged past her toward the opposite shore.

Even as the glacial chill invaded her limbs, Moira broke out in a cold sweat. It felt as though the river was pulling at her, desperately trying to tug her under.

Her horse took a step forward and every muscle in her body tightened. Moira gripped the saddle horn with both hands and hunched her back. The water surged along her thighs. Fear pumped through her veins, blinding her vision.

For a moment she worried she'd lose control, scream or cry or burst into a thousand pieces. She dug her heels into the horse's flanks once more. If John Elder saw her now, he'd know her weakness, her fear. If he realized her terror, he'd have a weapon against her. A reason to call a halt to the cattle drive.

She caught sight of Darcy waiting on the shore. She hadn't much farther. As the water rose around her, a tangle of mane hair swirled around her fingers. As she came abreast of Darcy, the girl leaned over and adjusted her foot in her stirrup. Her hat tumbled from her head, landing in the shallow water near the shore.

The cows rumbled past, stirring the water. Darcy reached out. A wave lapped at the brim, carrying the hat beneath the belly of an enormous bull.

Darcy cried out. "Grab my hat. It's going right past you!"

Moira peeled her fingers from around the saddle horn. The brim bobbed along the water just out of reach. She leaned forward.

Darcy huffed. "Reach for it! I haven't got a spare."

Moira stretched out her hand and touched the brim. Her mount slipped in the muddy embankment. She shrieked and groped for the saddle horn. Her fingers, stiff with cold, missed their purchase. The rushing water reached her shoulders and drew her beneath the dark surface.

Moira surged upward, gasping and sputtering. Her right leg slipped over the saddle while her left foot remained caught in the stirrup. Her stomach churned with terror and frustration. Reaching for her ankle, suffocating waves lapped over her head.

Panic scattered her thoughts. She flailed her arms and arched her back. For a brief moment her face breached the surface. She caught Darcy's horrified expression, the space between them separated by a dozen cattle, their lethal horns clicking together as they slipped up the embankment, falling to their knees and rising again in a powerful heave of muscles.

There was no way for Darcy to reach her. Not before the water pulled her under once more.

Moira kicked out and caught her horse's right flank. The animal started into motion, dragging her toward the shore.

Her boot slipped off and her foot sprang free. She thrashed her arms and felt for the bottom. The current snatched at her, dragging her into deeper water. She sucked in a mouthful of water. Gagging and coughing as her head bobbed.

The water closed around her, blurring her vision. Her heart thumped erratically as though clinging to the last vestiges of life.

She realized with a sudden clarity that she was going to die. She was going to drown before they even crossed the Snake River.

John had already started back when he heard the panicked shouts. Blood hammering in his ears, he kicked his horse into a gallop and found Darcy frantically pointing toward Moira's riderless horse.

"She's over there!" Darcy shouted. "She went under."

He urged his horse toward the water's edge and searched beneath the murky surface.

A tangle of brilliant red hair floated on the water. He slid from his mount and struggled toward the beacon. Reaching beneath the surface, he caught hold of Moira's limp body, then locked his arms around her waist and hauled her toward the embankment. She was heavier than when he'd held her before. The skirts of her waterlogged dress had nearly doubled her weight.

He clumsily made his way over the muddy shore and laid her on dry ground. She whimpered and spread her arms akimbo like a carelessly tossed rag doll. Her eyes remained half-open, dull and unresponsive. Icy fear twisted around his heart.

She coughed and gasped and her body spasmed. John sagged at the glorious sound. Crouching beside her, he slipped his hands behind her neck and turned her head aside, letting her expel the water she'd swallowed. When the retching calmed, he eased her head on his bent knee. Her mass of snarled red hair soaked his trousers.

He brushed the sodden strands from her forehead and

rested the back of his hand against her cool skin. Her face remained ashen. She moaned, her body trembling.

Darcy hovered over them, her hand over her mouth.

John searched the horizon. "Ride ahead and tell Tony what's happened, then fetch the wagon. We'll need a fire and warm blankets."

Darcy looked as though she might say something, then appeared to change her mind. She whirled and grasped the reins of her mount.

Moira's head lolled to one side and she puffed a weak breath. He lifted her into his embrace and she shivered violently.

Her eyes fluttered open and she coughed. "I'm all right now."

"Then you can walk back?"

She struggled partly upright and he pressed a gentle hand against her shoulder. "I was only teasing."

A bloom of color appeared on her cheeks. "I can't swim."

"I gathered as much."

She tugged limply on the buttons of her borrowed coat, the material plastered against her body, swollen with moisture and uncooperative against her fingers, nearly blue with cold.

He brushed her hands aside. "Let me help."

Together they worked her arms from the sodden sleeves. She sat upright and wrapped her arms around her legs, resting her chin on her bent knees, her teeth chattering. He shrugged out of his slickers and draped the heavy material around her shoulders.

She pulled one of the edges tighter together and trembled. "You were right, you know."

"About what?"

"I didn't even it make it twenty yards."

The woeful note in her voice tugged at something in his chest. "Actually, you managed about twenty-two yards."

She offered a weak chuckle.

Searching for kindling, he scratched in the dirt beneath the scrub trees lining the bank. "You're not the first person to fall in the river during a trail drive. My brother Matt once got his pant leg caught in some brush. Had to cut him out of his britches. Let me tell you, with six brothers, you never want to be caught in your drawers."

Moira rubbed her cheek against her bent knee. "I bet you never let him live that down."

"No. We did not."

He discovered the charred end of a log as big around as his leg. Considering this was the shallowest part of the river, it didn't surprise him that others had crossed here before. Other folks had obviously rested and warmed themselves here before pushing onward.

After gathering an armful of twigs and tinder, he removed a tin of matches from his breast pocket and struck a flame against the base. Some of the grass was partially green, sending up more smoke than flames. He got down on his hands and knees and blew at the spot till the embers glowed.

Shivering, Moira scooted nearer the fire. Without asking he kneeled beside her and gathered her against his chest. At that moment warmth was more important than manners and propriety. He held her stiffly, shielding her from a bitter wind that had kicked up as the day progressed. She relaxed into his embrace and he savored the feel of her in his arms. Tipping her head against his shoulder, her breath whispered in a sigh. His heartbeat pitched.

He chafed her upper arms and his fingers caught in a tangle of drenched hair. He wound the strands around his palm and wrung the moisture. With painstaking care he repeated the process on the rest of the soaking mass. Her eyes fluttered closed, her eyelashes casting soft shadows against her cheeks.

His perusal drifted toward her lips. This close, he could count each uneven freckle dusting her face. He noted how they were darker on the delightfully rounded tip of her nose and lighter as they flared over the pink apples of her cheeks.

He'd never been a man easily turned by a pretty face. He admired a beautiful woman as much as the next man, but he'd never felt the need to wax on like he'd heard other fellows. Studying Moira, he wished he had more words. More of the flowery descriptors he'd scoffed at in school.

He knew if he tried to put his thoughts to paper with pen and ink, he'd never do her justice.

A splash sounded, jerking him back to the present. Their horses had wandered nearer the river, snuffling along the bank and drinking the crisp water.

John cleared his throat and leaned back, putting some space between them, breaking whatever hold she had on his wayward thoughts. He pushed off from his knee and stood, then reached out a hand. She grasped his fingers, her own icy cold. He clasped them tighter, offering what bit of comfort he could.

"What happened to your gloves?"

She tugged on her hand, but he held firm.

"I lent them to Tony." Her voice was husky from her ordeal. "She's the only one of us who knows how to rope. She needed them more."

He flipped her palm over in his hand and rubbed his thumb along the raised marks, the skin abraded from working the reins. She curled her fingers into a fist.

All of the doubts he harbored about the cattle drive and his unlikely crew came rushing back. "Your hands are too delicate."

"They're not. They're rough and chapped. Not a lady's hands at all."

They both turned toward the sound of hoofbeats. Sarah reined her horse before them. "Is everything all right? Darcy said there'd been an accident."

Moira moved away from him, her steps halting. "I took a tumble into the water. It was my own fault."

John touched her elbow lightly, ensuring she was steady on her feet before putting some distance between them.

Sarah wasn't the best rider of the bunch. Not the worst, either. She appeared more comfortable in the saddle already. "Did you find the wagon?" Moira asked.

"We've caught up with them. We're having some trouble with the cattle, though. They scattered after crossing the river and we can't get 'em all back together. They've separated into two groups."

Moira plucked at her limp skirts. "You ride on and help, Mr. Elder. I'll stay here for a spell. See if I can dry out some more."

"I can't. You know that. I can't risk your safety. What if something happens?"

"It's only for a half an hour or so."

"In a half an hour you fell off your horse and nearly drowned in the river."

She tossed her head and gave an irritable tug at her damp hair. "It's not like I'm going to run afoul of anyone. We're in the middle of nowhere."

Leaving her all alone didn't sit right with him. "You'll get lost catching up."

"Really?" Moira gestured in a sweeping motion with one arm. "I can see halfway to Fort Preble. Don't know how I'd get lost."

"I don't like it."

"Then leave Champion. He'll keep watch."

"What if you don't put out the fire properly and you start a brushfire."

Moira lifted an eyebrow. "What? And ruin all this beautiful scenery?"

John scowled.

"It rained yesterday. It's not like we're in a drought."

She shivered and he realized she wasn't moving until he agreed. "I will build up the fire and leave you for precisely—" He fished out his pocket watch. "One hour. If you're not caught up, I'm sending someone back."

Moira's gaze remained transfixed on the pocket watch. She swallowed convulsively and jerked her head in a curt nod. He tucked his watch away and she appeared to relax.

The exchange was odd, leaving him uncertain. While he gathered more brush and stoked the flames, Moira removed her boot and stretched her stocking feet toward the heat. She wiggled her toes and leaned back on her elbows.

"You sure you're all right?"

"I'm certain."

He glanced at her askance, relieved her earlier wariness hadn't returned. "One hour."

"Yes, you mentioned that. One hour and you're sending a search party."

She closed her eyes, effectively dismissing him. He gazed into the distance, content there wasn't anything in sight except a few stray cattle and a couple of wild gobblers in the distance. He didn't see how anyone, even Miss Moira O'Mara, could possibly stir up trouble in this desolate environment.

Moira scrunched her hem beneath her fingers, feeling only a slight dampness. They'd set the fire well away from the cattle, though she didn't figure anything would spook those beasts. She heard the occasional whoops and hollers as the rest of the group rounded up the strays.

Her stockings were suspended by a stick she'd rigged near the fire. They weren't quite dry, but it appeared as though the rest of the team needed help gathering the herd once more. Champion's perpetual barking drifted over the wind. The dog returned occasionally, as though assuring itself of her safety, then darted off again.

The few cattle lingering near the river's edge wore perpetual expressions of boredom, with only the occasional grunt of discontent.

Darcy urged her horse into a trot and approached the fire, her expression glum. "I asked you to fetch my hat, not get yourself drowned."

"You're welcome," Moira replied with a wry grin. "Glad you appreciate the effort."

Darcy tossed her hair over her shoulder. "Are you dry yet? I'm tired of the drag. And there's still a couple of strays by the river."

Moira had been huddled before the warming fire for a mere twenty minutes. Despite the cowboy's gentle wringing, her hair dripped down her back and she had only one boot. She'd lost the other in the river.

She glanced at Darcy's sulky expression and back at the cheery flames. "I'm ready. I'll take over."

"Good. I'm tired of taking your turn." Darcy appeared almost triumphant as she galloped toward the line of cattle in the distance.

"Seems like your head is big enough to keep your hat on tight," Moira grumbled.

She doused the fire with three canteens full of water and kicked additional dirt over the embers, then doused them again. Heaven forbid a brushfire ignite the fresh grass. The cowboy would never let her live that down. She grappled onto her horse and glanced behind her.

A calf munched grass on the edge of the river. The animal was mottled a deep russet and red, with the darker color more pronounced around the head and shoulders haunches. Moira spurred her mount closer. Champion appeared once more and barked and bounced around the animal's legs. After a disgruntled snort, the calf lumbered up the embankment.

The calf labored and slipped, falling onto its forelegs with a bawl of distress.

Moira squinted into the distance. By the time she asked for the help, the poor animal would only dig itself deeper.

Champion splashed through the water, barking and nipping at the calf's hind legs.

The calf's eyes grew large, the whites showing stark against the red fur around its face. The animal brayed and snorted.

As the dog nipped at its hooves, the calf grew more agitated, thrashing from side to side. "Shoo," Moira ordered. "Give her some space, Champion."

She slipped off her horse and stumbled down the embankment. Moira pressed her palm against the animal's haunches and pushed. Though the calf was young, it still weighed several hundred pounds. Her feeble efforts were useless. "Easy there, big fellow. It's going to be all right."

Another animal appeared on the horizon. An enormous cow towered on the bank, flipping its head up and down and shaking the folds along its neck. The animal bawled, a lonesome sound that sent a shiver down Moira's spine.

"Go on, get up there," Moira urged the calf.

The cow at the top of the embankment lowered its head and snuffed. One sharp hoof pawed at the loose red soil.

A shot of fear skittered down Moira's spine. "You must be Mama. Well, Mama, tell your baby not to worry. We're going to get him out of here."

The mother threw back her head and bellowed.

Moira slid farther down the muddy embankment. She

fought through the muck and braced her hands against the calf's backside.

"Keep moving before your mama decides to come down and fetch you herself. Then you'll both be stuck."

The animal thrashed, kicking up mud and spattering Moira's already-damp dress. She brushed a smear of mud from her forehead with the back of her hand. "Thatta boy, keep it up."

Two things happened almost simultaneously. The calf pitched forward and Moira slipped on the slimy embankment. Her boot caught beneath the calf's leg. The animal dug its sharpened hoof into her ankle and surged forward.

Moira yelped.

The mama cow on the embankment brayed.

Champion barked.

The calf caught its footing and skittered up the hill. Moira pushed herself into a standing position and attempted to follow. Her boot stuck in the mud. She yanked and her stocking foot slipped out of her boot.

Moira groaned.

She reached elbow-deep in the slimy mud and felt around. Nothing. She grimaced. Her boot had disappeared beneath a layer of mud. She took one step toward the stream and winced. Her tender ankle screamed in protest. Crouching, she rubbed the sore spot.

The mama cow and her baby remained perched on the embankment, balefully watching her troubles.

"Go on now!" Moira shouted.

She limped up the hill and stumbled right into John Elder's arms. He took one look at her mud-splattered dress and his brows drew downward into a frown. "Why didn't you fetch help?"

"I didn't need help."

His gaze encompassed her disheveled appearance and

exasperation coasted across his face. "Yep. Doesn't look like you need any help at all."

He extended his hand and Moira grasped his fingers. He stretched out one leg and braced his foot against the embankment, then easily pulled her up the remaining distance. "You know," he said. "Stubbornness is not a virtue. It wouldn't kill you to ask for help once in a while."

Moira glanced down at the torn hem of her dress where the calf's hoof had shredded the material, and nearly wept. She didn't exactly have a warm bath and a change of clothing waiting for her back at camp.

She lifted her skirts and discovered the hole in her dress revealed her leg clear up past the knee. She dropped the material. "I didn't need help. I got the calf free all by myself."

The cowboy seemed singularly unimpressed by her accomplishment.

He grasped the reins of his mount and turned away. "And nearly got trampled in the process. You die, I gotta dig a hole for you."

His implacable expression was unnerving and her lips parted in shock.

"All right, maybe I'm taking this too far." The cowboy rolled his shoulders. "I'm used to giving this speech to men and the rules are different. Men respond to death and dismemberment and all that. I can see I'll have to take another approach."

Moira wrapped her arms around her body. "Dismemberment?"

"Forget that," John continued. "How about this? If you don't care about your own neck, think of those girls. They look up to you. They're counting on you. If you go and get yourself killed, I'll have a bunch of bawling girls back at camp."

Moira flushed but remained silent.

His mouth worked and he fisted his hand on his thigh. "Okay, I guess that wasn't much better either. Don't get yourself killed on my watch, all right? I'll feel bad."

"All right."

"Good. Then we're in agreement. Now finish drying off and take up the drag. We've still got a whole day ahead of us and this was your idea in the first place."

He dismounted and approached her horse. Moira made a face at his stiff back. There was no need to overact. *Dig a hole for her.* Indeed. He whipped around and she quickly resumed an implacable expression.

He led her horse nearer and she grasped the reins. Leaning down, he cupped his hands for her to step in. "Where is your boot?"

"In the river."

He glanced at her stocking feet. "Where is your other boot?"

"In the mud."

"Why doesn't that surprise me?"

He boosted her onto her mount and wiped his muddy hands against his pants. Moira adjusted her skirts and avoided his glower.

Together they set off for the herd in uneasy silence. Her leg throbbed and despite his dry slicker, she felt the cold seeping into bones. After his stern lecture on *death* and *dismemberment,* she wasn't giving him the satisfaction of showing her discomfort.

The herd appeared before them, the cattle back in line, the stream of bodies snaking over the horizon. Tony's hat bobbed along near the lead.

John slowed his horse. "Look, I shouldn't have yelled at you. When I came back to check and didn't see you, I guess I got a little scared. Might have pushed my temper."

"Thank you for the apology."

His head tilted upright. "It wasn't an apology. It was an explanation. And next time, ask for help."

Moira gaped at his retreating back. That infernal man had her all tied up in knots. One minute he was drying her hair and cradling her in his arms, the next minute he was shouting and carrying on.

John Elder sure made it difficult to like him sometimes. Which was probably a good thing. For a minute there, she'd been liking him a little too much.

The cowboy was a distraction she didn't need. Not now. Not ever.

Chapter Nine

John pushed the girls relentlessly. Better they realize the difficulties of the trail before they strayed too far from Fool's End. They'd realize soon enough the task they'd undertaken was easier said than done, and then he'd be finished with this crazy cattle drive. Keeping eight hundred head of cattle moving in one direction against the elements and the girls' inexperience wasn't a task for the weak at heart.

He cast a surreptitious glance at Moira. Of all the girls, she'd suffered the most that day. She'd been doused and muddied. She hadn't worn the gloves he'd lent her and her palms had already blistered. He'd resolved to treat them like men, and then he'd cradled her in his arms. Not the way he treated his men at all.

John impatiently drew his drifting thoughts away from Miss O'Mara and her troubles. The sooner he ended this debacle the better. His young crew was green and untried. As long as everything went well, they were fine. They weren't prepared for a disaster.

A form in the distance caught his attention and relief flooded his veins. They'd caught up with the chuck wagon and it appeared Pops already had a cook fire blazing. John's stomach rumbled in anticipation.

The girls had been on their horses for six hours and counting. By now they should be sore, hungry and ready to call it quits on the cattle drive. For good.

He dismounted and followed Moira as she limped before him. Not the weary gait of someone who'd spent too long in the saddle, she walked as though favoring one leg.

He jogged until he caught up with her and grasped her arm. "You okay? What happened to your leg?"

"It's nothing. It's been a long day, that's all."

With a tip of his head, he motioned toward the chuck wagon. "Why don't you sit? I'll take care of your horse."

She threw back her shoulders. "I carry my weight."

His steps slowed. "Suit yourself."

Sarah slid off her mount and her knees buckled briefly before she righted herself. She arched her back and rubbed her backside. "How can sitting all day hurt so much?"

"Because you're not sitting," Tony stated proudly. "You're riding."

"Well, I just discovered some muscles I never knew I had," Sarah said. "And those muscles are hurting."

"Don't get too comfortable. We've got to divvy up the watch."

Darcy hobbled into the campsite clutching the reins of her horse. "I don't know who's got the first watch, but it ain't me. I'm hungry, I'm tired, my back aches, the balls of my feet are sore, I'm sick of flies, and I'm sick of smelling cows."

"Well, ain't you just a ray of sunshine after a long, hard day." Tony chucked her on the shoulder. "A little hard work never killed anyone."

"If you don't shut your yapper I'm going to shut it for you."

Tony raised her arms. "Somebody got off on the wrong side of the horse today."

John stifled a grin. "We'll take two hour shifts. First shift will start right after dinner. Everyone else will stay behind and help set up camp. Any volunteers?"

"Not me," Darcy reaffirmed.

The others glanced around. Everyone was too tired or too nervous to speak up.

Tony snorted. "It's all right, I got this. Schoolhouse rules. Everyone put in a shoe and we'll figure this out fair and square."

As though on cue, the girls crowded around her, the tips of their boots touching. Tony motioned for Moira. "You too."

Moira touched her chest. Tony nodded. She hobbled toward the group and glanced around, and added her bootless foot to the press of pointed toes.

"First one out is the last one on watch and we go in order from there." Tony knelt and placed her fingers on the toe of her own boot. "One, two, the cow said moo."

She spoke in a singsong voice, and with each word in the rhyme, she touched the next shoe in the circle. "Three, four, the lions roar. Five, six, the monkey does a trick. Seven, eight, he's swinging on a gate. Nine, ten, big fat hen."

The word "hen" landed her on Sarah's foot.

Tony flapped her wrist. "Sarah's out. She takes the last watch." Tony rested her hand on the next one in line, Moira's stocking foot. "Apples, peaches, pears and plums. Tell me when your birthday comes."

The last word landed on Moira's toe once more.

"June," she replied.

"*J-U-N-E* spells June and you are not it. Darcy is out."

Darcy heaved a sigh of relief and flopped on the

ground. She tipped up her chin and let the setting sun warm her face.

"One potato, two potato, three potato, four. Five potato, six potato, seven potato more. I'm out." Tony sat back on her heels. "That means you take the first watch, Moira."

John waded through the seated girls. "Dinner first. Then watch."

Moira's shoulders slumped. "Food sounds wonderful."

"Hey," Darcy dug her heels in the dirt. "When is his watch?" She jerked her thumb in John's direction. "Ain't he the trail boss and all?"

"I'm the boss, all right, and I'll have you mind your tone." The sooner Darcy accepted his authority, the better. There might come a time when he needed a quick response from her, and he didn't want her constantly questioning his every move. "Pops and I will take midnight to two and two to four. We're used to the schedule and we'll stay awake."

Tony stuck out her chin. "We'll do our part. Same as the men."

"I know you will." He hooked his thumbs into his belt loops. "I've made my decision and I give the orders. My word is first, last and most binding."

"All right, boss. That puts Moira from six to eight, me from eight to ten, Darcy from ten to twelve. You and Pops have midnight to four which leaves Sarah from four to six."

Darcy grunted. "I should have taken the first watch. Six to eight sounds better than ten to twelve. I'm bushed."

"Yeah," Tony said. "You should have. But you didn't. Now let's eat."

As she walked past, John stuck out an elbow and lightly tapped her upper arm. "Good work doling out the watch assignments."

"That's how we decided who 'it' is in hide-and-seek. I figured it would work for this, too."

"Fair and unbiased. I like your style."

Her eyes lit up. "Thanks, boss. You're not so bad yourself."

She'd puffed beneath his meager praise and he made a mental note to offer more words of encouragement throughout the day. His men usually preferred good-natured insults and the occasional ribbing. Dealing with girls required a whole new set of skills.

John halted. He didn't need any new skills. This was the end of the line. No use planning for a future that was never coming around.

As he moved toward the wagon and dinner, an enticing aroma wafted through the air, a scent he didn't usually associate with a trail ride.

Pops appeared with a tin plate in his hand.

John peered over his shoulder. "What's that?" He caught sight of two-tone chunks of meat stirred through the beans. "Is that bacon in the beans?"

"Sure is. Sarah came up with the idea. Since the girls don't eat as much as the boys do in the morning, we figured we could spruce up the beans a bit with the bacon. Added some mustard and brown sugar. Mighty tasty, if I don't say so myself."

"Brown sugar? Mustard? This isn't some fancy hotel. This is a cattle drive." John's voice had taken on alarmingly high pitch. "How can we convince them to quit if you're serving them gourmet grub?"

"It ain't me serving them, it's Sarah." Pops scooped a forkful of doctored beans into his mouth and grinned. He chomped and swallowed, appearing as though he'd dug into a porterhouse steak and not a can of tinned beans with some flecks of fatted bacon. "I'm here to eat. Iff'in you want them to quit, that's your problem."

John's left eye ticked. The backboard of the chuck wagon had been flipped out into a makeshift buffet. A white handkerchief with embroidered pink roses and greenery at the corner had been folded into a triangle. A tin cup overflowing with wildflowers anchored the napkin in place.

John grunted. First bacon then black-eyed Susans. What was next?

He scooped the mouthwatering beans onto his plate and reached for a biscuit. His fingers sank into the soft bread.

"What's this?" He sniffed the unusually pleasant aroma and bit into the golden brown, flaky crust. A delicate tang infused the moist-textured grub. "If that's buttermilk I taste, I'm firing you on the spot. What happened to the hardtack? Where are the weevils?"

Sarah took a hesitant step forward. "Don't you like them? Pops had some buttermilk left from his supply trip into Fool's End."

Her crestfallen expression tugged at something in his chest.

He swallowed the delightful concoction. For a moment he feared his eyes would roll back in his head at the blissful flavor. "It's fine. Not bad at all. Just not what I'm used to."

Sarah beamed.

John stomped toward the fire. She needn't act as though he'd doled out some hefty praise. It was just a little buttermilk and some fatback.

He lifted his boot and hopped back. The girls had laid out a blanket and reclined on the surface.

He skirted the covering and plopped onto the prickly grass.

Pops held the handle of his Dutch oven and lifted the heavy cookware aloft. "Save room for peach cobbler."

"Are you pulling my leg?" John held his plate away from his body. "Peach cobbler? This is a cattle drive. No one serves peach cobbler on a cattle drive."

"Then I guess you won't be having any."

The cook meandered past and lifted the lid. A plume of steam drifted toward John. He held his breath and averted his gaze. Pops circled back around. The old coot wasn't playing fair. John exhaled his breath in noisy frustration and caught a hint of the succulent aroma. His mouth watered.

Sarah watched his reaction and plucked at the blanket. "Hazel helped make that special."

John suppressed the low growl in the back of his throat. He'd look surly if he didn't partake. "Well, um, if Hazel took all the time...I wouldn't want to be rude."

"I'm sure you wouldn't." Pops rolled his eyes. "Quite the thoughtful fellow all of a sudden, ain't ya?"

John lifted his fork and Hazel cleared her throat.

He paused.

She glanced pointedly at his hands. "Did you wash?"

"Did I wash what?"

"Your hands."

"Uh." Heat crept up cheeks beneath her watchful stare. "I forgot."

Hazel tsked. "There's water in the wreck pan."

He dutifully stood, crossed to the wagon, and rinsed his hands in the wreck pan of sudsy water. Upon sitting down, Hazel cleared her throat once more.

John tilted his head. "What did I do now?"

"You haven't said grace."

He mentally added another item to the list of things girls did differently than boys on a cattle drive. He supposed some of the changes weren't that bad.

After dropping his plate on the grass at his left, John folded his hands and bent his head. "Dear Lord, thank You for our safe crossing of the Snake River, thank You for this bountiful feast. Please continue to watch over us. Protect us from harm. And if there's any chance there's a stagecoach full of cattle hands just over the rise, tell 'em I can switch out with a bunch of girls."

Tony elbowed him in the gut.

John grinned.

As he reached for his discarded plate, a grasshopper leapt into his beans. He grimaced and flicked the insect off with his thumb.

Sarah raised an eyebrow. "The grasshoppers are as thick as cold porridge around here. That's why we're sitting on the blanket."

She smoothed her hand over the insect-free surface.

He gulped down another forkful of beans. "A little grasshopper never hurt anything."

Life on the trail was tough. Cattle drives weren't about cherry or peach cobbler and bacon baked beans. They were hard work and adversity. Throwing down a blanket and adding a little buttermilk to the biscuits didn't change the facts.

Keeping his head low, he stood and crossed back over to the chuck wagon. Pops had set out the peach cobbler and an additional set of tin plates. John filled his cup of coffee before scooping a dollop, then resumed his seat on the prickly scrub grass.

Each bite melted onto his tongue with the flavors melding in perfect harmony. Engrossed in the tasty dessert, he barely registered Moira rising and placing her dishes in the wreck pan.

He glanced up as she walked past, noting that same hitch in her gait.

She wore a pair of battered boots and he realized Tony was in her stocking feet.

"You sure you're all right?" he asked. "Looks like you're limping."

Her spine straightened. "I'm fine. Tony's feet are smaller than mine. There's nothing wrong."

John scraped his plate with tine edge of his fork. "You let me know. Pops has a kit for cuts and scrapes. You have to be careful out here. A wound can go septic real fast if it's not tended."

Tony perked up. "It's true. Back when I lived on the ranch, one of the cattle hands only had one leg. Said he lost it in the war. He got gangrene in his big toe and they cut off his leg below the knee."

Sarah's pale skin grew even whiter. "Because of his *toe?*"

"I know, right? I mean, can you imagine if it had been in his ankle. They probably would have sawed off his leg at the thigh." She chopped the edge of her hand against a spot high on her leg. "That bone is huge. I wouldn't want anybody sawing through that."

Sarah abandoned her plate of cobbler on the blanket. "Could we talk about something else?"

"Yes, let's talk about something else." John stood and dusted his pant legs. "Nobody is getting anything chopped, hacked or severed on my watch."

Sarah pressed her fingers against her mouth and heaved.

He threw up his arms. That was yet another problem with having women in the camp. A man had to watch what he said all the time.

Moira limped toward the remuda. Safely away from camp, she lifted her skirts and tugged down the flap of her borrowed boot, revealing a purpling bruise and an ugly red scrape on her ankle. The calf's sharp hoof had bitten into her flesh.

The injury was far too shallow to go septic.

A little scrape was the least of her worries. The sun was setting and it was her turn for watch. Weariness enveloped her and her whole body ached. While she'd never considered herself a sedentary person, the day had proved far more exhausting than she'd anticipated. Though she was accustomed to working late at night—her job as a maid at the hotel had been mostly after regular hours when the patrons were asleep and wouldn't be bothered by the presence of the staff—she'd been keeping a more regular schedule for the past week.

Her eyes burned drily from sleeplessness as she approached the remuda. The saddles were stacked on their pommels in a neat line as John had instructed when they'd made camp. Moira scooped her arm beneath the cumbersome saddle and staggered backward.

Tony appeared and grasped the other side. "You really should ask for help. These saddles are too big for one person."

"You already helped me this morning when you saddled my horse. It isn't fair to make someone else do my work all the time." Moira groaned. "I have to learn to do this by myself."

Tony pressed her lips together. "The way I see it, we're sharing the work. You help me, I help you."

Moira was saved from an answer as they heaved the saddle over the horse's back. She fished beneath the animal's belly and grasped the girth strap. Tugging her lower lip between her teeth, she clumsily threaded the leather belt through the D ring.

Tony sighed and brushed her hands away. "Not like that. This here is the latigo."

She pulled the leather through the D ring of the girth strap, back up through the D ring on the saddle and repeated the process. "Now you've got a double loop. See? The next thing we're going to do is tie the knot."

She ran her fingers beneath the leather. "Don't tighten it too much. Just push the tail end back through the D ring, pull it down and across, then up through the D ring again. See how you've made a loop? Now push the tail end of the leather through the loop and you've made a knot."

Exhaustion enveloped Moira as she tried to concentrate on the rapid-fire instructions.

Tony grinned and untied the knot. "Okay. Now your turn."

Watching the motions and actually performing the task were two entirely different things. Beneath Tony's watchful eyes, Moira repeated the instructions. Her back ached between her shoulder blades and her fingers worked, clumsy and uncoordinated.

Tony grasped the leather and ceased her fumbling efforts. "Not like that. You take the strap *under* the D ring."

Moira corrected her direction and looped the leather, then slid the end through, forming a knot.

Rubbing her chin, the younger girl nodded. "That'll do. Now you've got to tighten the strap, otherwise you'll end up beneath the horse's belly."

Tony grasped the outside layer of the long double loop they'd made with the leather strap and tugged, creating more slack. Then tightened the knot once more. At one point she reached beneath the horse and heaved on the strap.

Reaching up, she pulled on the saddle horn. "That'll hold firm." She glanced toward the horse's head. "Course, you're never gonna get anywhere unless you have a bridle."

She grasped what appeared to be a tangle of leather and expertly looped the halter over the horse's head, slid her thumb into the side of the animal's mouth and positioned the bit. "We'll save the bridle lesson for tomorrow. Mostly because I think you could use some instruction on horsemanship. You haven't ridden much, have you?"

"Once or twice, when I was very young."

When her parents were still together and they enjoyed

a few good times. The memories seemed far away, almost as though they belonged to someone else.

Tony tromped toward a second horse. "Let me saddle this one. I'll show you some stuff from the ground and then we'll mount up and I'll give you a few more lessons."

"That's really not necessary." Moira turned her attention toward the setting sun. "I need to start my watch."

"You fell off in the river today. If you fall off on the ground, it's gonna hurt a lot worse. Not to mention if you lose control of your mount and get yourself killed, that means we're a man down and it's more work for the rest of us."

Moira gaped. "You sound just like Mr. Elder."

"Good. He's an excellent trail boss. And have you seen the way he handles his horses? I barely see him move, but they follow his commands. I saw an Indian once in a show at the fairgrounds. That fellow rode bareback with only a single rawhide strap half hitched under the horse's jaw for guidance. I never saw anything like it. I bet John Elder is that good."

"He mentioned he trained all the horses himself."

"That's saying something. These are some of the best horses I've ever ridden."

A grudging admiration for the cowboy filtered through Moira's numbed thoughts. John Elder handled himself well. He was patient and kind and other than a few spots of annoyance, he kept his temper.

Mindful of her debt, Moira assisted Tony with lifting her saddle. The younger girl made quick work of the rigging before leading her horse near Moira.

"Always approach a horse from the left side."

"How come?"

"I dunno. That's just what you do. You're going to have to mount for real this time. There won't always be a rock or a fence around every time we stop. Anyway, approach on the left and grasp the reins and the saddle horn in your left hand, facing the horse's rump. Then place your left foot in the stirrup. This is where it gets a little tricky. You have to kind of lift yourself up until you're standing on that left foot, then throw your right leg over the horse's back."

She demonstrated the "tricky" move with remarkable ease.

Moira attempted the motion three times before successfully swinging her leg over the saddle. Safely perched upon her mount, she caught her breath and patted the animal's neck. "That wasn't so bad now, was it?"

Tony sidled her horse nearer. "Now for the lessons. We'll practice and keep watch at the same time."

For the next forty-five minutes, the two circled the herd while Tony barked out instructions and corrections. About a half an hour into the session, Moira sensed herself steadily improving. The animal responded better, turning with her movements. The progress was minor, but the control eased her anxiety.

Tony touched the brim of her hat. "I think you know enough to keep you in the saddle tonight. We can do the same thing tomorrow."

"Thank you. For everything."

"No problem. We're a team."

The cattle munched grass and dozed, mostly ignoring her quiet direction. Her horse had good instincts and the cattle appeared to recognize its authority. As the evening progressed, her exhaustion leveled out.

At the prescribed time, Tony rode up to relieve her. The younger girl appeared refreshed and almost cheerful to be riding again.

They dismounted and Moira switched out her boots. When she mounted again, it only took her two tries.

On Moira's way back to camp, John appeared in the glow of the three-quarter moon. He glanced at her seat, her back straight and tall in the saddle, and a look of approval coasted across his face. "You're a fast study."

"Tony helped me out."

"Well, you did a good job following instruction. Now get some sleep. It's another long day in the morning."

They hadn't made it far, only a few miles from their starting point, but the small gain felt like a victory. A victory dampened by the doubt she sensed in John's considering gaze.

"I know we didn't make it very far today, but we've made progress."

"You girls did well, but it doesn't change the facts. We're in Indian Territory. We're vulnerable. More so than most. I can't take the risk."

"I'm not asking you to make a decision. I only want you to consider all that we've accomplished today."

"No decisions until morning."

Moira hesitated in the purple glow of twilight. She felt as though she should say something, or do something. Offer some sort of gesture for all the trouble he'd gone to on their behalf.

Before she could gather her thoughts, John tipped his hat and rode away. Moira sighed. She'd try again tomorrow.

She appreciated his dilemma. The girls' safety remained at the forefront of her thoughts. Despite all the reasons they shouldn't go forward, she felt compelled. The empty space in her heart didn't bother her quite as much out here. The loneliness didn't have such a fervent pull.

She needed the money, they all needed the money. Lately she'd had doubts about her search. She'd pinned all of her hopes on a reunion. The more time passed, the more she worried her hopes were misplaced. All this time she'd thought if she could explain what had happened all those years ago, Tommy would understand. Hearing the sheriff talk had brought on new fears. Her brother hadn't just run away, he'd moved on with his life in ways she hadn't even considered. Would there be a place for her in his life? They'd always had each other. What if, when she finally found him, he didn't feel the same way anymore? She couldn't bear to lose him again. She was so tired of being alone.

Moira hung her head and prayed for guidance.

Chapter Ten

Moira woke with a start. She glanced around the tent and counted sleeping bodies. Hazel, Darcy and Tony were there but no Sarah. Panic snaked down her spine before she recalled that Sarah had taken the last watch. Moira took a few deep breaths, willing her heart to resume its normal beating once more.

Despite accounting for the girls' whereabouts, a sense of unease remained. She sat upright and kicked off the blankets, then straightened her rumpled clothing as best she could. Her dousing in the river the previous day hadn't done much for her by way of a bath, and she cautiously sniffed her sleeve. She didn't smell like a bed of roses, but she didn't smell quite as bad as a cow yet either. And that was saying something.

If there was one thing she missed from civilization, it was hot water. Her hair was a tangled mess, and she brushed through the gnarled strands with her fingers. When she'd braided the length into some semblance of restraint, she emerged into the brilliant morning sunlight. Sounds of the early dawn surrounded her. The call of birds, the low of the cattle and the clatter of the Dutch oven as Pops prepared the morning meal.

The sizzling scent of frying bacon filled the air. Moira inhaled a deep breath and froze. Sheer, black fright swept through her, paralyzing her limbs.

Perched on the hillside overlooking the camp were five Indians. Their stance was still and emotionless, chilling her fear into a cold knot in her chest. She couldn't make out much from the distance, but from their dress it appeared there were three females and two males in the group.

Moira backed away, keeping her eyes pinned on the distant group. She cautiously approached the tent John and Pops shared and scratched on the flap. For a moment she lost control of the spasmodic trembling in her hands. Pressing her fingers against her head, she tried to stop her brain from imagining what might happen to them, but the horrifying image crowded her thoughts.

"What is it?" a mumbled voice called.

"Trouble," Moira replied, her voice husky.

A moment later John stumbled from the tent, his hair mussed and the dark shadow of a beard covering his jaw. Her heart beat a rat-a-tat-tat at the sight. For a moment, she forgot the danger. Every time she thought she'd grown accustomed to his looks, he turned her tongue-tied and addled.

He frowned. "What's the trouble?"

Moira startled and pointed toward the hillside.

His throat worked. "Stay here."

Moira grasped his arm. "What are you doing?"

"I'm seeing what they want."

"Is that safe?"

"They've got their womenfolk with them. It's not a war party." He lifted the corner of his mouth in a half grin. "If it was a war party, we'd already be dead."

"That's hardly comforting."

Despite his assurances Moira sensed the fear pulsating through his body. Only yesterday he'd cautioned her against their vulnerabilities. Today his worst terrors were realized.

He set off up the hill and Moira trailed behind him. He turned once and she raised an eyebrow. "You said it was safe."

He appeared to consider her answer before nodding. "Chances are, they've already scouted us. It's not like I can hide the fact that I'm traveling with a bunch of women and children." He held out one arm. "Still, it's best if you stay behind me."

Moira chafed at the order before realizing the absurdity of any objection she might make. They were alone and helpless. Mr. Elder had a gun and Pops had his rifle. While the Indians didn't appear to be carrying weapons, there was no telling what was beyond the gently sloping hills or how many more of them waited in the distance.

Once they reached the top of the rise, she stumbled back a step. As Moira had observed before, there were three women and two men in the group. On the ride from St. Louis, she'd thought about Indians and wondered what they looked like, how they acted—if they were as savage as the newspapers and books had led her to believe.

The picture in her head didn't match up with reality. The elaborate headdresses and clothing she'd seen in drawings back home were absent. The men were dressed in simple buckskin pants with fringed sides, their chests bare. The women wore leather tunics decorated with intricate beadwork.

The three women and the younger man appeared to be from the same family, or at least the same tribe. Their faces were broad, their noses flat, their cheeks rounded. The oldest, a man with grayed hair at the temples, had a broader forehead and a slimmer hawklike nose. Instead of shoulder-length hair like the first man, he wore his in two long braids that dusted the tops of his knees.

Upon closer study, Moira noted the hair bound in the braids was two-tone, leading her to believe he'd wound horsehair or something similar into the braids to make them appear longer. He caught her staring and she flushed and looked away.

John Elder said a few words in language she didn't understand.

Moira whipped around. "You speak their language?"

"Some Apache. Let's hope they know Apache, too."

The oldest man spoke, his gaze fixed on Moira. John answered then turned toward her. "He likes your hair."

She grasped her braid and backed away.

The Indian chuckled and he and John exchanged more words.

John glanced at her from the corner of his eye. "He says not to be afraid. He's not going to scalp you. He said red hair is considered bad luck."

"That's comforting."

"Well." John scratched his head. "Come to think of it, he might have said good luck. My Apache is a bit rusty."

Moira pursed her lips. "Did you ask them why they're here?"

John gave a quick shake of his head. "That's not how this works. First we'll invite them to share our meal. Keep things friendly. Why don't you go down and let Pops know we're expecting company." He kept his face impassive. "And warn the girls. I don't want an uproar when they wake up and find Indians around the fire."

Hesitant, Moira nodded. She set off for the tent and caught sight of Sarah riding in from her watch. The girl's face was pale and she stared at the group gathered on the hillside. Moira waved her over and stood before the tent.

"It's all right. Mr. Elder is talking with them now. He's inviting them for breakfast. I'll let the others know."

"Who is going to take the next watch?"

"I think we'll skip the next watch. We should stick together. In case there's more."

"You think it's a trap?" Sarah wrapped her arms around her body. "What do they want from us? Are we going to die?"

Moira tamped down her own fears. "We can't think like that. We'll continue about our day as though everything is normal. There are still chores to be done."

"I'll feed and water the horse and join you." Sarah visibly calmed at having a task.

Moira rested her hand on her shoulder. "Stay sharp. If something happens, never mind the rest of us. If there's trouble, take whatever opening you can find and run. Don't look back."

"I will."

Moira ducked inside the tent and shook the girls awake. "We've got some special company in camp."

Tony blinked and yawned. "How special?"

"Indians."

Hazel squealed and Moira quickly shushed her. "Mr. Elder is talking with them now. Get ready and come out for breakfast. Try not to stare. Sarah is feeding and watering the horses. As far as we're concerned, this is just another day."

"Another day when we might all end up with arrows through our hides," Tony grumbled.

Moira shushed her. "Not now."

"Well I heard stories on the ranch. They'll cut you down and gut you without even a by-your-leave."

Hazel began to sob quietly and Moira hugged her against her side. "That's enough. Not one more word. If you can't keep a civil tongue in your mouth, Antonella, you should remain in this tent. We've trouble enough."

Moira stepped into the sunlight and stuttered to a halt. Seeing the Indians on the hill was one thing, having them clustered around the fire was quite another. She swallowed hard and forced her steps closer.

From the corner of her eye she watched as Pops added more bacon to the pan balanced over the cook fire. His hands wobbled.

The five Indians and John gathered in a neat half circle around the fire. They all sat cross-legged, their elbows resting on their bent knees. Even the cowboy. Moira brushed her skirts behind her knees and took the place beside him.

He tilted his head. "They think you're my wife. Let's keep it that way."

Moira glanced at the eldest Indian. He stared at her hair, his black eyes curious, his gaze intense, as though trying to peer into her soul. She turned away.

While John and the Indians spoke, Pops arrived with plates of bacon and rounds of cornbread fried in the leftover grease. The Indians accepted the food and ate with gusto, using their fingers. Pops must have realized they'd eat that way, since he hadn't offered up any utensils.

The girls emerged from the tent, Tony first, her face blank, clutching Hazel's hand. Darcy trailed behind them, her lips clenched in a thin white line. Sarah returned from caring for the horses and hovered uncertainly on the edge of the campsite. Moira motioned them over.

The two groups of people observed each other with wary curiosity. One of the women spoke, a mixture of English and Apache that Moira had difficulty following. John had a better time pulling out the words. He replied and turned toward the group.

"Most of the elderly and the children in their group

died last spring. An influenza outbreak. Brought by the settlers, no doubt. Near as I can tell, they were relocated by the army from a place farther south. I'm guessing with the settlers moving in and the buffalo hunters spread over the plains, resources are thin."

A portion of Moira's fear dissipated. On closer inspection she realized the Indians' cheeks were hollow, their ribs showing, their legs painfully slim. With a sudden, awful clarity she realized that she hadn't seen them as people up until this point. In her head she'd referred to them as savages, in her mind's eye she'd seen them as less than human. The stories she'd heard, the brutality, had created a myth.

The truth was much less savage. And much more tragic.

The woman who'd been doing the bulk of the talking clicked her tongue and nodded her head. "Safe passage," she said. "Safe passage."

John spoke a few words and she replied. He shook his head. The woman repeated something and the cowboy frowned. "I can't quite make out what she's saying, but I think they're on their way to Fort Preble for medicine."

The woman gestured and talked with her curious mixture of Apache and English.

John frowned in concentration. "Her only remaining child is ill. She believes it's a white man's illness and she's hoping the white man's medicine will cure the child."

The eldest Indian, the one with the long braids and the hawkish nose, shook his head and scowled. Clearly the plan had not met with his whole approval. The woman met his scowl, her gaze defiant.

John spoke and gestured. At one point the Indians stood and walked a distance away.

Moira leaned over and whispered in his ear. "What's going on?"

"A trade. I hope. I'm offering them the choice of several head of cattle in exchange for safe passage to Fort Preble."

Moira watched their guests. Hawk Nose made a great show of considering the plan. The younger man in the group replied sharply. The two Indians remained locked on each other, caught in a fierce battle of wills. Moira shivered. After a moment Hawk Nose spoke quietly and the younger Indian jerked his head in a nod.

Hawk Nose gestured toward her hair. "Mine." He spoke.

Her scalp tingled. "Oh dear. He wants to scalp me."

"No, no. He wants a lock of your hair is all."

She automatically reached for her braid. "What should I do?"

"It's up to you."

Tony leaned closer. "We're outnumbered and outgunned. I say we give 'em what they want before they take it by force."

"It's only hair." Darcy shrugged.

Sarah glanced between the two groups of people. "I don't see that there's any harm."

Moira chewed her lower lip and considered the Indians. After a long moment, she carefully unraveled her braid. Hawk Nose didn't show any sign one way or another whether or not he was pleased with her choice.

She faced the cowboy. "Can you help?"

John reached into his pocket and pulled out a knife. He unfolded the blade and grasped a handful of her hair. The strands were impossibly soft and springy beneath his fingers, as though her curls had a life of their own.

He stared into her eyes. Her pupils were dilated and her breath came in short, hollow gasps. She was terrified of the Indians and putting on a brave face.

Outnumbered and outgunned.

Tony had a way of sizing up the situation in her succinct, blunt fashion. Right now they were balancing on a fine line of good humor and dumb luck. Near as John could tell, the Indians saw them as some sort of novelty. They'd seen plenty of settlers, buffalo hunters and horse traders cross their land. He didn't suppose they'd ever seen eight hundred head of cattle led by five females, four of them children.

While he made a show of leisurely piercing through Moira's hair, he considered the outcome of the meeting. If the Indians rustled their cattle and tore off for the low country, they risked bringing down the army scouts. A decade past it might have been a fair fight. Now, the meeting was anything but unbiased. The Indians were short of able-bodied men, victims of disease and famine brought on by the dwindling land and buffalo.

As long as he mollified this bunch and sent them home with a nice steer, there was a good chance he and the girls had bought their safe passage.

Moira blinked. Her brilliant eyes were shadowed, yet trusting. Her fear kindled a fierce protectiveness in him.

He wrapped a hunk of hair around one finger and slid his knife blade near the base. "You sure?"

She licked her lips and his gaze dipped.

"If it'll keep old Hawk Nose from taking my whole scalp, I don't figure I have much choice."

Tony cleared her throat. "Maybe we shouldn't talk about them when they're sitting right in front of us."

"They don't understand," Darcy protested.

Tony's gaze slid across the group of Indians. "It's not something I want to bet my life on."

John's blade slid through the strands as easily as slicing through warm butter. He set down his knife and yanked a length of fringe from his buckskin chaps and wound the length around the base.

Hawk Nose reached across the distance and accepted the offering. He rubbed the hair between his thumb and forefinger, then lifted the strands toward the sunlight and tilted his head. John's stomach tightened. It hadn't seemed much of a sacrifice before, yet he didn't like the Indian having a part of Moira. Even something as simple as a lock of hair. The gesture felt personal, intimate.

The three women erupted into chatter and reached for the lock. They took turns studying the hair, holding it near their heads and speaking amongst themselves. Hawk Nose snatched the hair and stuffed the curiosity in the pouch at his hip, ending the commotion.

The Indian glanced between John, Moira and the girls. "Not your children," he said in his clipped Apache.

John shook his head and said, "Family." Or what he hoped meant family.

He must have gotten a close enough word because the Indian woman who spoke some broken English nodded her approval.

Hawk Nose blinked his approval. "Many fine sons to come."

John assumed he was referring to his and Moira's future as a "married couple." He swallowed. "Yes."

The situation was too complicated for his broken Apache. There'd be no explaining how he'd wound up with four orphans and a fiery redhead. Certainly not an explanation to satisfy his unexpected guests.

Moira tugged on his sleeve. "What did he say?"

"He said thank you for the meal." John didn't quite meet her eyes.

He needn't tell her the rest. He stood and motioned for the leader. Together they approached the herd and the younger Indian followed. The tall man wove through the cattle, unmindful of the clacking horns and the lethal hooves. Without asking he returned and grasped a coiled rope from the pile of gear near the chuck wagon. Once again he disappeared into the herd.

The girls stood and huddled behind John. For the first time since he'd met the girls, they remained unnaturally silent. The Indian returned, leading an enormous bull. John took a step back and bumped into Moira.

Hazel gasped. "He can't take Ironsides."

"Who?"

"Ironsides. That's the bull he's taking."

John rubbed his forehead. "Please tell me you did not name all eight hundred head of cattle."

"Only about twenty. And that's Ironsides."

"Well, your bull has a new home."

"They're gonna eat him." Tears welled in her dark eyes.

Tony scoffed. "What did you think was going to happen? They're all gonna get eaten sooner or later. That's why you don't go naming farm animals. Leastways you end up naming your dinner."

Hazel burst into tears and dove into the tent.

John pressed his fingertips into his eyelids until he saw stars.

"I'll see to her." Sarah patted his arm.

The Indian ignored the drama and led the bull away from the herd.

Pops moved to stand beside John. "I seen a lot of things in my life. I ain't never seen an Indian lead a bull like a trained dog."

John winced at the muffled sobs emanating from the tent. "He took my best rope."

"Probably the luckiest thing that will happen this day."

As the group of Indians faded into the distance, the tension in John's shoulders eased. If he'd ever been more terrified in his life, he couldn't recall the time. Pops wandered off and Moira moved toward the fire.

John touched her arm. "Should I talk with her? Hazel?"

"No. She's old enough to learn the truth. I think we all need a moment alone."

Moira trudged into the distance, disappearing behind a small copse of brush trees. Unsettled by the look in her eyes, he jogged the distance and found her sitting with her hands wrapped around her knees, her head bent and her shoulders trembling.

John knelt beside her and placed a hand on her shoulder. "What is it? What's wrong?"

She rocked forward. "I have never been so scared in my entire life."

"I was just thinking the same thing." He caught her around the shoulder, catching a bit of her loose hair in his grip.

Her head lifted. "Do you think they'll be back?"

"I doubt it. At their heart, they're an honorable people. They won't break their word."

"But what about all the raids? The massacres?"

"I don't like murder of any kind, that's for certain." John gathered his thoughts. "The settlers changed their way of life and they fought back. It's not much different than the War Between the States. Right or wrong, people will fight for their survival." He turned his head and his chin grazed the top of her hair. "One side wins and one side loses. That's how most things end."

"And so much death in between."

She turned her head and stared up at him. He lowered his head, brushing his lips against her forehead. Her eyes fluttered closed. He pressed a kiss against her temple, feeling the rapid pulse beneath her skin. Her pale ivory skin was creamy and smooth. Her cheeks matched the blush of a peach's skin. She tipped back her head and their lips met. He'd only meant to offer her a modicum of comfort, but her gentle sigh wreaked havoc on his resolve. He pulled away and cupped her face, searching her eyes. The sweet, misty look on her face drew him forward.

His lips moved tentatively over hers. She swayed against him. He continued his leisurely exploration, giving her every chance to pull away. Her trembling hands wound around his neck and pulled him closer.

A shrill scream split the air.

Moira's forehead bumped his nose. "The Indians. They've come back."

John's stomach dropped. He leapt to his feet and glanced around. "It's not the Indians."

He'd expected more trouble. Just not this soon.

Chapter Eleven

Moira reached the commotion mere paces after John. "What's wrong? What's happened?"

The girls had gathered around an outcropping of rock on the edge of a shallow dip in the grassland. A narrow overhang of ragged weeds indicated the presence of a tiny cave, an opening fit only for an animal. The mouth of the hole opened beneath a ledge at the base of a flat rock. About the size of a barrel, the darkened mouth stretched into the embankment. Out of the opening came Champion's steady barking.

Hazel clasped her hands together. "It all happened too fast. I was standing here when Champion started barking. Then it brushed past my leg."

Tony tilted her head. "When what came past?"

"An animal."

"A possum?"

"No. It was soft with a fluffy tail. I think it's a cat. Champion chased it in there." She cast an accusing glare at John. "Now it won't come out."

"Well, uh." John adjusted his hat. "I suppose we best leave whatever it is alone. Once we're all gone, it'll come out soon enough."

"I think it's hurt."

John hesitated. "Even more reason to leave it alone. A frightened animal is dangerous."

"It's a cat."

"It's not a cat. We're too far from town for strays."

Hazel set her jaw. "I'm sure it's a cat."

"Trust me. It's not a cat. I've been walking this trail for twenty years and I can guarantee you that."

Moira studied the determined set of Hazel's shoulders. She had a bad feeling if he didn't check out the animal, Hazel would go in after he turned his back.

John caught her gaze and an unspoken communication passed between them. He must have come to the same conclusion.

"If I prove it's not a cat, will you leave it alone?"

"I promise. But it's a cat. I'm certain."

Smothering a sigh, John knelt.

Moira edged closer. The hollowed-out area stretched deep into the ground, narrowing until the dog disappeared into the darkness. Stale dust and the rank scent of a wild animal sent her nose wrinkling.

Muffled barks echoed through the recesses of the tiny cave.

She didn't know much about nature, but this didn't seem like a good idea. "John is right, Hazel. If we all leave it alone, the animal will come out on its own."

Sarah patted the younger girl's back. "They're right. We shouldn't go messing with wild animals. For all we know it's a bunch of shoats."

Hazel remained stubbornly silent.

John gave a slight shrug. "It can't be very big. I'm guessing it's a prairie dog Champion chased out of its den. I'll take a quick look." He doffed his hat. "This won't take long."

Moira accepted the hat and clutched it to her chest.

A tingle of apprehension danced along her spine. "I still don't think it's such a good idea."

The cowboy angled his head and glanced up at her. "I'll be quick. We don't have much time. Looks like there's a storm coming."

Moira followed his gaze.

She'd been so engrossed in the excitement over the Indians and then distracted by John's kiss, she hadn't noticed the growing wall of white, fluffy clouds in the distance. "They don't look so bad."

Her cheeks warmed beneath his glance and she unconsciously touched her lips. Somehow, in that moment, everything had changed. Of course she'd thought he was handsome, what girl wouldn't? She'd known he was kind, considerate. Now she was thinking about him in a whole new way.

Had anything changed for him? She couldn't read his inscrutable expression.

"Those clouds will get worse, trust me," he said. "They'll get bigger and taller and darker. Then we'll have a storm on our hands. At least we're out of harm's way from the river. It's late in the season, but we're still risking a flash flood. The more we talk, the more time we waste."

Moira huffed at his quiet rebuke. Her earlier sterling thoughts of him tarnished a bit. "I'm only trying to save you from a bite. Or worse."

John reclined onto his left hip. He leaned in, positioning his body until he held most of his weight on this left elbow and shoulder. With the heel of his boot he pushed off, scooting into the darkness. His head and shoulders disappeared.

Moira held her breath.

"Oh no."

His boots kicked a furious tarantella in the dust.

The cowboy rolled out of the cave as though he'd been

shot out of a cannon. A flurry of fur and squealing followed close behind. As John scrambled to his feet, the ball of fur flattened him back against the ground.

A screech sounded, immediately followed by an ear-splitting yelp. Champion leapt onto the pile.

"I told you it was a cat!" Hazel shouted.

"Stay back," John shouted. "It's a bobcat."

Champion and the angered cat rolled in the dust. The dog soon realized he was outmatched with a painful yowl. Champion released his clenched jaw from the animal's neck and sprang backward.

Dazed, the bobcat shook its head a few times before streaking into the distance. Moira caught sight of the cowboy sprawled on the ground, an angry slash across his cheek with two drips of blood sliding beneath his chin. He swiped at the blood with the back of his hand and made to push himself off the dirt.

His hand landed smack on the back of a startled skunk.

Moira clapped her hands over her mouth and stumbled away.

Champion had chased the bobcat into a den with a previous occupant. A burst of noxious odor hit Moira like a wall. John lunged. He clutched his face and staggered upright. The girls shrieked and scattered like shrapnel. Champion whimpered, tail tucked between its legs, slinking away, muzzle down.

Hazel pinched her nose. "That's not a cat."

Her eyes watering, Moira clutched John's arm. "Skunk."

"Skunk," he repeated, his voice hoarse. "I didn't think of that."

Pops appeared on the hill, then halted, waving his hand before his face. "Who got skunked?"

"That would be me." John coughed and sputtered.

"Well, don't just stand there," Pops shouted. "There's a watering hole about fifty paces ahead. Go rinse off."

John held his hands before him like a blind man. "My eyes are swelling shut. I can't see a thing."

Moira buried her nose in the crook of her elbow. "I'll lead you."

The odor was alive, slithering down her throat and coating her mouth. Moira coughed.

John groped along his puffy cheeks. "What's happening to my face?"

Her own eyes watered profusely, tears running down her face. She pried them open and got a good look at the cowboy. His cheeks were swollen, the sockets around his eyes puffy and misshapen, even his lips were bloated. His face was rapidly becoming unrecognizable.

"Take my hand." Moira linked her left hand with his and wrapped her right arm around his waist.

Sightless, he extended his right hand, feeling his way. Together they stumbled toward the creek.

Tony jogged toward them, stopping a safe distance and pinching her nose. "You need help?"

Moira glanced over her shoulder. "Get some rags. Have Darcy catch up with Pops and Hazel. He's gonna need a change of clothes and some soap."

"Soap isn't going to help with that stench."

Moira swiped at her runny nose. "Well, it sure can't hurt."

She spotted the depression and followed it down to a stagnant puddle left by the wet fall weather. John tripped through the muddy hoofprints and waded in to his waist. Moira followed close behind, worried at his lack of sight. He pressed his face into the shallow water and threw back his head, showering Moira with water droplets.

"Hey!"

"Sorry," he mumbled.

Moira wiped the moisture from her cheeks. "You're not sorry at all."

"Nope."

She laughed and skimmed the heel of her hand along the water, kicking up a splash.

He waded deeper and Moira splashed after him, catching his elbow. "Not too far."

Halting, he turned and grazed her shoulder with his elbow. "Sorry." He reached for her and stumbled, threw out his arms, and sank deeper into the water.

Moira struggled, pulling them toward the bank until the water grazed her waist. She snatched his hat and filled the crown with water, then dumped the contents over his head.

The cowboy gasped and sputtered. "You might give me a warning next time."

Moira laughed. "Where's the fun in all that?"

John reached beneath the water. After a moment his hand emerged clutching his familiar, faded blue bandanna.

He mopped at his face "Another."

Moira obliged, dumping a hatful of water over his head. After ten or twelve dousing, the odor abated somewhat and Moira stepped back. The swelling in his face had gone down, though his eyes remained blistered and closed.

Keeping her arms above her waist she circled until she was upwind of the cowboy. He turned in her direction, running his hands down his face.

His reaction had her worried. "Have you ever been sprayed by a skunk?" she asked.

"I'm happy to say I've never had the pleasure."

"I think you had a reaction. I've never seen a swelling like that before. Mrs. Gifford only had a bit of red after she was sprayed."

"Who is Mrs. Gifford?"

"My foster mother. I worked for Mr. and Mrs. Gifford for years."

"Wait, I don't understand. You worked for them? I thought you said they were your foster family."

Moira smirked. Since he couldn't see her face, she didn't have to hide her reactions. "Orphans are little more than indentured servants, serving out our time until we come of age."

"Surely it's not like that for everyone."

"Too many. It's a hard life out west. It makes people hard. I could spread out blame, but what's the point. Folks shouldn't have children if they're not going to care for them."

His whole body stilled. "Your parents couldn't help dying, Moira. You must see that."

"My parents weren't dead, Mr. Elder. Not right away. My pa ran off. He figured his money went further supporting one man instead of a family. My mother was sick. Tuberculosis. She couldn't care for us."

"I'm sorry, I didn't mean—"

"It's all right. They're both gone now. My brother left the Giffords first." A sharp pain gripped her heart. "I stayed. I thought he'd come back for me. He never did. When I came of age, I set off on my own, too. I got a job cleaning rooms after hours at a hotel not far from the Giffords and waited. If Tommy came looking…well, I didn't want to be far."

Except he'd never come. And the longer she'd waited, the less hope she had. The more she worried he couldn't forgive her, the more she realized she had to find him and set things right.

"Moira, I'm sorry for bringing up the past. Of reminding you of the pain. Truly I am."

He stepped closer, blindly reaching out his hand. Moira flinched away. She didn't want his pity. There were truths in life, that was all.

"I've been looking for Tommy ever since. Once we're together, we'll be a family again, things will be different."

He'd make her whole again. She wouldn't be a burden

or a charity. She'd be family. He'd forgive her for what had happened.

"That's an awful lot of responsibility to put on a person. An awful lot of hope to pin on someone."

"It's not worth talking about. You wouldn't understand."

He *couldn't* understand. He was a loner, but Moira needed family. She needed love and belonging. She needed something to fill the empty parts of her soul. There was no use explaining loneliness to someone who'd never been lonely.

John sank deeper, tipping back his head. "I thought you were afraid of the water." His shirt plastered to his body, outlining the muscles of his shoulders, the corded strength of his arms.

Moira shivered.

"I'm afraid of running water."

"You're afraid of indoor plumbing?"

"No!" She chuckled. "Ponds and lakes don't bother me so much. It's the rivers and streams. I'm afraid I'll be swept away."

"We're not getting very far today. Why don't we call it quits and let everyone rest. We'll pull out the washtub and give everything at camp a good scouring."

Moira blushed. She'd gone forty-eight long, hard hours in the same clothing. She'd been soaked twice, but that was different. She needed soap and water and a good scrubbing. A thorough washing sounded wonderful.

"How do I look?" John asked suddenly.

"Horrible!" She replied quickly, grateful for the change of subject. In the two days since she'd let go of civilization, she hadn't yet adjusted. "You look like you've gone three rounds at the fights. And lost."

"What else do you see?"

"That's an odd question."

"It's strange, not being able to see." He turned a lazy circle, sending ripples toward her. "I can't see you, but I'm picturing you. It makes a fellow think about things. Reminds me of playing blindman's buff as a kid. When I think of you, you're very serious. You're always looking at where you're going, never what's around you."

"I don't want to trip."

"We're not walking now. Humor me. Tell me what you see?"

"No Man's Land."

"And what does No Man's Land look like?"

"Red."

"You're terrible at this, you know?" John raked his hands through his damp hair. "Haven't you ever played I Spy? I spy with my little eye, something green. You'd be surprised at how much people never notice. Look at us right now. My eyes are closed and even I see more than you do. I see black clouds."

"They're gray."

The cowboy shot her a look of pure disgruntlement. "You lost your turn. Don't interrupt."

"Fine."

"The sun is reflecting off the water, shimmering, there's catfish."

"This pond is too small for catfish. Besides, how can you see a catfish if you're blinded?"

"I didn't see it, it bit my toe."

A twitch of a smile flickered around the edges of her mouth. Grateful he couldn't see her reaction, she clamped shut her lips. "I hope it hurt."

His face distorted in a way that told her clearly he was attempting not to smile. "Of course you don't."

The fool man didn't even have the sense to be embarrassed. Moira chewed her lip and glanced over her shoulder. Where on earth were the others with the supplies? The soap and the change of clothes.

"The water is cold," John said. "So it must be spring fed. Which means there are trees around. The trees are spindly, already losing their leaves. A storm is coming, but the clouds aren't dark enough yet. They're building in the sky like mountains."

"Your mouth has been leaded, not gilded."

"I hear the cattle. They're gathering, too. Trampling down the hill looking for water. Pretty soon that old bull will wade right in up to his waist. I never once saw a bull who liked water as much as that old lazybones."

He was right, already the cattle dotted the area around the watering hole. They were keeping a wary eye on John and Moira, waiting for their turn.

Instead of admitting that, she said, "It's a good thing you're a cowboy. You'd make a terrible poet."

"Keep your voice down, you're disrupting my artistic genius. And they're not cows," he said with exaggerated patience. "They're long-horned Texas steer, and they'll gore you for mocking them. If you're going to be a trail boss, you should talk like a trail boss."

Her cheeks warmed despite the chill water. It suddenly occurred to her what a ridiculous turn her life had taken. A simple twist of fate had stranded her in Indian Territory on a cattle drive with a reluctant cowboy.

"My brother Tommy and I had a game, too. We'd imagine where we'd be if we could be anywhere in the world at any time in history. What about you? If you could be anywhere, where else would you be?"

"I'd pick a week from now. In Cimarron Springs," he announced immediately. "Warming my feet before my own fire with my boots set firmly on my own stool."

"But what about your family? Wouldn't you rather be with them?"

John guffawed. "Only once a year at Christmas. When it's too cold for hunting and the women are around making sure we're all on our best behavior."

Her smile faded. "Don't you miss them?"

"Of course I do. But that's the way of things. People grow. They move on. Jack and Robert have their own families now."

"But you could still be a part of their lives."

"Of course. But things change. We can't go on like we're still kids."

"Things don't have to change," she said.

"You know what would happen to this pond if the spring dried up? If the water didn't keep pumping out? It would go stagnant. Moss would grow on the surface and all the tadpoles would die. The whole place would turn rank. Life is like that. Things have to change to stay alive."

Is that what she'd done? Had she grown stagnant? No. That wasn't it at all. She was preserving her family. That was an honorable goal.

He had everything. He had a home. And he didn't want it. He didn't understand and he never could. He was carefree and unencumbered, waxing on about shimmering streams and imaginary catfish. He'd lived his safe life near the ground, never understanding what it was like to live up high, inching along a thin wire without a net. Never knowing where your next meal would come from or where you'd sleep that night.

Even with his face swollen and the faint stench of skunk drifting over the rushing stream, he was handsome. It wasn't just his looks, there was something compelling about him, a pull that kept her waist-deep in a freezing pond when she could be curled up before a warm fire instead.

He had effortless charm and an easy way. Perhaps that

was the problem. He was right about her. She always kept her head down. She was drawn to his sense of adventure.

He ran his hand down his face and for a moment she sensed a rare vulnerability. In that instant his shoulders appeared less broad, his expression worried, though muddled by the swelling, distracted. She'd come to think of him as invincible, certainly indefatigable. His patience never lagged, his temper rarely flared.

He'd taken a rotten situation and put a humorous spin on the events, and not for his own benefit.

John took a step forward and stumbled. Moira reached out and steadied him. His shirt was soaked through, plastered against his torso. The heat of his shoulder radiated through the chill water, warming her hand.

Her breath grew shallow and uneven.

She took the bandanna from his free hand and dipped it into the water, wringing out the excess. Her touch cautious, she laid the cool cloth against his creased eyes. He winced and Moira pulled back.

His hand covered hers, pressing the cloth into place. "It's all right."

Moira shivered against the husky timbre of his voice.

"You're freezing." He wrapped his arm around her shoulder. "Lead me toward the bank. If we don't get you out of this water, you'll catch your death."

Together they struggled through the thick mud toward the bank, then collapsed on the dry, prickly grass.

Moira glanced up. "It looks like the cavalry is coming."

Pops appeared on the horizon, his bulky form moving faster than Moira had thought possible. Sarah and Hazel jogged beside him.

John touched her hand. "You haven't told me where you'd rather be."

"I'd go back in time and right a wrong."

His head jerked around. "What wrong?"

"It's nothing. Never mind."

"Has anyone ever told you that you're stubborn as all get-out?"

"They tell me all the time. I just never listen."

"That's because you're stubborn," he replied gruffly.

John accepted the blanket Pops draped around his shoulders. "Someday I'll get my answer, Miss O'Mara."

She tightened the blanket Sarah had given her and glanced at the sky. True to John's prediction, the clouds had grown and darkened. They hadn't made any progress yet that day and they were going to be halted by a thunderstorm.

Pops swung his arm in an arc. "Get yourselves back to camp. I've got a surprise waiting."

John sighed. "Please tell me it's not another skunk. This day can't get any worse."

A clap of thunder met John's muttered question.

"Yep," Pops replied. "Looks like this day just might get a touch worse at that."

Moira trailed behind the group. When she was with John, he consumed her thoughts, her focus. She hadn't thought about Tommy in hours. She hadn't considered what she'd do next. She hadn't even thought about the sheriff's promise or what she might find at the telegraph office in Cimarron Springs. Moira scoffed. She hadn't thought of anything beyond the present. The oversight felt like a betrayal.

When she'd lived with the Giffords, she'd felt trapped. At least the choice of searching for Tommy had been taken from her. Not anymore. She had no excuses for faltering in her goal. Glancing in John's direction, she shook her head. She'd vowed not to be distracted and it was time to keep that vow.

No more kisses. No more banter. This was business.

They were driving a herd of cattle. Once they reached Cimarron Springs, they'd never see each other again.

John groaned. He still couldn't see well. Despite a good dose of Pops's magic cure-all, a syrupy concoction with a foul aftertaste, his eyes remained swollen and his vision blurred. "You didn't tell me the surprise."

"The drummer caught up with us." Pops muttered something unintelligible. "Now where is my ladle?" John heard the distinctive clink of tin cups and cutlery as Pops searched his chuck wagon. "That's funny. I don't remember putting it there. Anyway, he's unhitched his horses. Looks like he plans on sticking around a while."

"The girls must be chomping at the bit."

"Not like you'd think. You gotta remember, they've got no money. They're not getting their hopes up. Don't know how they'll get outfitted. I think they're afraid to ask. They've got their pride you know."

John absorbed the quiet rebuke. Of all the roadblocks he'd considered, pride hadn't been on the list. "Two days ago I had a crew of men. I didn't have to worry about this stuff."

"That was two days ago. This is now. You've got other problems."

"Point taken." John pressed his bandanna against his swollen eyes. "Make up some nonsense about a gear allowance. Buy him out of gloves and anything else they need."

Pops clicked his tongue. "We've only got another day or two before Fort Preble. That's a lot of money spent without much chance of return."

John thought of Moira's hands, the blisters already forming on her palms. "I guess I owe them something. They've gotten us this far. I can always sell off a bull or two, or wire the bank for money."

"Robert will wonder why you're wiring for money."

"Let him wonder. It's none of his business."

The jingling of bells signaled the arrival of the peddler and John tensed. "I still don't like the idea of a stranger in camp. I don't need word getting out. We're too far from Fort Preble."

"Don't worry. I've crossed paths with Swede before. He's harmless."

John pulled the bandanna from his face and squinted. "Is there anyone you don't know?"

"I've been walking this trail for thirty years. You're bound to run into the same faces. Don't worry about Swede. We go way back. He'll keep your secrets. He won't be spreading rumors about our crew. And he's promised me a deal on a new frying pan for bringing in the business."

"I knew it. You have an addiction to frying pans."

"And taken a liking to good food."

"At least we agree on one thing."

By the time the drummer lumbered into camp, John could open his left eye and make out hazy images. He couldn't recall a time when he'd felt more helpless, more inadequate. While the girls set up camp and made use of the washtub, he'd bathed and changed his clothes at the nearby watering hole. He'd worn the bar of soap to a whittling, but he still felt the skunk's odor glazing the back of his throat and saturating his hair.

The others steered clear, giving him a wide berth. Someone had pressed a steaming hot cup of coffee into his hands and quickly retreated. Someone else had slapped a tray of food before him. Tony, judging by the forceful presentation.

Having a stranger in camp while he wasn't at his best force left him feeling exposed. Since he'd discovered that rubbing his eyes only made them worse, he'd forced his hands back to his sides. No matter how much they itched and annoyed him, he remained stoic.

With his eyesight impaired, the rest of his senses heightened. The air had turned heavy and he feared an oncoming storm. Voices swirled around him and he felt disconnected and out of sorts.

He pushed off from one knee and stood. The girls remained huddled around the campfire.

"I need you outfitted," John declared. "All my men have full kits. You'll need hats, coats, gloves, a change of clothes and sundries. It's part of crew pay."

Tony sat up. "No fooling."

"No fooling. A crew can't function without gear. You're my crew. Every one of you should have a canteen and a pocketknife as well as a box of matches. You'll carry them with you in your saddle bags at all times. Jerky as well. If we get separated, those items are the difference in survival."

Tony sidled nearer the wagon, keeping a wary eye out. Her hesitation confounded him. A look passed between Darcy and Tony, raising his hackles. Darcy had performed well on the ride, but a certain rebellion in her demeanor kept him wary. While he didn't know the source of his unease, he trusted his instincts.

Sarah held Hazel's hand and they both kept their heads bent. He searched the surrounding area and realized Moira had taken her turn caring for the horses.

A man rounded the corner of the wagon. He sported a dark, scruffy beard that covered his face and stretched well down his neck. His black hair was parted down the middle and hung slightly over his collar. He wore mud-brown trousers held in place by a pair of suspenders, and his red union suit showed beneath the rolled-up sleeves of his chambray shirt.

Hazel buried her head in Sarah's shoulder.

The movement caught the newcomer's attention. His gaze narrowed. Darcy scooted away.

The newcomer stalked toward the girls.

John blocked the man's progress and caught him by the collar.

The newcomer spun around. "Are you John Elder?"

"I am."

"I'm Swede. Sheriff Taylor sent me."

"I figured as much." John kept his grip on the man's collar. "You want to explain what you're all fired up about?"

Swede jabbed a finger at the cowering girls. "I ain't letting them near my wagon. That one stole an apple off me cart not two days ago."

Hazel cowered into Sarah's arms.

John's suspicions crystallized. Even before the sheriff's arrival, he'd suspected they were thieves working together. Without proof either way, he'd let the issue remain unresolved. The arrival of the drummer had forced his hand.

John released his hold on the man's collar. "Surely you can forgive a slight transgression."

"The apple is what I know'd about. Who knows what else they took when I wasn't looking."

"They're children." John recalled his thoughts from that first day. "Starving children forced into desperate measures."

Swede wiped his nose on the back of his sleeve. "That ain't my problem."

John glanced to the hinged door on the wagon, already propped open, revealing a colorful array of wares. "You've come a long way to leave empty-handed."

The drummer tore his gaze from Hazel. "I ain't letting them girls pilfer my stock either."

John considered his options. As he mulled his choices, Moira appeared.

His breath hitched. Her hair remained damp, the curls darker and lanky at her shoulders. Her cheeks were flushed from her time spent in the sun and her eyes sparkled with curiosity. She wore the same dress she'd been wearing since the moment she'd dropped from the sky. The blue was faded from washing, the fabric worn thin. And she was the most captivating sight he'd ever laid eyes on. She glanced between the two men and a wrinkle appeared between her cinnamon-colored brows.

Swede's attention flicked in her direction and he appeared to quickly dismiss her. John didn't realize he'd been holding his breath until he released the pent-up air in his lungs.

"I'll vouch for them," John announced.

Darcy's eyes widened. Hazel raised her head. Sarah and Tony turned in his direction.

John shrugged. "I'll vouch for them. They're my crew. They're my responsibility. They'll do right by you."

Tony fisted her hands on her hips. "You'd do that? You'd trust us. Even after what he said?"

John mulled over the question, the implications of his answer. "I want an honest day's work for an honest day's wage. You've done that. You've never given me any reason to believe I can't trust you."

He considered the earlier reticence from the girls. They weren't afraid Swede would recognize them, they were afraid John's assistance came with a cost. They'd been conditioned throughout their lives, trained that their worth came with a price. Even among the four of them there were uneasy allegiances. Snatches of remembered conversation filtered through his memory.

They didn't entirely trust one another. They certainly didn't trust him.

What about Moira?

The deeper he dug, the more he realized he didn't know

much about their pasts. They were young enough he figured he didn't need to dig far. He couldn't unravel the
events that had led them to this point. One thought hadn't
escaped him: Fool's End was an odd place for a bunch of
orphans.

While he couldn't change what had brought them to
this point, he could offer them his trust.

Moira remained motionless near the tent, sensing the
undercurrents, no doubt.

Swede tugged on his suspenders. "You'll vouch for
them girls with your wallet. If I find anything missing,
I'll hunt you down for payment."

"I consider that fair."

The drummer puffed up.

"You needn't act like you've done anything special."
Sarah flipped the hair from her eyes. "Mr. Elder has given
us leave to purchase whatever we need. Why would any
of us steal from you?"

The drummer squinted one eye. "Because you're
thieves, that's why. It's all you know. Once a body gets a
taste for thievin' he don't wanna work no more. You're
like a bunch of magpies, you are, always looking for something shiny."

Moira gasped. "What is the meaning of this? Who
are you and what gives you the right to say such horrid
things?"

John tossed her a sharp glance. "We all need each other.
The girls need new gear and Swede has stock. The sooner
we get the girls outfitted the better. We can all be on our
way again."

"I got my eye on ya'." Swede pointed at his face and
then at Hazel. "You most of all."

Pops lumbered around the wagon carrying the Dutch
oven by a hooked metal pole attached to the lid, his gait
hitched against the heavy load. He glanced at the new-

comer. "Taking over the business from your father, are you, Swede?"

The drummer blanched. "I didn't know you was part of all this."

"Swede, you've got your dad's beard and your mother's coloring," Pops spoke to the drummer. "I thought you were working out of Silver Springs."

"We moved up to Fool's End. More business."

"You'll not be getting any business by insulting your patrons. That's for certain. Why don't you keep an eye on this stew instead?" Pops wrinkled his nose and glanced at John. "Wouldn't hurt to buy yourself a new slicker. You're still sending off a powerful stench."

John lifted his elbow and caught a nauseating whiff of his sleeve. "Will do."

He'd placed his trust in the girls. He sure hoped his faith wasn't misguided.

Chapter Twelve

Moira glared at the drummer. He ate his stew with gusto, filling his bowl twice more while the girls rummaged through his wagonful of supplies. She snatched a pair of denim trousers and held them at her waist. The hem stretched well beyond her feet. She'd need four rolls in the cuffs, but at least she'd be able to ride more freely. Satisfied with the fit, she added another pair to her pile.

Hazel's clothing proved the most difficult. The drummer had brought a selection of clothing suitable for an adolescent boy.

The smallest of the group held up a pair of trousers over her head and the cuffs reached the dirt at her feet. "Everything is too big."

"Don't worry," Tony said. "We'll find you something."

Moira caught sight of a beautiful leather case. She flipped open the hinged lid and discovered a sewing kit nestled in the velvet-lined interior. The kit contained a pair of silver scissors with ornate detailing on the handles, a delicate thimble and wheels of cardboard with the spokes wrapped in a colorful array of thread. There was even a lidded cylinder for needles.

Tempted for a moment, she glanced over her shoulder.

Would John balk at the expense? The men remained in deep conversation around the campfire.

Darcy caught her gaze. "Don't do it."

Moira started. "I beg your pardon?"

"You're thinking of stealing that. I can see it in your eyes. You can't. It's too big."

Moira slammed the lid over on the kit and set it aside. "Don't be absurd."

A hint of skunk caught her attention. She turned and found the cowboy leaning over her shoulder. He glanced at the kit then at Hazel.

She'd tugged a chambray shirt over her head and the hem reached well below her knees. John reached for the kit. "Looks as though we're going to need this."

He rested the leather case atop Moira's pile of clothing before setting off toward the cattle in the distance.

Darcy's expression turned speculative. "I think he likes you."

"Don't be silly."

"It's not a bad thing. Having someone like that take a shine to you. Could be real useful. For all of us."

Moira tensed. "What are you implying?"

The girl raised one shoulder in a slight shrug. "Well, he's not bad-looking and he seems nice enough. A girl doesn't have much choice out here. You could do worse."

"I'm doing fine on my own. I don't like the direction of your thoughts."

"You're not doing any better than the rest of us. You're just faking it better. You might have fooled Mr. Elder, but you haven't fooled me. I know your kind."

"You don't know me." Moira shoved the sewing kit off her pile of clothing and stacked her new boots on top instead. "You don't know anything about me."

She grasped her bundle against her chest and walked a few paces away from the wagon. Her heartbeat raced and her hands tingled. She thought of Mr. Gifford, how he'd once sidled up to her in the hallway and pressed her against the wainscoting, his hot breath on her cheek.

John wasn't like that. Their relationship was different. Her thoughts scattered. What was she thinking? They didn't have a relationship.

Moira glanced over one shoulder at Darcy. "Find yourself something to wear. We have a job to do."

Keeping his eyes open was exhausting. John rested his head against the wheel of the chuck wagon. A heavy weight landed near his bent knee.

He groped and discovered the pitted leather of a well-used valise with the word O'Mara stamped on a brass plate. "Give it to the redhead."

"My orders were to give it to you. That's what I'm doing."

John inclined his head. "Hope it wasn't hard finding us."

The man cackled. "I'd sooner track a slug. I left shortly after Sheriff Taylor found me. After that I took the road out of town. I cut off the path and circled back. Still beat you to the watering hole."

John felt his ears heat. "My crew did well considering they'd never seen a longhorn before two days ago."

"At least you're going in a straight line. That's something."

"Yep. That's something."

Swede tugged on his suspenders. "The sheriff filled me in on your situation, and I added a few extras to the stock. Things that appeal to the girls."

"Put it on my tab."

In for a penny, in for a pound.

The girls' chatter ebbed and flowed around him. After a moment, he sensed someone else approaching.

He knew it was Moira before she spoke. There was something about her. Her footfalls, the way she smelled like peony blossoms. He didn't quite understand the connection, but since that first moment, something sparked between them when she was near.

"Is there anything I can get you?" she asked.

"Nah. I'm fine. You get everything you need?"

"You've set the girls free in a candy store. I don't think any of them have had anything new in ages."

"Send his wagon back empty. Everyone should have something new once in a while."

She touched his forehead, her fingertips featherlight. He sucked in a breath.

"The swelling has gone down," she said. "Can you see?"

"It's better. How's the smell?"

"Better."

"You're not much of a liar, Miss Moira O'Mara."

She laughed and he recalled what Swede had brought. "There's something special for you."

He hooked his hand through the handle and hoisted the valise over his lap.

Moira gasped. She immediately knelt on the ground and rummaged through the bag, emerging with a dogeared sketchbook. She flipped through the pages then hugged the book to her chest.

Curious, he glanced over her shoulder. "What have you got there?"

"My sketchbook."

She proudly displayed a page featuring a young boy. The details were flawless, delicately formed and perfectly displayed. He forced his sore eyes further open. "You're very talented. That's truly wonderful."

Moira blushed. "I practiced a lot."

He took the book from her hands and flipped through

the pages. Every inch of every page was covered in sketches. Her subjects were disparate: people, animals, flowers, anything and everything. She had a great eye for particulars and an excellent sense of perspective. John angled the paper and realized the sketches covered both sides.

Moira tugged the book from his hands. "I don't like to waste space."

"You're good. Real good. You're running out of pages, though."

"I still have some space in the back."

John cast a surreptitious glance at her bag. She didn't have much.

She clutched the handles to her chest. "How did you talk the sheriff into sending this along?"

"I asked."

"I can't believe he agreed."

"He's not such a bad guy."

Moira snorted. "Did you have to pay him?"

"Nope. He wanted information."

"About what?"

"Land. He was looking to buy some land suitable for raising horses. Wondered if I had any leads where I was heading. I put him onto a parcel down the creek in Cimarron Springs."

Moira laughed. "Wouldn't that be the way? You'll be neighbors with the man who kicked you out of Fool's End."

"He saved those girls' lives."

"He did no such thing! We could have gone back into town but for him."

John had considered the events of that first evening over the past few days, and he had a bad feeling the girls hadn't acted alone. "Those girls weren't safe there and you know it. Not after, well, you know."

"I don't think we should paint Sheriff Taylor as the hero of this story."

"Heroes don't always look like we expect them to."

"I never expected you to defend the man. Especially after he ran you out of town."

"I had a lot of time to think today. It occurs to me that maybe I was wrong about some things."

Moira stood. "Well, I'll leave you to your thinking. It's my turn for watch and I can't be late or Darcy will pitch a fit."

He found himself longing for her return. When another moment passed, he let his thoughts drift. John enjoyed the silence for five whole minutes before Pops appeared.

The older man sipped on his ever-present tin cup of coffee. "We've gotten the girls outfitted. They've set up the tents and worked out a watch list. It's going to storm tonight. Looks like it's gonna be a real humdinger. We've got extra stakes on the tents in case there's wind."

"All right."

"Look, John. I'm sorry about setting this whole thing into motion. I know you're sore. And maybe you're right. After this morning, well, we got real lucky. I can't help but think if it had been the old crew and us, things might not have gone so well. As it stands, we're lucky we made it out with our scalps. Maybe it's too dangerous for these girls out here. But I didn't see any way of stopping them. And I sure didn't want them out here alone."

"I get it."

"You sure you're all right?"

"I lost my men, my herd and my horses. One of my orphan crew nearly drowned. I got sprayed by a skunk and can't see out of my left eye. I assaulted a deputy sheriff and got kicked out of Fool's End. No mean feat considering it's a town with as many outlaws as law-abiding citizens. It's about to rain and I've got a leaky tent full of females. Oh, and my slicker is in the fire because it smells like skunk. Other than that, I'm doing all right."

"It doesn't sound all right when you say it like that." Pops rummaged through the drawers lining the sides of the chuck wagon. "You're starting to sound like Jack before he settled down and relaxed a bit."

John bolted upright. "What's that supposed to mean?"

"Easy there. It don't mean nothing except you sounded like Jack just then, you know, back before he met Elizabeth. There's something about a woman that changes a man. Jack was all full of right and wrong. He was all black and white. Always trying to force things his way. Not the sort of fellow who'd marry the widow of an outlaw."

"He must have changed all right, because that's just what he did," John said.

When Jack had set out after their sister-in-law's killer, he never expected the man would already be dead, or that he'd left a widow and child behind. Jack had fallen in love with the widow and child and brought them back to Paris, Texas. He was definitely a changed man, that was certain.

He and Jack hadn't gotten along well, before Jack married Elizabeth. They'd grown closer of late. While Jack hadn't encouraged him to leave after the fight with Robert, he hadn't questioned his decision to leave either. It was as though Jack understood his need to put some space between him and Robert.

No matter what Jack was like now, John didn't appreciate the comparison to the "old" Jack. The stubborn, hardheaded Jack.

Pops shook his head and continued his work.

John pressed the backs of his knuckles against his swollen eyes, thankful they weren't nearly as sore as an hour before. At the low rumble of thunder in the distance, he turned up his collar. They wouldn't make any progress today. Not with the rain and his green crew. He'd send out the boys in this weather, but he didn't dare risk the younger girls.

While he enjoyed the rare respite from his duties, a drizzle misted the air. Instead of wind and lightning, the drops were barely more than a haze. The girls disappeared into their tent and John sidled into the narrow space in the center of the chuck wagon, his knees bent against the sideboard. He laced his hands behind his head and stared at the overhang. Pops's words kept ringing in his ears. He was behaving like Jack. He was forcing the situation into a preordained shape. He was stubbornly jamming the pieces together when he knew good and well the puzzle had changed.

Just because his new crew was different from his old crew didn't make them better or worse. They were simply *different*. As the trail boss, it was his job to bring out the best in his men, even if they were women.

It was high time he did his job.

After the drummer's exit and after everyone had washed and changed into a fresh set of clothes, they'd made the decision to set out on the trail once more. The clouds had moved north and the rain had let up. The time had gone past one in the afternoon, but Moira figured some progress was better than no progress. Even Hazel could tell John was chafing at the bit. Despite the Indians and the skunk, he'd made the decision to press onward.

The rest of the day passed beneath the monotonous drone of flies and the plodding of hoofbeats. The terrain remained even and unchanged, the horizon a faint line in the distance. Once she'd jerked upright, realizing she'd fallen into a slight slumber.

Tony circled around. "Look sharp. No sleeping on the job."

Moira yawned. "I always thought falling asleep in the saddle was a tall tale. I think different now.

Clouds covered the sun and kept the air cool. Moira's horse mostly took the lead. Better trained than her, the horse seemed to realize when one of the cattle was about to stray out of line. After what seemed like hours, John lifted his fisted hand and called them to a halt.

Moira slumped. "How far was that?"

"About six miles."

"Six? Is that all? Seems like we've gone fifty."

"We lost half the day. That's half the distance."

Since they'd had an easy day, she wasn't near as sore as she'd been the first. Already her muscles were accommodating the change in activity. That evening they gathered around the campfire. They'd rotated the watch backward from the night before, which meant Sarah had the first watch and Moira the last.

The air had a chill and Pops added extra logs to the fire, building the flames higher than normal. The sun sank in the distance, leaving behind the darkened haze of twilight.

Tony splayed out, her feet stretched toward the warmth, her head propped on a saddle. "You know what this night needs? Some good scary stories."

"I don't think it's a good idea," Moira said. "You girls won't sleep a wink after a round of scary stories."

"Nah." Tony had perked right up with the idea. "We'll be fine."

"I love scary stories," Darcy added.

Hazel plopped down. "Me too."

"Good." Tony grinned. "I'll get started. Everyone gather around."

The girls giggled and pulled their rough wool blankets around their shoulders against the cold.

"Go on," Hazel urged. "Tell us the story."

"I heard tell why all the soil in the Indian Territory is red," Tony whispered.

Even Darcy leaned in closer. "How come?"

Tony spread her arms. "A thousand years ago, a great monster roamed the plains."

"What did it look like?" Hazel gasped.

"It was big as a two-story building." Tony gauged her rapt audience. "As big as a four-story building. It was black as night, with enormous claws like a bear and horns that stretched as wide as main street. It had razor-sharp fangs as tall as a grown man, that stuck out of its jaws. The beast roamed the plains in the dark of night, searching for prey. The monster ate buffalo like they were no bigger than spring peas. And everywhere the beast hunted, the blood of its victims spilled on the earth and left the whole territory red."

"Oooh." Hazel wrinkled her nose. "What happened to the beast?"

"Don't know. Maybe it's still around."

"That's dumb." Darcy scoffed. "That's not even a scary story."

"You got a better one?"

"I heard a whole family in Mississippi was murdered with an ax—"

"That's a tale for another time," John broke in. "Moira's right. You won't sleep a wink with that kind of talk."

A coyote howled in the distance. The girls shivered and huddled closer. "Are we in danger?"

"Nah," the cowboy continued. "It's probably just the Ivory Coyote."

"What's that?" Hazel sat up straighter.

"The Indians say every five hundred years an Ivory Coyote is born. Its fur is as white as an elephant's tusk and its eyes are as red as a garnet. See, the coyotes never howled until the most recent Ivory Coyote was born, must be going on two or three hundred years ago."

"They live that long?"

"They live for five hundred years."

A stump popped in the fire, collapsing in a shower of embers. The air around the flames shimmered in a mirage, turning everything outside their vision hazy and muddled.

Moira rubbed her upper arms.

Tony kicked back on her saddle pillow. "What started them howling, then?"

"Well, a bunch of settler children found the Ivory Coyote and her litter of pups. They'd never seen the like before. It was too tempting. When the Ivory Coyote went out hunting that night, they stole the pups away."

"They stole her pups?" Hazel exclaimed. "That's so sad."

"Is that why she's howling then?" Darcy asked. "For her lost pups?"

"Those coyotes will howl for another two-hundred years, until the next Ivory Coyote comes to take its place."

"That still ain't scary." Darcy huffed. "Who cares if some old coyote is howling for her lost pups?"

"Because she's also looking for revenge."

Moira turned. "What kind of revenge?"

"She snatches the settler's children."

The cowboy goosed Hazel in the arm. The little girl shrieked and giggled. The girls yelped and laughed.

"I knew you were only fooling." Darcy grumbled.

Drawn toward the commotion, Champion trotted into the firelight. The animal wove its way among the girls, sniffing each one in turn, as though assuring their safety. Once satisfied with the inspection, Champion lay near Moira, pressing its entire body against the length of her thigh.

She stiffened and held her hands out of reach. Champion rested his snout on her knee and stared at her with velvety-brown eyes. She cautiously brought down one hand, gently stroking the top of the dog's head.

Hazel crawled closer and scratched behind the animal's ear. "He likes it when you do this."

Moira repeated the gesture on the opposite ear. If she didn't know better, she'd think the dog was grinning at her.

"See," Hazel said. "He's smiling."

Moira studied the girls. They'd worked hard over the past two days, stretched beyond their skills.

Hazel tired of petting the dog and joined Tony. They played a game, clapping their hands together and repeating a singsong rhyme.

"My mother told me to open the door,
But I didn't want to.
I opened the door, he fell through the floor,
That silly old man from China.
My mother told me to take off his coat,
But I didn't want to.
I took off his coat, and out jumped a goat.
That silly old man from China."

Moira shivered. John leaned over, extending his hand, the handle of a tin cup full of Pop's ubiquitous coffee clutched between his fingers.

"You cold?"

"No." Moira wrapped her fingers around the cup for warmth. "It's the rhyme. I never did like the words."

"My mother told me to take off his hat,
But I didn't want to.
I took off his hat, and out jumped a cat.
That silly old man from China."

John shrugged. "Seems simple enough to me."

Darcy joined the group, and Hazel and Tony rearranged to accommodate her.

The three resumed their clapping with another song.

"Three sailors went to sea, sea, sea
To see what they could see, see, see,
But all that they could see, see, see,
Was the bottom of the deep blue sea, sea, sea."

John caught her gaze. "How are you holding up?"

"I've never been more miserable," she answered truthfully. "Or more satisfied. I'm exhausted, sore, and my hands are raw. I've got an itchy sunburn on the tip of my nose and the back of my neck. I'm more tired than I ever recall being in my life, yet I'm not ready for sleeping. I want to be right here, under the stars, listening to the girls play and laugh."

Something inside her was shifting. Her beliefs about herself, about the world. She'd set out with a goal: find her brother, reunite their family. The steps in her life had been simple and straight. She wasn't the sort of woman who drove cattle or told scary stories around a fire.

"I think I understand what you're saying. A hard day's work can make a man feel useful. Needed."

"Not always." Moira sipped her coffee and recalled her life with the Giffords. "Did you know it takes three different kinds of leaves to make a proper cigar?"

"Nope. I did not know that. You don't seem the type of woman to imbibe."

"It's how the Giffords earned their money."

"The foster family that took you in?"

Moira nodded. "Mr. Gifford never had much of a job. He was always looking for a way to get rich quick. They had a maid and a cook because everyone who was anyone in St. Louis had a maid and a cook. They took in Tommy and me because they didn't have their own children, and children made a man look respectable. That's what Mr. Gifford said, anyway. Success and fame were always just around the corner for Mr. Gifford. In a way I suppose I admired his optimism. No matter how many times his schemes failed, he was always ready for another. Always staying one step ahead of the debtors."

"That's not optimism. That's idiocy."

"The cigars were his one, steady source of income. The tobacco farms paid us piecemeal."

She pictured his gold watch, the links of the chain stretched between his brocade-vest pockets. The steady tick, tick, tick. The monotony that gave her too much time for thinking. Too much time for dreaming.

Tick, tick, tick.

"That's how your foster family earned a living then, rolling cigars?"

"No." Moira stood and dusted her pant legs. "Mrs. Gifford didn't like how the tobacco left her fingers yellowed. Mr. Gifford felt he lacked the dexterity for such delicate work. Which meant the work fell to Tommy and me."

She laughed, the sound hollow even to her own ears. "I suppose it seems perfectly normal to you. Growing up on a ranch, you must have worked hard. Even as a child."

"I suppose," John began. "But what you're speaking of sounds more like child labor than chores. Is that what you were talking about earlier? When you said you'd like to right a wrong."

"Something like that."

She couldn't admit what she'd done. The more she knew about the cowboy, the less she wanted him to know about her life. She wanted him to like her, to respect her. He might regret kissing her, he certainly hadn't brought up the subject, but she didn't want him to regret knowing her. She'd gotten him all wrong from the beginning.

He might be separated from his family, but at least he hadn't betrayed them.

Chapter Thirteen

Two nights later, following supper, the girls lounged around the fire once more. In a few short days they'd fallen into a regular routine. They went about their chores without fuss. Most of the animosity from the first few days had withered away beneath the weight of exhaustion. John was even growing accustomed to the improvement in the food.

Hazel sat cross-legged, her elbows propped on her knees, her chin cradled in her hands. "Why aren't you married yet?"

"Well, uh. I'm just not," John replied.

Tony whittled at a stick. "She means, what's wrong with you?"

"Nothing is wrong with me. Why would you think something is wrong with me?"

"You're a good-looking fellow. Got yourself a nice herd of cattle. You're plenty old enough. Why ain't you got a wife and kids by now?"

He caught Moira watching him and a flash of heat crept up his neck. "I guess I haven't found the right lady yet."

"Or you're not looking."

"I think he's doing something wrong." Tony eyeballed

the sharpened end of her stick. "Maybe you're not approaching things the right way."

"What things?" John glanced around. "I'm not approaching anything. I just haven't gotten around to courting anyone yet."

"You better get around to it soon," Tony replied. "You're not getting any younger. And where you're going, there's not too many available women."

"How do you know?"

"Well, it stands to figure. The farther west you go, the fewer women. My pa used to say, there's a woman behind every tree in Kansas. Both of 'em."

"Well, I don't see the need to force anything." John didn't like the direction of this conversation. Lately he'd been thinking more and more about settling down, having a family of his own. He didn't need the girls goading him. "If the right woman comes along, well, we'll see."

Pops appeared in the firelight, a tin of raw bread dough in his hands. "What about that girl you was dating back in Texas?"

John fidgeted. "Ruth Ann?"

"Yeah, that's the one. Whatever happened with her?"

"You remember well enough." Moira had finally ceased looking at him as though he was about to disappoint her at any moment. He didn't need Pops dredging up the past and casting him in a bad light. "She married Alex Stillwell. They've got a pecan farm and five children."

"I didn't ask *who* she married. I asked *why* she didn't marry you."

"That's personal." Best to end this conversation here and now. He didn't need Moira wondering what was wrong with him. "What have you got there?"

"A bit of bread for cooking over the fire. Sarah got it started this morning." Pops handed him the pan.

"What am I supposed to do with this?"

"Give me a minute."

Pops set off for the chuck wagon and returned a moment later with several slender twigs about two feet long apiece. He handed each of the girls a stick. "These are for cooking. Let me show you what to do."

He sat next to John and pinched off a fistful of the bread dough, then rolled it into a rope between his palms. Keeping hold of the bread with one hand, he grasped the stick with the other, then wound the dough around one end. "Be sure to pinch the ends together so it stays put."

He held the stick over the fire. "Just keep twirling it till the dough gets nice and golden brown."

The girls crowded around John, reaching for the dough. In short order, only a marble-sized ball of dough remained. With much giggling, the dough was formed into long snakes. More than one piece hit the dirt and had to be discarded. The activity kept the girls distracted, but not for long.

After Moira left for her watch, Hazel nudged him. "Why didn't you marry Ruth Ann?"

"Well, it's not so much why didn't I marry her, but why didn't she marry me."

"So?" Tony lifted her eyebrows. "Why wouldn't she?"

With Moira gone, he wasn't as self-conscious about opening up. "We were too young. Or at least I was too young. She didn't think I could care for her properly."

"Did you draw her a picture?" Hazel asked.

"Um. No. Can't say that I did."

"I'd like it if someone drew me a picture. I think Moira would like it, too. She likes to draw a lot."

"A picture," Pops said. "Never would have thought of that. But it's not a bad idea."

"I'll keep that under consideration." John twirled his piece of dough over the fire. "Although I don't see how drawing pictures can make someone like you."

"Sure can't hurt," Tony said. "Doesn't seem like what you're doing so far is working out all that well."

"I can always count on you to put things into perspective."

While the girls laughed and talked, John considered his future. The girls had obviously decided he and Moira belonged together. Considering their odd circumstances, the assumption fit. They were relatively close in age, they were both single. Other than Pops, they were the two adults in camp that the girls relied on.

He tried on the notion for size, letting the idea roll around in his head. He'd never felt for anyone what he felt for Moira. Not even Ruth Ann. His childhood sweetheart had been a friend. In retrospect, he realized their parting had been inevitable. Neither of them had felt deeply enough for the other to fight for their relationship.

Maybe in a year or two, when his ranch was up and running and he had a steady source of income—when he proved he could care for Moira—maybe he'd see if she was interested in the idea as well.

He wasn't making the same mistake twice. He wasn't courting a woman until he knew well and sure he could care for her.

The breakfast bell clanged the following morning. Tony stuck her face in the tent. "Mr. Elder says we're pulling out in twenty minutes. With or without you sleepyheads."

Moira glanced around. "You certain? I just went to bed."

The nights were cooling yet Moira kicked off the covers and wiped at the fine sheen of sweat on her forehead.

"It's morning, all right. You can tell by the sun."

Moira tossed a shoe in her direction, but the girl ducked out of the tent and avoided the blow.

Moira slipped into her denim trousers and tugged her

blue chambray shirt over her head, knotting the long tail ends at her waist. Even those simple tasks left her winded and she sat back on her heels. After closing her eyes and counting to ten, she reached for her boots and pulled them on, wincing as the new, stiff leather brushed against her right ankle.

The scratch on her ankle had healed well at first, then yesterday she'd scraped it and reopened the wound. The previous day she'd sweated despite the cooler weather. She'd hardly slept the previous evening for the throbbing.

She rested for another few moments and stood, then stepped toward the tent flap. The world spun and she paused, pressing two fingers against her temple. After sucking in a few more breaths, she emerged into the morning sunlight.

Four faces stood in a half circle around the tent opening.

Sarah crossed her arms over her chest. "If you don't ask for help, that wound is going to go septic and then we'll have to cut off your leg at the thigh."

Moira's eyes widened. "Don't be silly. It's only a scratch. I'm fine." She steadied herself with a hand against the tent.

"Well, we're not going anywhere until you let us have a look."

"We're wasting time." Moira spoke in her most commanding voice. "Mr. Elder will be none too pleased."

"Mr. Elder is the one who called this meeting," a masculine voice spoke.

Moira groaned. "If it's that big of a deal, you can take a look."

The group disbanded, appearing disappointed at her easy capitulation.

Sarah brushed past. "It's not a crime to ask for help, you know."

"I don't need any help."

"Whatever."

John cleared his throat. "Have a seat over here. Let's look at that ankle."

She dutifully took her place on the edge of the chuck wagon and stuck out her leg.

John crouched before her and tugged off her boot. "You should have showed this to someone sooner. This appears infected."

"Do what you need to do. There's no call for a lecture."

He rested his forearm on his bent knee. "Actually, there's every need for a lecture. You're part of my crew. If I tell you to have a scrape checked out, you check it out. Our success is dependent on the health of the crew."

Moira bit her lip and looked away. "I am sufficiently chastised."

He held her ankle and turned her leg from side to side and his hands dwarfed her foot. She'd never considered herself particularly dainty. Next to John she felt positively tiny.

The cowboy took a bottle of liniment from a kit at his elbow and unstopped the cork. He poured a measure onto his bandanna and pressed it against the scrape.

Moira hissed.

"It'll only burn for a minute."

True to his word, after the initial sting, the pain slowly faded. He pulled away the bandanna and examined the wound once again.

"I'm going to wrap this. Keep the dirt out."

"Make it quick. We've a whole day ahead of us."

He grasped a roll of binding and carefully wound the bandage around her ankle. "I'll change this tonight and check for infection."

Moira stared at the top of his hat. "Thank you."

She couldn't recall the last time someone had looked out for her this well.

The brim lifted, revealing his dark eyes. "You're welcome. Say, I wanted to ask you something. Would you like it if someone drew a picture for you?"

"What kind of a picture?"

"Maybe a tree or something."

"I, ah, I suppose. Why do you ask?"

"I just wondered."

Her heart skittered a beat. Covering her unease, she reached for her boot and tugged the leather back over her ankle.

The cowboy held out his hand. Moira tentatively reached out her fingertips. He clasped them, helping her balance as she stood. She put some weight on her foot, testing the bandage.

"It's better."

He threaded their fingers together and stared at their clasped hands. "You don't have to be strong for everyone. You don't even have to be strong for yourself all the time. We're a crew together, we help each other. Support each other."

"And what happens when we reach Fort Preble?"

"What do you mean?"

"What happens when I become dependent on you and then you're not there anymore?"

"Well, it'll be different, that's for sure. Town life is quite a bit different from trail life."

"It's not only that." She'd promised herself she'd remain aloof from the girls. The more time they spent together, the more difficult keeping her promise became. "Once we're back in town, everyone will go their separate ways."

"You can write letters."

"That'll never happen. Out of sight is out of mind for

people. Once this is over, we'll never even think of each other again."

"Do you really think that?"

"Don't you?" She avoided his dark gaze. Lately she worried that she'd miss the cowboy most of all.

She didn't understand her feelings for him, but she recognized they were strong. And they frightened her.

"I think it's important to enjoy the time we have together. Here. Now. If you're worrying about the future, or living in the past, you can't properly enjoy the present."

"Strange words coming from a man who's running from his own family."

Hurt flickered across his face, quickly masked by his easy grin. "Don't forget. Check with me tonight. We'll change the dressing."

He turned and strode away. An unexpected burst of anger flared through her chest. She'd expected him to fight back. Defend himself. Defend his actions. Instead, he'd closed the subject and left her feeling like a first-rate heel.

He was kind to the girls, good to the animals. He was fair and open-minded. And he didn't care a whit about moving hundreds of miles from his family. How did all those contradictory things exist in one man? Last night the girls had teased him. He'd had a sweetheart, Ruth Ann. The admission had shocked her.

Almost as much as realizing she was jealous.

John's crew had finally picked up speed. The next two days took on a rhythm and they made good time, fifteen miles each day. There was little need for instruction.

He'd pulled a watch in the middle of the night during a brief squall, letting the rain sluice off his hat and dribble into his boots. Despite the discomfort, he slept better than he had in weeks. The following morning the smell of frying bacon teased his nostrils and pulled him from a restful slumber. Circling around the wagon, he stretched and yawned. A quick look in the mirror attached to the wagon post showed his face had returned to normal. He opened and closed his eyes a few times. They were still a mite bloodshot, but he no longer looked like he could scare a rattler out of its skin.

It had taken seven days to make the trip. Fort Preble sat in the distance, tall chimneys puffing smoke from cook fires. He hadn't expected they'd make it this far. Suddenly the idea of going the distance didn't seem so far-fetched. They were a few days from the Kansas boarder and a few more from Cimarron Springs.

He shook off the idea. The closer his destination came, the farther it seemed. He'd closed his mind against the dangers of the trip. With each day, he realized the chances of a disaster grew.

The more he got to know the girls, the more he worried that something would happen. This morning his unlikely crew had crouched before the cook fire. They were filthy and exhausted, and, quite possibly, the best crew he'd ever had. The idea of putting together another crew at Fort Preble to make the rest of the distance soured his stomach.

Moira rode into view, her new hat low on her head. She slid off her mount and approached him. "We've got riders. Two of them. They're coming toward camp. Fast."

John reached for his gun. "Let me handle this."

At the rebellious gleam in Moira's eyes, he set his jaw. "Let me handle this," he repeated.

Keeping his fingers on the stock, he watched as the two riders approached. They could be anyone with their enveloping slickers and their hats pulled low against the rain. John widened his stance.

"What business do you have here?"

The first rider lifted his head and glanced around. "That's not the crew you left with."

John's jaw dropped. Of all the people he'd expected to see, he wasn't prepared for his brother Jack.

John reached out, clasped his hand in a quick shake. "You're a long way from home. Did you run out of fugitives in Texas or did Elizabeth send you to check up on me?"

"Both. Elizabeth is beside herself with worry. She'd probably faint dead away if she saw you now."

John shielded his eyes from the sun and met his brother's steady gaze. "I sure am glad you're here."

Relief coursed through him. His thoughts came into focus. He'd come all this way to prove his point, when the answer was already in sight. He'd inherited his share of the ranch from their father before he was ready, before he'd broken free of childish jealousies and developed the confidence and conviction that came with maturity.

Looking back on the past few days, he realized he'd sacrifice his pride if it meant the girls' safety. Nothing else mattered.

All this time he'd fought hardest with Robert, and the truth was humbling. Robert had lost his wife, he lived with guilt, and he struggled beneath the weight of responsibility that came with raising two children alone. Robert hadn't saved his wife, so he was driven to save the rest of them. He just went about it the wrong way sometimes.

A good man knew his strengths, but it took a bigger man to admit his weaknesses.

John had lectured Moira because her stubborn pride prevented her from asking for help, when he had been guilty of the same offense.

He'd set out on this journey filled with pride, and he'd discovered humility in the process.

"I sure am glad you're here," John repeated. "I could use the help."

Chapter Fourteen

Moira glanced between the two men. "Do you two know each other?"

"You could say that," John said. "Meet my brother, Jack Elder. Jack, this is Miss Moira O'Mara."

The resemblance was unmistakable. John was an inch taller than his brother was and wider in the shoulders, though they both shared the same rugged good looks. Jack was clearly the older of the two. Gray hair showed at his temples and deep lines tracked across his forehead.

"Pleased to meet you, Miss O'Mara." Jack faced his brother. "You and I need to talk about your crew. Alone."

Moira held up her hands. "No. Absolutely not. Those girls are my responsibility. Anything you have to say to John you can say to me."

The cowboy jerked his head in a nod. "This concerns her, too."

"Your call," Jack replied.

Moira glanced uneasily at the second rider. Jack followed her gaze. "That's Sergeant Baker from Fort Preble."

The second man braced his hands against his saddle horn. "I'm just along for the ride. This is Sheriff Elder's show."

Pops rounded the corner of the chuck wagon and his eyes widened. "What brings you this far from Texas, Jack? You missed the cows?"

The senior Elder brother dismounted and the two men clasped shoulders in a quick, perfunctory embrace that clearly demonstrated their affection.

"You old coon dog," Jack Elder teased. "Aren't you too old to be trailing across the country?"

"I'm not that much older than you, and don't you forget it."

"Well, I *am* too old." Sheriff Elder rubbed his hip. "I think I'm getting a bit of the rheumatism."

"I've got some of my cure-all."

"How about some coffee instead?"

"There's always coffee over the fire when I'm in charge."

Moira watched the three men from a distance. They shared a history and their easy affection kept her isolated, staring in from the outside like a child pressing her nose against an ice cream shop window. With their easy relationship, the distance separating them might have been miles instead of a few feet.

Pops poured steaming hot brew into a tin cup. "How is Elizabeth? What about your young'uns?"

"Elizabeth is fit and healthy. We're expecting another child before Christmas."

John slapped his brother on the shoulder with a grin. "You never said."

"We were waiting to be sure. It's been five years since our last was born."

"You're awful cheerful for a man who's about to give up sleep for the next year."

"I wouldn't have it any other way." Sheriff Elder's expression sobered. "Which is why I can't stay long. I don't know what you did, but you've made a stubborn enemy. Some deputy sheriff wants your head on a platter."

Moira groaned. "Wendell."

"He sounds like a real weasel. He's claiming one of your crew stole from him. Says he's got plenty of other people willing to say the same."

John braced one shoulder against the metal ribs of the chuck wagon. "I was afraid something like this might happen. Still doesn't explain how you got roped into all this."

"I had some business up in Cimarron Springs. Elizabeth and I were worried when you didn't show. I figure you're a grown man who can ask for help when he needs it, but once Elizabeth is worried, there's no going back."

John snorted softly. "I remember."

"Anyway, it was pretty easy to backtrack. I figured you'd be stopping at the fort for supplies. They'd heard of you all right. They'd been warned about your arrival. Wendell wants you all arrested and sent back to Fool's End." Jack waved his coffee cup through the air. "I expected a more dangerous-looking crew after the deputy's dustup. And boys."

Moira made a sound of frustration. "This isn't fair. We cleared everything with the sheriff."

"Evidently, the sheriff was only temporary. He's been transferred to another town. I pulled some strings with the boys at the fort," Jack continued. "I did what I could. Since it's a state official making the case, I had the jurisdiction transferred to the U.S. Marshals. That means we can take the girls across the Kansas border. Marshal Garrett Cain has agreed to take over the case for me."

"Couldn't you handle this?" John asked. "Throw out the whole nonsense?"

"The deputy knows you came up through Indian Territory with longhorns. He'd have kicked up a fit if I sent them back to Texas."

"I still don't like it," Moira said. "What do we know about the marshal? Can we trust him?"

"Don't worry. I've met Marshal Cain. He's a good man. If there's anything that can be done, he'll figure it out."

Moira paced before the brothers. "They're children. Who cares about a few apples they've taken for survival? Where is the forgiveness?"

"Wait." Jack held out his hands. "Let's go back a step. How did y'all end up together anyway?"

John sketched out the story. He kept to the facts, downplaying his own role. Moira glanced between the two men. Jack Elder remained respectfully quiet during the explanation, yet she sensed he had more questions.

"If you weren't my own flesh and blood," Sheriff Elder said, "I'd say you were lying."

John grinned. "I gave them the idea. I told them about Gramps in forty-nine."

"Not sure how much of that story I believe."

"I believe more of it now."

"You did good, John."

The cowboy didn't reply, yet Moira sensed his pride.

The two brothers exchanged a glance. John studied his boots. "Moira, I can't shake the belief that Wendell is after you for some reason. Something personal."

"Me?"

Her thoughts flew back over their encounter in Fool's End. This had gone beyond a bit of revenge for whatever disturbance her brother had caused.

Sheriff Elder rubbed his chin. "Can you think of any reason the deputy would want you back in Fool's End. What brought you there in the first place?"

"I was searching for my brother. He sent a telegraph from there. Part of the message was missing, but I made out *Fool's End* and the name *Grey*. It was the first I'd heard from my brother in almost four years. I came as soon as I could. Mr. Grey said he'd never met Tommy. Something didn't sit right."

"It doesn't make any sense." John tugged on his ear. "Why wouldn't he admit that he knew your brother? If he's exacting some sort of revenge, what for? And we're certain your brother wasn't in Fool's End the whole time?"

Moira's stomach plummeted. "I don't know. I didn't check. Mr. Grey said he was gone…I took him at his word."

"Let's not panic until we think about this." John touched her cheek. The gesture was comforting. "The sheriff had heard of your brother. He said he'd moved on. There's no reason to believe Tommy was still there at the same time."

Her breathing came in quick, shallow gasps. "What do we know about Sheriff Taylor? What if he was working with Mr. Grey? He said there had been a dustup over Mr. Grey's daughter. What if he was lying?"

"No. I don't think so. The sheriff let us leave without much of a fuss. Wendell was the one who wanted your return. If Sheriff Taylor was involved, he wouldn't have let you leave that easily."

Moira shifted and Jack turned in her direction.

"And the telegram didn't say anything else?"

"Not much. I brought it along. Would you like me to fetch it?"

"Wouldn't hurt."

Moira retrieved the telegram and returned in short order.

Jack held the singed pieces between his thumb and forefinger. "What do you make of that word?"

The cowboy leaned closer. "Looks like it starts with a *w*."

Jack tucked the papers back into the envelope and

handed it back. "I can do some digging on my way back to Texas."

"I don't know if that's such a good idea," Moira said. "I don't trust Wendell. If you start asking questions, who knows what he'll do."

"Don't worry about me, miss. I've been dealing with men like the deputy my whole career. I'll be careful."

An awkward silence descended and Moira realized the brothers were looking in her direction. She stood and dusted her pants. "I'll leave you two gentlemen."

Jack clasped her hand in both of his. "Pleasure to meet you."

Moira returned his easy grin. She wouldn't have thought it possible, what with all the trouble the girls had caused for his brother, yet he seemed genuinely at ease with her presence.

"Pleased to meet you as well."

And she was pleased. Watching the two men together filled her with warmth.

She left more confused than she had been all week. If the brothers got along so well, why was John traveling four hundred miles to get away from them?

When Moira moved out of earshot, Jack's expression sobered. "You're lucky you made it this far without a catastrophe. There are rivers and Indians and who knows what else. Not to mention those cattle are deadly if spooked."

"Bobcats and skunks."

"Huh?"

"That's what else is out here. Moira nearly drowned in the Snake River, Champion was almost mauled by a bobcat. And I got skunked."

"Who is Champion?"

"The dog."

"I thought the dog's name was Dog."

"Not anymore."

"I'll bet you didn't come up with that name. You've never been real imaginative when it came to naming things."

"No," John conceded. "Actually the girls came up with that name. And now he won't answer to anything else."

"Well, it's better than Dog. That's for certain."

"Which reminds me, we also ran into a group of Indians," John said.

"You ran into Indians." Jack shook his head. "It's fortunate Elizabeth didn't know what was happening. She'd have pitched a fit."

"I thought I'd planned for everything," John said. "I sure hadn't planned for any of this."

Of all his brothers, he'd known Jack the least growing up. His brother's job as a Texas Ranger had taken him to all corners of the state. He hadn't been around much. When he'd married and taken over the role of sheriff in Paris, Texas, they'd grown closer.

Jack glanced at the cattle. "You realize things might be hostile at the border."

"I know." John blew out a hard breath. "Any chance of lenience?"

"None. The ranchers and farmers will meet you at the border with rifles. They're taming the West one farm at a time. They don't want cattle chewing through their crops and bringing disease."

"What do you think about Texas fever? When I left, I figure the stories were exaggerated. You know, because the farmers and ranchers didn't want the cattle trampling through their fences and grazing on their land. After our stop in Fool's End, I'm not so certain. I heard a few things that had me worried."

"It's real, all right, and getting worse. I think in the beginning there might have been a question. Not anymore. Texas cattle carry something that's killing off the Midwestern stock."

"But our stock is immune?"

"Looks that way."

John pressed two fingers against his temple "I'll see if I can sell the herd in Fort Preble. Winter is coming. I'm hoping they'll need the stock."

"I'm sorry," Jack continued. "I know the boys give you a hard time. None of us wanted this."

"I took a shot. It didn't work out."

"You know you can always turn around and go home. There are able-bodied men for driving cattle out here."

"No. Robert has enough to worry about. I couldn't see that before."

Jack dropped his head and stared at the reins clasped in his hands. "It changed him, losing Doreen. It changed all of us. You were probably too young to remember, but he wasn't always like he is now."

"I'm only four years younger. I was old enough to remember, and too young to understand."

"He's hard on you. I've seen that. That's why I didn't stop this cattle drive. I figured both of you could use the distance."

John didn't mind losing face to his brothers, but starting over took time. What if Moira wasn't willing to wait? Anything might happen between now and then.

And he hadn't even gotten the courage to ask her if she'd even consider courting sometime down the road. "Selling the herd is the best choice. I don't see how kicking and screaming is going to change anything."

"You're unencumbered. You can travel. You'll have a bit of money from the sale of the herd. Go to Europe. See the continent like them fancy fellows back east. Worse comes to worst, I'll put the homestead on the market. I can't seem to shake that property. It's gone through two owners and it always comes back into Elizabeth's name."

John rubbed his face. "Don't sell the property. I'll still take over the deed."

"Suit yourself."

"I won't need much."

Jack slapped his gloves against his leg and stared into the distance. "What are going to do with the horses?"

John blinked. "The remuda?"

"Yeah. You're selling the herd. What about the horses?"

"Hadn't thought about it yet."

"Let me know. I have buyers. And they *will* pay top dollar."

"I might take you up on that offer."

"It's none of my business, but you were always more of a horseman than a cattleman." Jack patted his horse's neck.

"There's more money in cattle than there is in horses."

"A man doesn't need much."

"I need security if I want to build a future. If I want a family." The words escaped before John could call them back.

Jack faced his mount and adjusted the saddle. "Taking care of someone is more than putting a roof over their heads. That's probably the easiest part. The hard part of taking care of someone is building their trust."

John kicked at the dirt. The girls had trusted him. How would they feel once they realized he was quitting? Probably they'd be happy. They'd have their pay, they were out of Fool's End. There was help for them in Cimarron Springs.

Jack faced him once more. "You're doing the right thing by those girls. They're young, they're defenseless. You've gotten lucky this far. Maybe someone higher up is watching out for you. I don't know. But anything can happen. It's best they're not riding the trail anymore."

"Believe me, I've thought of that."

"Marshal Cain is a good man. You can leave the girls in his hands. You've done more than most men already."

Hadn't John said the same thing to himself a week before? "I have to see this through. Some of those girls have families. If I can reunite them, *then* I'll have done a good thing."

"Even Miss Moira O'Mara?"

"Especially Moira."

John didn't want his brother reading anything into the relationship. He might have had a chance before he lost the herd. A chance of building a future for them. Now he was starting over. Moira deserved better. No matter what Jack said, she deserved someone who could provide for her. Until he knew whether or not a horse ranch was viable, he couldn't make her any promises.

He'd help her find her brother. That much he could do. Once they were reunited she wouldn't have much use for a failed rancher anyway.

John stuck his hands in his back pockets. "Can you make arrangements for us in town?"

"They've got barracks set aside for visitors." Jack led his horse toward the remuda. "You'll hardly recognize the place. It's doubled in size since we drove that herd up to Wichita in seventy-one." His brother halted. "Do you trust them?"

"How do you mean?"

"They're pickpockets. And how long have you known Miss O'Mara? Maybe the deputy isn't lying after all. You think she knows more than she's saying."

"She's not lying."

"I trust your instincts."

John grinned. "I've been waiting my whole life for one of you to say that."

"If Dad had lived longer, he'd have taught us better.

We tried to fill in for him. We did the best we could, but we were too young ourselves."

"I know that."

Jack strapped a feed bag onto his horse. "What's the story on Miss O'Mara? You think she'll settle in Cimarron Springs?"

John sensed a deeper meaning behind the question. By the time he built up the homestead, she'd probably be married and starting a family of her own. There was no reason to believe she'd wait for him. No reason to believe the idea had ever even crossed her mind.

"I doubt she'll stay around long," John replied. "I'm guessing she'll make sure the girls are settled, then she'll be gone again. She won't quit until she finds her brother."

"Loyalty is an admirable trait in a person."

"Yep."

"And you don't think she was working with the girls? That's the one part of Wendell's story that rang true. Those girls were organized. Feels to me like there was an adult involved. Someone older. More savvy."

"Those girls were definitely working together, but Moira wasn't a part of it. I've had my doubts about Darcy. Something's not right there. But Moira's problems begin and end with Grey. He wants revenge for something. And I have to wonder how bad does he want it? How far is he willing to go?"

"I'll check it out. You know, we're all assuming this goes back to Mr. Grey on account of the telegram. Maybe we should be taking a look at Wendell."

"He doesn't seem smart enough to start something on his own."

"I still think it's worth checking up on." Jack glanced at the chuck wagon. "That does not smell like Pops's usual mash."

"The food is different when you bring girls on the trip."

John patted his stomach. "I've never gained weight on a cattle drive before."

"Are those flowers?" His brother squinted at the posy of black-eyed Susans on the back of the chuck wagon.

"Wildflowers. Wherever we go, they always seem to find wildflowers. I can't figure it out."

"That's because you're not looking."

"I'm a man."

"Tell you what. I'll send Sergeant Baker on ahead and stick around for lunch. You've been on the trail for six, almost seven days? We'll take the girls into town. Let them get cleaned up and sleep with a roof over their heads. We can all eat dinner in town."

"They'd like that."

"You said some of the girls have family. I can start digging up information at the fort."

"I haven't thought that far ahead." John scratched his forehead. "I know Tony has an uncle. Sarah has family, but I'm not certain she's welcome with them. There's no one for Hazel."

"What about the dark-haired girl?"

"Darcy. That's the one I told you about before."

"Cimarron Springs is a nice town. Good people. You might find your solution up there."

"I tried to take a shortcut, Jack. I should have taken the long way."

"You were in that alley for a reason." His brother looped the reins around his fist. "Sometimes you have to sit back and trust in God's plan. Stop pushing and step back a pace. He'll lead you where you need to be."

John kept his silence. He might be the most easygoing of the Elders, but he'd never been one to sit back and wait for anything once an idea got hold of him.

Sarah approached them, a plate in each hand. "Would

you like a scoop of peach cobbler? We didn't have any fresh so I used some tinned."

"Peach cobbler?" Jack's face lightened.

"I'm telling you, this isn't your normal cattle drive," John said.

Jack accepted the plate with a grin. "I could get used to this."

Wishing he felt as optimistic, John glanced at the place where the girls had gathered around the chuck wagon. They'd known all along that the end of the line was Fort Preble. He'd pay them fair and square, but there was no way he was leaving them on their own. He had a bad feeling his new plan wasn't going to go over well.

Chapter Fifteen

"His brother is going to change everything," Darcy declared. "You mark my words. They're up to something, the Elders, I can tell."

Moira had the uneasy feeling that Darcy was correct. "I have an idea, but I'm not entirely certain."

She searched for the cowboy. Somewhere along the way she'd begun to think of them as a team. With the arrival of his brother, the balance had shifted. He wasn't consulting her any longer. Once again she felt an unaccustomed prick of jealousy. Outside of the cattle drive, he had a whole other life. A life that didn't include her.

John strode toward them, his shoulders squared, his dark hat low on his forehead. The muscles rippling beneath his chambray shirt quickened her pulse.

Moira looked away. "The girls would like to know what's next."

John Elder stood beside her, as though they were still a team. "We're driving the cattle into town this afternoon. I'm fixing to sell."

"No!"

"You can't."

"But we've come this far!"

"What will you do?"

"Wait." John raised his voice, silencing the protests. "I know I considered hiring a short crew and pushing onto Cimarron Springs. This is the right thing. I can't guarantee my herd isn't carrying disease. If I sell them here, at the fort, I won't be risking an outbreak. We talked about the risk before. Jack has been up north. Texas fever is real."

Tony stuck out her chin. "We're on our own after that, right?"

"No," John said. "You're underage. The deputy from Fool's End is stirring up trouble. The fort is too small, but the train goes through here. We'll regroup in Cimarron Springs together. I won't leave until everyone is settled."

John sketched out his plan. While Moira didn't like leaving the cattle any more than the rest of the girls did, she admired his principles. How had one week altered the course of her life? When she'd set out on her journey, she'd known exactly what she wanted, exactly what she was seeking.

Not anymore.

Oh, she still wanted to find Tommy. She'd never give up on that. Except she wondered if there was room for something more. Had she closed herself off too much?

After John completed his speech, Tony remained defiant. "There's no chance you would let us set out on our own? I ain't ending up on that orphan train again."

"Just because I'm selling the herd doesn't mean I'm giving up on you guys. We're a team. You're my Calico Cowboys."

Hazel tugged on his sleeve. "How did you know that was our name?"

"Because I listen. Because it fits. We'll break down the camp this afternoon and drive the herd into town. Jack is going on ahead and he'll let the boys at the stockyards know we're coming."

"Then what?" Sarah asked.

"There's a train to Cimarron Springs tomorrow. That'll give everyone a chance to clean up and get a good night's rest."

Hazel raised her hand. "What about Moira?"

"That's up to her. She's of age and she's free to do as she pleases. The rest of you are still minors and under the care of Marshal Garrett Cain until other arrangements can be made."

Moira straightened. "I'm coming with you. We're in this together. We'll search for Tony's uncle."

"What about the rest of us?" Sarah asked.

"I don't know." John didn't like the unpredictability any better than the girls did. None of their futures were certain. "But I meant what I said. I'm fixing to make Cimarron Springs my home. I'll be there to make sure everyone is settled."

John clasped Moira's hand. His fingers were rough and strong and gave her a sense of protection. "You're sure this is what you want?"

"I'll keep looking for Tommy while we settle the girls in Cimarron Springs. Maybe Sheriff Taylor will think of something. Anyway, it doesn't matter. We're talking about the Calico Cowboys, right?"

John jerked his head in a nod. "That's settled. I don't think anybody at Fort Preble has seen an all-girl crew before. I want you sitting high and proud in the saddle. You've done something amazing. Let's give those army boys a show they won't forget."

Moira felt the tug on her heart once more. She clutched this precious time together, knowing it would be over all too soon.

With practiced efficiency the girls finished lunch, broke down the campsite, saddled their horses and took their places with the herd. They worked quickly, with few words. A sense of mourning permeated their routine. For a short time they'd been a part of something bigger. They'd strapped together their meager skills and accomplished something that was larger than any of them alone.

The accomplishment had stretched Moira's endurance to the breaking. She'd been tested again, only this time she'd proven worthy of the test. For the first time in a long time her life had possibilities. She wasn't trapped by circumstances.

Once the horses were saddled and ready and the tents and equipment stowed, the girls mounted and gathered. Hazel resumed her position next to Pops on the chuck wagon.

John gave the signal and sent up a whistle. Champion barked and nipped at the cattle's heels. Their hooves rumbled into motion while Pops kept the wagon to the side and watched them pass, a great river of cattle.

Moira whooped and hollered, pushing the cattle into action. She paused and drank in the scene. She catalogued everything in her memory: the sights, the sounds, the smells. Even the ever-present buzz of the flies. She didn't know the future, but she didn't figure she'd ever see the like again. After seven monotonous days on the trail, her life had blazed into motion once more.

As they neared the town, Tony circled back from the point. "I think you should lead the herd when we go through town."

Moira adjusted her hat. "You're more experienced. It should be you."

"We voted already and we all decided. None of us would have made it this far if it weren't for you."

"I didn't do anything."

"Are you fooling? You did everything. You came up

with the plan to get us out of the brothel. You were the one who decided we should drive the cattle."

Emotion burned behind Moira's eyes. "What about Mr. Elder—John?"

"He's agreed. He's taking the drag." Tony lifted the corner of her mouth in a smile. "It would mean a lot to us."

Moira fisted her hands on the reins. "Then I'd be honored."

Her heart pounded as they approached the town. The cattle kept up their steady pace, nose to tail, unaware of the monumental occasion. Moira straightened her collar and adjusted her hat. She tugged her new gloves over her wrists and sat tall in the saddle.

Enormous timber walls rose before her; the great doors of the fort were propped open. The enclosure had no windows, only narrow slits for rifles. They'd contained the settlement inside the walls, safe from Indian attacks. A dirt road bisected the two sides. The only way to the stockyards on the far side of the fort was straight through town.

Moira lifted her face toward the sky and offered a brief prayer of thanks for their safe arrival. They had done something amazing.

The area inside the fort teemed with activity. Uniformed men and bustled women walked the narrow boardwalks. Smaller buildings dotted the parade grounds. An armory, no doubt, and what appeared to be a blacksmith's shop.

A young boy jogged toward them. "It's true! You're girls, ain't ya?"

Moira grinned. "Yep."

"I gotta go tell my pop it's true."

He dashed off and Moira waved to Sarah across the herd. As they moved down the dusty street, she noticed a small knot of folks standing before the blacksmith shop. They pointed and elbowed each other. Moira felt her cheeks burn. With each building they passed, more folks emerged onto the boardwalk.

A man waved his hand and shouted. "Look over here!"

Moira turned and a sudden burst of light blinded her. As her eyes slowly adjusted once more, she realized the man had taken a photograph.

The cattle, seasoned by weeks on the trail, barely twitched an ear at the commotion.

Moira figured by the time Hazel and Pops brought up the drag with John, the whole town would be watching them pass.

The stockyards appeared and Tony kicked her horse into a canter and joined her at the point. The young boy who'd spotted them on the edge of town sprinted toward the gate. He quickly released the chain and hopped on the lowest rung as the gate glided open.

The first steer rumbled into the enclosure.

The boy balancing on the fence gaped at her. "I never seen a girl riding point before."

"You have now."

"My dad thought it was a joke."

"Girls are just as capable as boys."

"Never would have thought it if I hadn't seen it with my own eyes."

"Don't you forget it."

The cattle filed in and eventually Darcy and Sarah joined Tony at the gate. The gentleman with the camera rushed toward them, his progress burdened by his cumbersome photographic equipment.

He quickly plopped his three-legged box onto the dirt packed street and held up his arms. "Don't move. This picture is going to make me famous." He leaned around the black draping. "It'll make all of you famous."

"I don't want to be famous, mister," Tony declared. "I could go with a hot meal, though."

* * *

Four hours later, Moira sat in the dining area off the barracks in her faded blue poplin. The other girls had purchased new dresses with their earnings that afternoon. They'd all taken long, hot baths and were upstairs trying on their new finery. Since she already had a perfectly good dress, Moira had saved her money for her uncertain future. Slipping into her worn outfit wasn't exactly difficult, and she'd arrived for dinner ahead of the others.

An elegant lady sashayed past in a bustled acid green poplin and Moira cupped the worn patches at her elbows. Sheriff Jack Elder appeared, his broad shoulders filling the doorway. He doffed his hat and ducked beneath the transom.

He searched the room and Moira stood, tugging her skirts over her ankles. This dress wasn't as short as the other was, but the difference brought a flush of heat into her cheeks.

He raked his hands through his hair. "Miss O'Mara. John should be along any moment."

"The girls are running late as well." She motioned toward the bustling restaurant area. "Shall we wait for them at a table?"

Once seated, the tension in her neck muscles eased. At least with her legs tucked beneath the table her skirts touched the floor. Seated, the sheriff wasn't quite as intimidating either.

Jack folded his hands on the table. "Must be nice to be back in civilization again."

"Yes and no," Moira answered honestly. "It's difficult to explain."

"Try me."

"I once took a riverboat ride up the Mississippi. It was windy and the boat swayed through the whole trip. Even after I was back on shore, I felt like I was still moving. I suppose that's what it's like. Like I'm still in motion."

"I know what you mean. Back before the trains criss-crossed the country, I rode for days on end. Same kind of thing. You get used to the motion and you can't hardly sit still anymore."

Moira smoothed her collar and tucked a stray curl behind one ear. Jack Elder wasn't the man she'd expected. His relationship with his brother wasn't what she'd expected either. There was an unspoken respect between the two men.

He smoothed the dark hair from his forehead. "My wife, Elizabeth, is never going to believe me when I tell her what happened. How you and John found each other in Fool's End."

She felt her cheeks heat. "I promise you I never stole anything from Mr. Grey."

"I believe you. A man has to trust his instincts in this job."

While his announcement was hardly a stellar endorsement, at least he believed her. "Thank you."

"I'll stop through Fool's End and see what I can dig up. Chances are someone knows why Wendell is fired up about you and the girls."

Moira recalled the sheriff's pregnant wife. "You mustn't go to all that trouble. I'm sure you want to be home."

Something shifted in his expression. A look she didn't quite understand. "I'm anxious for home, that's for certain. A few inquiries won't take long."

"What's it like? Your ranch?"

"Elizabeth and I don't live on the ranch. We live in town."

Moira started. "Oh, I just assumed…"

"I left early. I knew even as a boy I couldn't stay. I've never been a cattleman. Besides, men have a way of fighting for their territory. There were seven of us boys on that ranch. And if a man doesn't like fighting, he'd best make his own way. It's hard though, setting out on your own."

"Like John?"

"He never had much of a chance winning with our brothers. He was the baby. Sometimes in a family people get set on roles. That's what happened with John. Ma always told us to look out for him. I guess after she died we took the job too serious. If we let him grow up, it was like we lost a part of her."

Moira folded her hands in her lap. She'd been wrong about him the whole time. She'd framed his actions based on her own experiences, and she'd been misguided. He'd cared for them all, his unlikely crew, watched out for them, risked his reputation and his life for them.

Jack cleared his throat. "I don't mean to frighten you away from our family. We're a noisy bunch, but we look out for each other."

And she had absolutely nothing to offer him in return. She was an orphan with fifty-six dollars to her name. Moira snorted softly. Fifty of the dollars she now possessed had come from John for their work on the cattle drive.

A sound caught her attention and she turned. Three of the four girls crowded the archway of the restaurant. Jack rose from his seat.

They were like a posy of wildflowers. Sarah wore a simple two-piece outfit in delicate pink calico. She had a lace collar and new kid boots peeked out from beneath her hem. Hazel had chosen a yellow party dress with several flounces. The ensemble was a touch too formal for the occasion, but Moira didn't suppose anyone cared. Tony appeared uncomfortable in her simple shirtwaist and dark navy skirt. She ran her finger around her collar and tugged.

Tears sprang into Moira's eyes. Sarah hovered on the edge of womanhood, not quite an adult, yet not quite a child either. Tony and Hazel wore the bright-eyed enthusiasm of youth.

Moira checked the stairwell. "Where's Darcy?"

"She didn't feel well." Sarah swept her pink skirts aside and approached the table. "She said she wanted to rest."

Moira half rose from her chair. "Maybe I should check on her."

"She's fine." Tony flapped her hand dismissively. "She's been acting strange since we left the mercantile."

"I suppose." Moira resumed her seat. Darcy had been quiet after their shopping trip. And goodness knew the past few days had been exhausting for all of them. "I'll check on her after dinner."

Content that Darcy was old enough to seek them out if she needed assistance, Moira once again studied the three remaining girls. With each new pair of shoes, with each new piece of clothing, the experience which had brought them together was slipping further into the past, further out of reach. They were all beautiful, all filled with the promise of a new beginning. Who knew what would happen after today?

Everything had changed and Moira's heart ached for the loss. Despite the hardships, the past several days had been wondrous.

Hazel rushed over. She paused before the table and twirled, her new yellow skirts fluttering. "Isn't my dress beautiful?"

Moira pinched one of her braids. "It's lovely. You're lovely."

Tony flopped onto a chair and planted her elbow on the table, rattling the cups and saucers perched at each setting. "I miss my other clothes."

Sarah sniffed. "I never thought I'd say this, but me too."

Moira thought of her trail outfit carefully tucked in the bottom of her valise beneath a stack of newspaper. She'd captured the wild smell, the moment and the feelings the scent recalled.

Hazel took her seat and shrugged. "I don't know which I like better. I think I like them both equal."

"Me too," Moira replied softly.

"I'll be the envy of Fort Preble," a familiar voice spoke.

Moira glanced up and gasped. John stood behind her, one hand braced on her chair, one hand on Hazel's chair. He'd shaved and his dark hair was neatly trimmed over his ears. He wore a dark gray coat with fabric-covered buttons and matching waistcoat, black trousers and a white turnover shirt collar with a black string tie.

She'd thought him handsome in his work clothes. In his formal attire, he snatched the breath from her lungs. Glancing down, she discreetely covered the careful mending on her sleeve where she'd torn the thin fabric.

They might have been a family. A big, noisy, loving family. He inquired about Darcy before taking the empty chair on Moira's right, across from his brother. For the next several minutes, their banter circled the table. Succulent dishes came and went, tea and coffee were served. The girls, decked out in their finery, displayed their best manners.

As the conversation ebbed and flowed around her, Moira's thoughts drifted further away.

"I can't believe you're passing on chocolate cake," John spoke beside her.

She pushed the plate toward him. "I couldn't eat another bite."

He accepted the offering with a boyish grin that sent her heart fluttering.

Sheriff Elder pushed back his chair and crossed his

arms over his chest. He had a naturally commanding presence. The girls quieted and their expressions grew somber.

"I'll miss you girls after tomorrow," he said, his voice gruff.

John rested his fork on his plate. "The next stop is Cimarron Springs. It's a chance for a new beginning. A fresh start for everyone. I've got business in Fort Preble. Looks like I'll be able to sell the cattle for a fair price. I'm looking at using the money to purchase a few more horses. I'll be a week or two behind the rest of you."

Sarah gripped her hands together on the table. "No matter what happens, we're not going back on the orphan train."

The two brothers exchanged a look. "We're all in agreement on that. There's a boardinghouse in town and the landlady is willing to keep you for the next few weeks in exchange for some help around the place. She needs help with canning and yard work."

Sarah's face brightened. "I've never canned before, but I like to cook."

Tony stuck out her chin. "I don't know. Sounds like a trick."

"It's the best we can do right now," John said. "I'll finish my business in Fort Preble and we'll take another look at the situation. Give it a chance. It's better than sleeping on the street and stealing your dinner."

Tony's cheek bloomed pink at the reminder. "And you'll help me find my uncle?"

"I promise. You have my word. I have the information I need on your uncle. I'll do everything I can to find them. What I can't do is make promises about the results. All I can do is try."

Sarah glanced away.

Tony brushed at her eyes. "I trust you."

"What's going to happen to Champion?" Hazel spoke. "Can we take him with us?"

"I need him for a little while longer," John replied. "Don't worry. I'll take good care of him. You'll see him again."

Hazel's lower lip trembled. "I'll miss him."

"He's going to miss you, too. Don't worry. We'll be back before you know it."

After dinner the two brothers set off to complete the business Jack had mentioned earlier and the other girls retired to their rooms, chattering amongst themselves. Moira hovered in the restaurant after the others, feeling lost. Everything was settled. Everything but her future.

Recalling Darcy's absence, she took the steps two at a time and paused outside her room. She rapped three times.

"Go away," Darcy called.

Moira leaned her shoulder against the doorjamb. "No. I'm not leaving until I know you're all right."

"I'm fine. Don't worry. Just a touch of the collywobbles is all."

"Can I bring you something to drink? You must be thirsty."

"Maybe later."

The hairs on the back of Moira's neck stirred. There was something off about Darcy's voice. A certain hesitation in the other girl's answers. Looking left and right, she took a step closer and leaned her ear against the door.

A thump sounded from inside the room. Alarmed, Moira twisted the knob.

A male voice spoke, "Get a move on."

Moira shoved open the door and found a blond-haired cowboy sprawled on the chair in Darcy's room, his hands linked behind his head, his feet crossed at the ankles.

"What is the meaning of this?" she demanded.

Darcy leaped to her feet. "It's not what you think."

Glancing between the two, Moira tightened her lips. "Actually, I don't know what to think. Who are you, sir?"

The man smirked. "Who are you, sir," he mocked in falsetto voice. "Why don't you mind your own business?"

"This girl is my business. She's in my charge."

"Well, she and I are getting married." He smacked his lips. "It ain't your business anymore, is it?"

Hazel appeared in the doorway. "Is everything all right?"

"See if you can find Mr. Elder and his brother," Moira ordered.

Hazel scooted away and the man guffawed. "They ain't gonna help you none."

"What is this all about?" Moira faced Darcy. "I need an explanation. Something..."

Darcy wrung her hands together. "He's my fiancé. We met in Texas before travelling to Fool's End."

"But you're only fifteen."

"I lied. I'm eighteen this month." Her gaze skittered away. "You've got no hold on me."

Staggering back a step, Moira pressed her hand against the wall for support. She didn't know much, but she could make a few assumptions. "You were the one who recruited those girls, weren't you?"

Darcy stuffed a hairbrush into a bag at her feet and shut the top. "It's none of your business what I done."

The answer cemented Moira's suspicions. "You recruited Hazel, Sarah and Tony," Moira repeated. She glared at the cowboy who was picking beneath his fingernails with the pointed tip of his knife.

He smirked. "She couldn't even get that right, could you, Darcy?"

Moira touched her throbbing temple. Bits of conversation flitted through her head. She recalled the glances exchanged between Darcy and Tony. The animosity, the feeling that something else had been going on the whole time. "The whole thing was planned. You gave the girls shelter and food for stealing for you. Then, when people grew suspicious, you made certain they were caught. That way you could slip away and no one would be looking for you. Except it didn't work out that way, did it?"

The man grunted. "Darcy got herself caught. I lost seven days, I did. Been waiting in this two-bit fort full of stiff collars. I overheard the sheriff talking about your crazy plan. Never thought I'd see girls leading a bunch of cows." He chuckled. "That's the funniest thing I ever heard."

Darcy glared. "It wasn't stupid. We did it. We drove that herd."

"Took you long enough. And it's not like it's that far." He nudged her hip with the toe of his boot. "Them cows could have walked on their own and gotten here faster."

Moira blocked the door. "You don't have to go with him. You're with us now."

"It's over, Moira. I'm not like the rest of you." Darcy lifted her bag. "I love Preston. I belong with him."

The man stood. "Yeah. She belongs with me."

He was young, not much older than Moira, exuding a certain shifty charm with his blond hair and lanky frame. While a girl might be taken by his glib manner, she doubted he'd fool anyone for long. She'd thought Darcy smarter than someone like Preston, but everyone had a blind spot.

They pushed past her toward the door. As though unwilling to look her in the eye, Darcy rushed ahead, skirting the banister and rushing down the stairs. Moira made to follow her, but the cowboy grasped her shoulder.

"Get your hands off of me," Moira spoke, her teeth clenched.

"Don't you get uppity with me, you little troublemaker."

He leaned closer, his breath whispering against her cheek. "Unless you want to come along."

Moira strained away. "Never."

The man laughed and shoved her. Moira stumbled and cracked her head against the doorjamb. Stars exploded in her head before the whole world went black.

Chapter Sixteen

His blood boiling, John took the stairs two at time; Jack pounded close behind. Moira lay on the floor of Darcy's room, her eyes closed and her face unnaturally pale. He knelt and cradled her head with his hands. His brother crouched on the opposite side.

Moira groaned and her eyes fluttered open. "What happened?"

He felt along her head and discovered a raised knot. "I was hoping you could tell me. Hazel said there was a man in Darcy's room."

Moira limply raised one arm. "She says he's her fiancé. She went with him willingly."

"Then how'd you end up on the floor?"

"He pushed me and I tripped. It's not as bad as it looks."

John cursed his inattention. He'd known something was suspicious about Darcy the whole time. She'd seemed older, more mature than the other girls. More worldly. He should have realized there was a man involved.

John met his brother's concerned gaze. "Find them."

With a communication born of family connections, Jack tightened his jaw and stood.

John slid his hand beneath Moira's knees and hoisted

her into his arms. After what he'd heard from Hazel, he didn't want to leave her alone in the room. Sarah reached the top of the stairs and gasped.

"Which room belongs to Moira?"

Sarah led the way and opened the door to the sparsely furnished room. John carefully rested her on the bed.

Tony hovered near. "They're sending for a doctor."

"I'll be all right," Moira said. "I feel more foolish than anything."

She struggled upright and he gathered pillows behind her back. "Did you get his name?"

"Preston," Tony answered from the door. "His name is Preston. We never did know much else about him."

Moira pressed her hand against her head. "How long were you working for him?"

"I never figured he'd follow us," Sarah said. "I always thought... Well, I always thought Darcy sorta liked him more than he liked her. I figured once we were caught and he didn't come for us, well, you know. I figured Darcy would forget about him. That's why Darcy was reluctant about the escape."

"At first, anyway," Tony said. "Once she figured out he saved his own hide, she took her chances the same as the rest of us."

"Then she didn't know Preston was at the fort?" John watched the girls for any sign of deception.

"No. I don't think she knew until she saw him today. That's when she started acting strange."

Moira touched the back of her head and winced. "I sure am tired of feeling unsafe all the time."

John tucked two fingers beneath her chin. "If the doc checks you out and says you're okay, and if you rest a while, I'll show you a couple of tricks for defending yourself."

Seeing Moira hurt had ignited a rage in him he'd never

felt before. He fought against the guilt and anger; he might have had his suspicions, but he hadn't seen this coming.

He tucked a curl behind her ear. "Promise you'll never scare me like that again. It took ten years off my life, finding you like that."

Moira offered a shy smile. "You must be getting tired of rescuing me."

"Never."

His chest swelled. He may not be a hero, but she sure made him feel like one.

After receiving a clean bill of health from the doctor and a good night's rest, Moira and the girls met John back in the barracks' restaurant.

Tony had donned her trail drive clothing and was itching for the instruction on self-defense that John had promised earlier. "It isn't fair that we're not safe. That other people can take advantage of us just because we're smaller. No one tells the boys they can't go out alone at night."

"The question isn't whether it's fair or not," John replied. "The point is keeping you girls safe."

"I wish I had been packing a gun. I'd have shot him," Tony declared.

"We're going to use the resources we have," John said. "And those resources are brains and common sense. We'll need some space to work."

Moira helped Sarah push the chairs against the wall. While she didn't have much confidence in learning skills to outmuscle a grown man, she was willing to listen. Once they'd cleared the room, the girls took their seats on the line of chairs while Moira stood a distance away.

John Elder paced before them, his arms crossed over his chest. "I grew up with six older brothers and I learned a few things. First off, don't make yourself a victim. A bully isn't looking for a fair fight, he's looking for an easy win. Look how Miss O'Mara is standing."

Moira started at her name.

"She's got her arms crossed over her chest, her chin is tucked. She's making herself smaller. She doesn't want to be noticed. You know what a bully sees? He sees a victim. Stand up straighter."

Moira glared and planted her hands on her hips. "Like this."

"That's much better. Her head is up and she's taking up more space. Showing confidence. She's less of a target."

Tony fisted her hands. "Are you saying it's our fault?"

"No. No." John waved his hands. "I'm offering you tools. The most important thing to remember is that fighting is your last option. When you're fighting a larger opponent, chances are, you're not going to win. You have two other choices before fighting back." He held up his thumb. "You can run." He stuck out his index finger. "Or you can hide. When you're in a vulnerable place, stay alert. That means being aware of your surroundings. Know your escapes, know your hiding places. If your head is up, you're aware."

Sarah folded her hands. "What if you don't feel very confident?"

"Fake it. People believe what they see. If you have to fight, get your attacker on your level. Use what you have. An elbow in the stomach doubles your attacker over and you've got a clean shot at a face. Don't forget to scream. Make noise. It's not time for being ladylike."

"I'm not sure if I could do that." Sarah glanced around.

"Of course you can. This is your life. It's not Sunday tea in the parlor. Use everything you have."

"Wendell caught me off guard," Tony spoke. "Otherwise I would have socked him." She swung her arm in a wide arc.

"And chances are, he'd have socked you back. Men are bigger and stronger than you are. Your best defense is a good offense. Watch his hands. You can duck out of the way if you see him cock back his elbow."

Tony swung her arm again.

"No," John admonished. "Not like that."

He searched the group and his gaze lit on Moira. "Watch me, I'll show you." He carefully pulled her around beside him. "Stay on the balls of your feet, that way you're ready to run at the first sign of trouble. Keep your hands up and protect your face."

Moira lifted her arms and John shook his head.

"I feel ridiculous."

"Not like that." He circled around behind her and wrapped his arms around her waist, not touching, but she could feel the heat of his body through her clothing. "Keep your elbows tight to your body and hands up."

Moira swallowed around the lump in her throat. "Like this?"

"That's it." He stepped to her right. "You're looking for an opening, a chance for escape. Go for the vulnerable spots. Eyes, ears, nose, throat."

Moira tightened her fist.

"The best way to win a fight is to avoid it altogether," the cowboy continued. "I can't repeat this enough—trust your instincts. If someone is making you uncomfortable, put as much distance as you can between you and that person. If you have to be out at night, make certain you're not alone. All of you were picked up when you were alone."

"I walked right into him," Moira mumbled.

"What was that?"

"The deputy. I walked right into him. I was distracted, I had my head down. I bumped into him. Then he looked at me and he just kept looking. Like he was studying me or something. I could have run or hollered. I knew there was something strange about the way he kept staring at me. But I didn't do anything. I just stood there."

"That's what I'm talking about." John clapped. "Moira brings up a great example of why it's so important to be aware of your surroundings. It's also a good case of why you should trust your instincts. I never trust a man who's mean to dogs or children. Anybody who picks on somebody more vulnerable isn't trustworthy."

"But what if that person seems nice at first?" Sarah asked, her voice low.

"Most folks can't hide their true natures for very long. Even when they're charming, you can see bits and pieces of the real person showing through the cracks. Never settle for a man who drinks too much or treats you bad. You're better than that."

"But what if you're not?" Sarah asked. "What if you're not better than that?"

The cowboy grew serious. "We're all God's creatures. You're all worthy of love and acceptance, and anybody who tells you any different is wrong. Just wrong."

"Even if you've done something bad? Even if you messed up?"

"What would the world be without forgiveness?"

Tony stepped forward. "This is a lesson on defense. Y'all want to hash up the past, that's fine. But I don't feel bad. I did what I had to do. We all did. There wasn't much other choice."

Moira dropped her arms. "Is this about Preston?"

Hazel sat in one of the abandoned chairs pressed against the wall. "It was Darcy's boyfriend that got us into trouble."

Moira had already pieced together the circumstances, but she wanted to hear it from the girls. "How?"

Sarah squirmed in her seat. "I guess we were drawn

to each other from the beginning. Darcy had been on her own the longest. She was confident. She knew things."

"She had nice clothes. She knew stuff." Tony hung her head. "At first we were just taking food. Then she convinced us we should take more."

Sarah heaved a sigh. "You can convince yourself of anything, I suppose, if you try hard enough. The stealing was getting out of hand, but I didn't know how to back out. I tried once, but Darcy said she'd turn me in."

"Preston was the worst," Hazel said and the group turned in her direction. "Darcy wanted him to like her."

Moira pressed a hand against her throbbing forehead. "You're probably right."

Having seen Darcy's boyfriend, Moira didn't doubt the draw he had over her.

Sarah stared at her hands. "What do we do now?"

"What do you mean?"

"What about Darcy?"

"I don't think there's much we can do," John said. "Jack searched. He didn't find a trace of either of them. They're of age. You can't save someone who doesn't want to be saved."

Moira glared at him. "We should at least try."

"If we drag her back here, she'll only run away again."

"But we'll be abandoning her."

Tony snorted. "She abandoned us first."

Moira gaped. "Matthew says, 'If a man have an hundred sheep, and one of them be gone astray, doth he not leave the ninety and nine, and goeth into the mountains, and seeketh that which is gone astray?'"

They stared at her, their looks pitying.

John spoke first. "We don't even know where to look. And she doesn't want to be found. We only know their first names. They're adults according to the law. They may have gone in any number of directions."

"It's not right. It's like we're leaving her behind. Abandoning her. I shouldn't have started this. If we'd never gone on the cattle drive…"

"Then what?" Tony shook her head. "She would have caught up with Preston earlier."

Sarah toyed with the embroidered cuff of her sleeve. "She knows where we're going. She knows we'll be in Cimarron Springs. The town can't be that big. If she wants help, she knows where to find us."

"Someone should care." Moira choked off a sob. "We should care."

"We do care." Sarah touched her arm. "But she doesn't want our help. She never did."

Not for the first time Moira recognized the gulf separating them. Never once had they mentioned Preston or his involvement. The girls had known why they were being held, yet they hadn't trusted her with the truth. Even John had suspected the real story long before she had. He'd been trying to tell her all along, only she hadn't listened.

She'd mistaken his easy nature for apathy. She'd been wrong. He was more watchful, more attuned to the needs of everyone around him. Even *her* needs.

Tony perched near Hazel. "Darcy always kept a wall between us. I knew she wasn't going to stick around long. She was with us, but not. We all knew she was going to leave sooner or later. You must have realized that?"

Somewhere Moira *had* realized that. She'd pushed the truth aside, because she knew if she accepted that Darcy didn't belong, she'd have to admit that she didn't belong either.

John pulled a chair out and straddled the seat. "We've all done bad things at one time or another. Doesn't mean we're bad people."

"Do you think God forgives us?"

"Of course He does. The hard part is forgiving yourself.

Tomorrow you're getting on a train for Cimarron Springs. It's a new start. For everyone."

Moira's throat tightened. She'd started over more than once in her life. Always before she'd seen a new beginning as a challenge. Not anymore. She didn't want anything to change. Because once they reached Cimarron Springs they'd no longer be the Calico Cowboys. John Elder didn't need them anymore.

She wanted him to need *her*.

Chapter Seventeen

Moira spent the first week in Cimarron Springs sketching. She splurged on a new sketchpad and pencils. The pictures poured from her fingers in a frenzy. Normally sketching was her hobby. As the leaves fell and the brisk fall air tinted her cheeks pink, the drawings became her obsession.

A full month had passed since they'd arrived in Cimarron Springs. September had turned into October, and the weather was temperate. She hadn't seen much of John Elder in that time. He was traveling more often than not, though he did check up on the girls when he was in town.

She captured the memories as quickly as her fingers allowed, whittling her pencils down to the nub. The work kept her from thinking. About the past, about the future, about anything. She didn't have to think about how she didn't belong. While the other girls had flourished, Moira puttered around without a clear direction.

Sarah backed her way through the door from the kitchen and spun around, a mason jar in each of her hands. "Look! We've finished canning the peaches."

Moira flashed an indulgent grin. "Is there any room next to the tomatoes and the apple butter?"

"I can't help it. This is the most fun I've had in ages. You should come and join us."

"That's all right. I'm sketching."

Sarah whistled her way back into the kitchen. She and the boardinghouse owner, Agnes, had been inseparable almost from the day the girls arrived. The two shared a love of cooking and baking, and, most recently, canning. They'd spent the past week in the kitchen whipping up dish after dish.

A knock sounded. Realizing Agnes was up to her elbow in peaches, Moira answered the door and discovered Deputy McCoy. The young man was tall with jet-black hair and brilliant green eyes. From what Moira had gathered, all of the McCoys shared the distinctive coloring. From the few snatches of gossip she'd heard, David had recently married his sweetheart, a pretty blonde with blue eyes and a smile that must have broken more than one heart before she fell in love with David.

He gripped his hat brim. "The marshal has some news. For Tony."

The younger girl appeared in the doorway. "About my uncle?"

"He didn't say. I can walk you over."

Tony glanced at Moira. "Will you come along?"

"Of course."

Moira quickly donned her bonnet and the three of them walked the short distance to the marshal's offices. A few people tipped their hats along the way, smiling greetings. She returned their good wishes with a hesitant wave, always feeling like a bit of a fraud. The girls were a novelty around here.

Upon arriving at the offices, the marshal motioned them toward the two sturdy wooden chairs before his desk.

They exchanged greetings and Moira took the chance to study the marshal. He was older than his deputy was and more world-weary. As though sensing a kindred spirit, she knew instinctively he'd seen more in his life than his young deputy.

He brushed the mahogany hair from his coffee-colored eyes, took his own seat behind the desk. She caught the scent of fresh paint and wood shavings.

The marshal noted her curiosity. "We had a fire not long ago. Had to take the place down to the studs and start over."

"Oh dear. Was anybody hurt?"

"Nope. It all worked out. Rather well, if I do say so myself."

He grinned and Moira shook her head. "You seem awfully pleased," she commented.

"Well, got myself a wife out of the deal."

"JoBeth, from the telegraph office?"

"That's the one."

Moira recalled seeing her once or twice when she visited Agnes. "Your Cora is quite precious."

The girl often accompanied JoBeth on her visits.

"That's my niece. Although we'll have a baby around the house next spring." Flaming color infused his cheeks. "Uh, shouldn't have let that slip. We haven't told anyone yet."

Moira hid a grin at his mixture of pride and embarrassment. "Your secret is safe with me."

Tony shifted impatiently. "Enough with the chitchat. How come you called us in?"

Marshal Cain smiled indulgently. "Of course. You should be aware that while I have some good news, I have some bad news as well. I think we've found your uncle. My wife sent out a few inquiries since she works at the telegraph office. Anyway, we found him in El Paso. He's out of work right now and doesn't feel he can properly care for you."

Tony blinked rapidly. "Well. It's not like I need much. I can work, too."

"As to that," a voice spoke from the doorway. "I might have a solution."

Moira bolted upright. John Elder stood in the doorway. His welcoming grin sent her heart beating erratically and her palms dampened. "Mr. Elder. I didn't realize you'd returned," Moira said.

"Only got in this morning."

"You're chitchatting again." Tony crossed her arms over her chest. "What's your idea, cowboy?"

"Marshal Cain told me about your problem this morning. I need some extra hands at the ranch. I'm building up a stock of horses. You'll have to live in Cimarron Springs. But if your uncle agrees, you'll be together."

Tony launched herself from the chair and threw her arms around the cowboy. He staggered backward and patted her back.

The girl sprang away. "I have to tell Hazel and Sarah." She dashed toward the door and paused. "You coming?" she asked Moira.

"In a minute," Moira replied. "I won't be far behind."

Tony slammed out the door in a flurry of petticoats. Moira smiled at the cowboy. "Thank you. That was a very kind thing for you to do."

He propped one shoulder against the doorjamb. "Not really. Works out for both of us."

"How many horses have you acquired so far?"

She was falling in love with him.

She'd been skirting the truth for ages. For a time she'd wondered if her feelings would fade, if she was confusing her blossoming love for him with the adventure they'd shared. She'd convinced herself that she'd kept her feelings in check. She couldn't have been more wrong.

He was always polite and deferential toward her, and

sometimes she wondered if he liked her as well. Yet he hadn't tried to kiss her again. And they hadn't been alone since the cattle drive.

There were things she needed to settle. With Tommy. With the Giffords. She had nothing to offer John Elder. She was a twenty-two-year-old woman who could roll cigars and drive a herd of cattle. Two skills John had little need of. And even if she did declare her feelings, was there a chance he might return them? The risk terrified her into silence.

"I've acquired thirty-four more horses," John said. "I've got a line on another twenty up north. Mustangs. Good stock."

The marshal cleared his throat and Moira started. She'd forgotten he was even there. When John was in the room, he captured her attention. A sheen of sweat covered her forehead. She'd nearly blurted out her feelings before a near stranger.

She grasped a newspaper from the marshal's desk and fanned herself. "That sounds like quite a herd. You've got a lot of work ahead of you."

"I do. It'll take a while. Building up the ranch." The tips of his ears turned red. "It'll be worth the wait."

What was he saying? *It'll be worth the wait.* Was he trying to tell her something?

The marshal's chair creaked and Moira jerked upright. She'd forgotten about him again. He didn't appear annoyed at the oversight.

"What about Sarah?" Moira changed the subject. "Have you found her sister yet?"

"Well, that's the thing." The marshal straightened the cup of coffee resting on the corner of his desk. "I don't think Sarah wants her sister found. All the information she's given me has been vague. I discovered a gentleman I thought might be her brother-in-law, but he didn't seem real interested in answering my queries. I'm just not certain how much more I should look."

Moira fanned herself more vigorously. "Her sister's husband didn't want her before. I suppose she's worried that's still the case."

"It's a good assumption." The marshal sipped his coffee.

The sight sent a sudden rush of melancholy through her. She missed Pops drinking coffee over the cook fire. She saw him once in a while, around Cimarron Springs. He'd stayed in town. He'd said he needed the rest, but Moira had the feeling he couldn't leave until they were all sorted out. Until everyone had a place. But the relationship was different now, more formal. Just as she knew it would be when they'd parted ways at Fort Preble.

The marshal lifted one shoulder in a careless shrug. "I don't see why Sarah can't stick around Cimarron Springs. She sure has taken a shine to Agnes. The feeling appears to be mutual."

John pushed off from the doorway. "Would you be willing to speak with Agnes before we set something into motion? I don't want Sarah disappointed again."

"I'll have my wife take care of it. She and Agnes go way back. Wouldn't be surprised if she brings up the subject first."

Moira didn't have any doubt of the outcome. The solution was ideal—for both of them. Despite her confidence, she was grateful for John's careful handling of the situation. He was correct, the girls had suffered enough disappointments. They didn't need any more.

John crossed his arms over his chest. "That leaves Hazel."

"And Darcy," Moira added quickly.

The cowboy frowned. "We've talked about this. She's

an adult. She's getting married. There's nothing we can do unless she wants our help. Near as I can tell, she doesn't."

"He's right." The marshal kicked back in his chair. "I've gotten some reports out of Illinois. Could be a coincidence, but there's a couple that matches the description of your friend and her fiancé. Appears Preston likes to cheat at poker. He's going to meet a bad end if he's not careful."

"Keep us informed," Moira pleaded. "I know Darcy is a touch prickly, but she was a good worker. She pulled her weight along with the rest of us. I don't like the hold that man has on her. She was different when she wasn't around him."

"I'll let you know if I find out anything else. I wouldn't get your hopes up, Miss O'Mara. Love has a way of making people do strange things."

Afraid she might reveal something in her expression, Moira kept her gaze firmly affixed on her lap. Any moment she'd blurt out the words and shock them both.

I'm falling in love with you.

Then what would she say? *Would you like to go for ice cream?* She'd gone and lost her wits like Sarah's Great-Aunt Sylvia.

"That leaves us with Hazel," John said.

The marshal braced his hands against his desk. "My wife and I could take her in. She's not much older than our little one."

"No." Moira half rose from her seat, caught the startled gazes of the two gentlemen and plopped back down again. "That is to say, I don't think we should disrupt her life just yet."

"The offer stands. There's always room for her with us."

"Thank you. That's very kind."

The obvious question hung in the air. What was she going to do? For the past month she hadn't let herself think about much of anything concerning the future. The more time passed, the more she worried she'd never find her brother, Tommy.

I love you. How do you feel about a wife who betrayed her own brother?

"I should go." Before she blurted out something revealing and embarrassed all of them. "If you discover anything else of importance…"

"Don't leave just yet." The marshal lifted a hand. "I haven't showed you the best part. You're famous. Check that paper you're fanning yourself with."

She loosened her death grip on the paper enough to read the headline. The Calico Cowboys of Cimarron Springs. Her jaw dropped. "Where did you get this?"

"A reporter from the *St. Louis Chronicle* was at Fort Preble when you came through. They even sketched your picture."

Moira recognized the four girls on their horses before the stockyard gates. "He never said he was a reporter."

"Either way, the *Omaha Bee* picked up the story as well." The marshal slid a second newspaper across his desk. "You and the girls are quite a sensation."

John tugged the newspaper from her limp fingers and read, "'Led by a feisty redhead, the girls arrived at Fort Preble under the watchful eye of their stoic trail boss, John Elder.' Huh. You're feisty and I'm stoic?"

"That's enough." Moira touched her warm cheeks. "I'd rather absorb this news in private." Never in her wildest imagination had she thought about the story appearing publicly. "It's quite odd, discovering that one has become a sensation."

Was that why people were tipping their hats and waving on the boardwalk? Because some overzealous reporter had fashioned them into a sideshow?

The marshal took one look at her face and flipped over the newspaper. "It'll blow over soon enough. I'd warn the girls to keep up their guard. I've seen things like this happen before, and we're bound to have a few reporters showing up."

Moira groaned. "Reporters? You really think so?"

"Don't worry. My deputy will keep a watch out. As long as we don't add any fuel, this will blow over soon enough."

"I suppose that's not the worst thing. If there's nothing more…" She wanted nothing more than to escape and gather her thoughts in private.

The marshal's expression grew somber. "There is one more thing."

The cowboy straightened. "You need a moment alone?"

"No. You better stay. This concerns you, too."

Moira rested her forehead on the edge of the desk. "I don't think I can handle any more surprises."

John didn't like the tone of the marshal's voice. "Well, spit it out. What's so serious?"

"It's Hazel. She's been stealing from the mercantile."

"That's outrageous." Moira snatched John's hand. "Are you certain?"

He glanced at their intertwined fingers. Had she taken his hint? Did she understand that he was building up his ranch before he courted her? He wasn't certain. He'd dropped enough clues to his feelings. When he'd spoken earlier, she'd had an odd expression on her face. Was that a good sign or a bad sign?

"I'm certain," the marshal continued. "Mr. Stuart complained. Then Agnes found a stash of candy and baubles when she was cleaning out the girl's room."

He lifted a sack from the floor and dumped the contents on the table. Contraband scattered across the surface. Beads and ribbons and penny candies.

Moira lifted a peppermint drop. "Why steal something if she's not even going to eat it?"

"I don't know. But it's got to stop. I've given her some leeway considering what she's been through. I don't think we're doing her any favors by not addressing the problem."

John squeezed Moira's trembling hand. "We'll handle this."

Together they crossed the distance to the boarding-house. The girls and Agnes had gathered in the parlor, laughing and chattering about the discovery of Tony's uncle.

Agnes lifted her head when they entered. "This calls for a celebration, wouldn't you say?"

"I think we should make a cake." Sarah stood and dusted her hands. "Chocolate."

Tony nodded. "That's my favorite."

The girls bustled into the kitchen and Moira placed a hand on Hazel's shoulder. "Why don't you stay behind?"

The young girl paled. "This is about Mr. Stuart's store, isn't it?"

Moira nodded.

Hazel sat on the divan and Moira and John flanked her. Moira spread the contents of the bag on the table. "These things were discovered in your room."

A single fat tear rolled down the little girl's cheek. "Are you going to send me away?"

"Absolutely not," Moira declared.

John admired the fierce note of protectiveness in her tone.

Hazel's face brightened, then fell once more. "Sarah and Tony have a family. I don't have anything."

"That doesn't give you the right to take things."

"Am I a bad person?"

Moira sighed. "No. Remember what Mr. Elder said at the fort? Well, he was right. We have to forgive ourselves before we can move on. I have my own confession to make. I stole something too once."

Hazel gasped.

John gaped. His memory flitted over something she'd said the day he'd gotten skunked on the trail. If she could go back to any time in history, *she'd right a wrong.*

"What did you steal?" Hazel asked.

"I stole a watch." Moira snapped open her reticule and fished out a brass watch. "When I was your age I lived with a family that wasn't very nice to me."

"Like Mrs. Vicky?"

"Very much like Mrs. Vicky. This watch belonged to Mr. Gifford. My brother and I rolled cigars and Mr. Gifford timed us. I hated the sound of the ticking. One day, I couldn't stand it anymore. When he left it on the table, I took it. I don't even know why. It happened so quickly. I hid it in the pantry behind a tin of crackers."

"What happened then?"

"Mrs. Gifford and I went to the store that morning. When I came back, my brother was gone." Moira's voice grew thick with emotion. "You see, Mr. Gifford thought Tommy had stolen the watch. They fought and..." Her voice broke. "They fought and Tommy ran away. I figured Tommy would come back and I could explain things, admit what I'd done. Only he never came back."

John's throat tightened. Her obsession over her brother crystallized in his mind. No wonder she wouldn't be at peace until she found him.

Hazel blinked. "Did you ever find him?"

"No. I'm still looking. I kept this watch because I didn't know what else to do. After so much time had passed, I was afraid of admitting the truth. Of confessing what I'd done. It's time I returned the watch. It isn't right, keeping it after all this time."

"What if he's mad?"

"I have to take responsibility for my own actions."

Hazel stared at the table. "I guess I should return these things."

"Mr. Elder and I will accompany you. But I think it's important we set things straight before we move on. For both of our sakes."

"Can I help make the cake?" Hazel said.

"Of course," Moira said.

She left the room, and Moira kept her face averted.

John ached to reach across the distance, but he was afraid she'd pull away. "That was a very brave thing you just did."

"I should have done it a long time ago. I was holding on to the past, I guess."

"I think you still are."

She tucked her chin to her chest. "What else would you like me to do?"

"Forgive yourself."

"I can't. You must see that. Tommy has to forgive me."

"What happened with Tommy wasn't your fault." John touched her chin and turned her face toward him. "Listen to me. You weren't there when Tommy and Mr. Gifford fought. You don't know what happened between them."

"I know I set the whole event in motion." Tears welled in her eyes. "And Tommy must blame me. I haven't heard from him since that day."

"You mustn't give up hope."

"If it wasn't the watch, then it was just me."

"No, it wasn't you."

John had been relentlessly searching for her brother since before they'd left Fort Preble. Two days ago they'd received a telegram from a man who'd seen their story in the paper. A man who claimed to be her brother. The marshal thought it was legitimate, but no one wanted to see Moira disappointed.

Her words added fuel to his hunt. He thought of his brothers, of Jack and Robert, their children and their wives. Anything could happen. There were no guarantees in life. He wasn't waiting until he had a successful ranch before he'd court Moira, he was only waiting until she squared things with her brother. He didn't know what the future held for the siblings, and he didn't want Moira torn between the love of her brother and his love. If they needed time together, he'd wait. Only he loved her and he didn't want to wait. He wanted to start their lives together right then. He'd trust in God's plan. If the timing was right, he'd know.

If he found her brother, if he proved to her she could forgive herself...after that, he'd campaign in earnest. Maybe she'd have him, maybe she wouldn't, but he wasn't giving up without a fight.

"I almost forgot," he said. "I have something for you."

Moira sat with hands folded in her lap, her knuckles white. What did he have for her? She couldn't tell from his expression if the delivery was a good thing or a bad thing.

John returned a short while later with two enormous fabric-wrapped boxes.

He set the colorful packages on the low table before her and stepped back.

Moira tilted her head. "What are they?"

"You have to open them to find out."

She hesitantly lifted the lid from the first box and gasped. A beautiful porcelain doll rested in the satin lining.

John cleared his throat. "It took me a while to find one with red hair."

Of all the things she'd been expecting, this had never crossed her mind. The exquisite doll wore an emerald green velvet coat with tiny brass buttons.

He gestured toward the other box. "There's more stuff in there. Clothes and things."

He rubbed the back of his neck.

She reverently lifted the doll free, enchanted by the details of her painted face and elaborate clothing. Keeping the doll firmly tucked at her side, she lifted the lid from the second box and revealed a trove of tiny clothing in satins and velvets, as well as several tiny pairs of shoes.

Her throat dry, she blinked several times. "I don't understand. Is this a mistake? Shouldn't this be for one of the girls?"

He reached for the box. "It was a dumb idea," he spoke gruffly. "I'll take it back."

Moira leaned away. "No you won't."

"Then you like the doll?"

If she didn't know better, she'd think he was embarrassed.

"I love her. She's beautiful. How did you find something so perfect?"

"I saw how much you liked Hazel's doll. I thought you'd like one of your own."

Moira opened her mouth to speak, but emotion caught her words.

He gestured again. "I bought one for Hazel, too. Didn't want her to be jealous. And I got Tony a rifle and Sarah a fancy comb and brush."

"You didn't have to get us anything."

"I wanted to thank you."

"For what?"

"For reminding me of what's important. I don't regret coming out here. I'm where I need to be. But I'm a whole lot more thankful for the things I have. I'm not taking things for granted anymore."

She'd been wrong about her feelings. She wasn't *falling* in love with him. She was *in* love with him.

He paced before the fireplace. "Uh, well, looks like the girls will start school next week."

"Tony's not real pleased."

"She doesn't like being cooped up inside for too long."

Moira stared at the doll's lovely face, the eyes a shade of green she was used to seeing in the mirror. If she didn't know better, she'd think the doll had been specially made in her likeness. "I only went to school until I was twelve."

After the admission, she kept her eyes averted.

"That's better than me," John said. "I went to school until I was sixteen, but I stopped paying attention around eleven." He offered a lopsided grin. "You know that whatever happens, there will always be a place for you here."

Her chest tightened. She was foolish to read anything special into his words. She was simply another responsibility. Sheriff Taylor had called him an honorable cowboy. Of course he was looking out for her. He was looking out for her the same as he'd looked out for the other girls.

She cleared her throat. "How are things for you?"

"Good. Real good. The house needs work. The pastures are good, though. I need more hands. It'll be a proper working ranch soon."

"I guess things turned out okay."

"They did." He paused. "They'll work out for you, too. You'll see."

He knelt before her and cupped her face with both hands. "I'm fixing to kiss you, if you don't mind."

Too startled for thinking clear, Moira nodded.

The pull between them sparked into a flame as his lips found hers and his hands slipped around her waist. A fierce yearning took hold and she wrapped her arms around his neck, pulling him closer as she tried to pour her feelings into the kiss. The moment stretched out and new wondrous feelings surged through her heart.

He stood, stepped back a pace and planted his hands on his hips.

She gaped at his sudden withdrawal. "Did I do something wrong?"

Had her enthusiasm embarrassed him?

"Of course not, but I can't think while we're kissing and I have something I need to say." He crossed his arms over his chest. "I love you and I want to marry you. It'll be hard. I'm just starting out. I don't know what the years will bring, but I'll always take care of you. I don't want you to answer yet. Think on it for a couple of days." He heaved a breath. "This is harder than I thought it would be."

Her thoughts tumbled in confusion. He loved her, but he didn't want an answer. Why was he waiting? "Are you certain?"

"Of course I'm certain. I mean it though, I don't want your answer until next week. I need to know you're with me all the way.

"All…all right." She wasn't sure what else to say.

He huffed out a breath as though he'd just run a mile. "Well, that's settled then."

After his hasty retreat, Moira sat in stunned silence.

He loved her, he wanted to marry her, yet he didn't want an answer yet. Was he uncertain of her feelings, or his?

Chapter Eighteen

A week following John's startling marriage proposal, Moira plucked weeds from the garden behind the boardinghouse. She had to make her decision today. Confusion had her thoughts jumbled. She kept waiting for a sign to give her some indication of why John had wanted her to wait before giving her answer. She was no closer to figuring out her next move and she'd decided to avoid people altogether. Part of her wanted to march right over to John's ranch and give him a piece of her mind. Why had he put her off? Was he having doubts? She'd snatched her bonnet from the peg three times this morning, and three times her courage had faltered before she reached the door.

When the gate squeaked open, she kept her head bent, hoping the person would note her lack of interest and move on. Footsteps padded through the rows of vegetables—late tomatoes and squash. She should have told John that if he didn't want an answer right then, he shouldn't have asked the question. She should have let the Cains take custody of Hazel. Should, should, should. Despite all the things she should be doing, here she was, crouching between the rows of pea vines, plucking weeds while wearing the gloves she'd kept from the cattle drive like a sentimental fool.

"Moira?"

At the familiar voice, her breath caught and her vision blurred. Certain she was mistaken, she kept her head bent and yanked another weed from the soft-tilled earth.

"Moira," her brother whispered. "Aren't you going to turn around?"

She lifted her hand above her head and swiped the moisture from her face on her shoulder. "I can't."

Tommy stepped closer and extended his hand. "Sure you can."

Moira grasped his fingers and he pulled her to her feet. She stared at him, searching his face, cataloging the changes the years had wrought. He wasn't the image of a gangly teen she'd locked away in her memory. He was inches taller and his face had changed. His cheeks were thinner and his shoulders broader than when she'd seen him last.

Her heartbeat raced and her stomach clenched. She'd waited four years for this moment and couldn't think of a single thing to say.

The corner of his mouth turned up in a hesitant grin. "Aren't you happy to see me?"

Collapsing into his arms, Moira sobbed. "I can't believe you're here."

He tightened his hold and murmured soothing words against the top her head.

Gathering herself, she stepped back and pinched off her gloves, then brushed at her dress. "I wish I'd have known you were coming. I would have worn something different. You should come inside. We'll have a cup of tea."

They stepped back through the kitchen. After hasty introductions and more tears, Agnes hustled them into the parlor with promises of tea and cakes.

They sat across from each other on the chintz-covered

chairs flanking the fire. After all the anticipation, Moira found herself uncertain. "I'm sorry," she blurted.

Tommy rested his ankle on his bent knee. "For what?"

"It's my fault you ran away. And then you never came back."

"That wasn't your fault." He tipped forward and gripped the arms of her chair.

"But I stole Mr. Gifford's watch. Then he accused you."

Her brother collapsed back into his seat. "That wasn't the reason. Not the whole of it, anyway. I just figured the old fool lost his own watch. Never even occurred to me you might have taken it. We were going to have it out sooner or later. That part was inevitable. I was so full of anger. It wouldn't have mattered what he accused me of that day. I was leaving one way or another."

Nausea rose in the back of her throat. She was relieved and hurt at the same time. Questions filled her head. "Then you didn't stay away because you blamed me?"

"I stayed away because I knew I would only make things worse for you. Those first few months were rough. I found what work I could. Most times I was sleeping out in the fields."

"Why didn't you ever come for me?"

"I did. Must have been a year and a half ago. But you'd already left the Giffords."

For a moment she didn't believe him. Searching his face, she realized the truth. "Then you *did* try and find me?"

"I wrote every few months that first year. When I never received a reply, I stopped writing."

"They never gave me your letters."

"I should have guessed as much." He clasped his hands together and lifted his thumbs. "But I was struggling for my own survival."

"How did you finally find me?"

"This." He held up a copy of the *Omaha Bee*. "I read the story. I knew from the description and the name it had to be you. How in the world did you wind up on a cattle drive?"

"Looking for you, of course. One of the maids at the Gifford house found part of your telegram in the fireplace. I made out the name Mr. Grey and Fool's End."

"I only wish that maid had had the guts to bring you my letters sooner."

Moira waved his complaints aside. "You have to tell me. Why were you in Fool's End?"

Another knock sounded at the door. She made to rise and Tommy waved her down. "That's the reason now. She was waiting. Giving us a few moments alone."

Who was waiting?

Moira brushed at her skirts and straightened her collar. The door opened revealing a young woman with honey-colored hair pulled into a simple knot at the back of her head. She wore a smart gingham dress in shades of yellow with puffed sleeves and a high waist. With her hovering in the open door, the wind whipped at her skirts, plastering them against her belly and revealing the slight bulge of her stomach.

Moira's eyes widened. "Is this your…"

"Wife. Yes. This is Ava Grey. Well." He grinned. "Used to be Grey. Now it's Ava O'Mara."

The woman smiled shyly and rubbed her belly.

Moira rose unsteadily to her feet. "It's, uh, it's a pleasure to meet you, Mrs. O'Mara."

"Call me Ava. We're sisters now."

"Uhhh…well…uhhh…where are you staying?"

Tommy wrapped his arm possessively around his wife's waist. "Over at the hotel. Can you believe it? We're living up in Wichita. That's not too far. We can see each other as often as we want. Say, you should come by the hotel for dinner."

"Dinner?"

"Yes. And bring that fellow, what was his name?"

"John Elder," Ava replied in her breathy voice.

Moira's tongue felt thick and uncooperative. "How do you know Mr. Elder?"

"I wired looking for you." Tommy appeared sheepish. "I hadn't planned on coming out, but he sent the money. Sent enough for both of us. I told him I'd pay him back, but he wouldn't hear about it. Told me that he owed you and you didn't like asking for help."

Don't answer just yet, John had said. He was waiting. Not because he was uncertain of his feelings for her, but because he wasn't certain of her feelings for *him*.

Ava pressed a hand into the small of her back. "My father didn't approve of our marriage. That's why we left Fool's End."

"And that other fellow." Tommy's expression darkened. "This fellow Wendell had a crush on her. Kept stirring up trouble."

All the pieces of the puzzle fit together. Mr. Grey's feigned ignorance. Wendell's anger.

Her head reeled and her attention scattered as they chatted for a few more minutes, catching up on the lost years. When Ava's eyelids drooped with fatigue, Tommy quickly wrapped up the pleasantries.

He caught Moira in a quick shoulder embrace without releasing his wife. "I'll see you tonight. Can't wait to catch up."

Ava tucked herself against her husband's side. "I'm sorry about everything that happened. I knew my dad was angry. I never expected him to act so outrageously."

"Don't apologize," Moira said. "You can do me a favor, though."

"What's that?"

"Make your peace with him. Your father."

"But after what he did—"

Moira held up a hand. "He was frightened. He was scared he'd never see you again. Sometimes people do crazy things when they're scared."

"I don't know." Ava hesitated. "He was awfully mad when we left. He disowned me."

"At least let him know where you are. That there's a baby on the way."

The two exchanged a look.

"She's right," John said. "Moira is right."

"If you think so." Ava gazed adoringly at her husband.

The pair stared at each other with such devotion, Moira felt her own cheeks heat.

A few moments later, Moira stepped onto the porch and followed their progress. What had she been expecting? Tommy had moved on with his life. She'd been hanging on to her guilt for years. Using it like a wall to keep her from living. From truly experiencing life. She'd been afraid.

The watch had been returned and she didn't expect a reply.

She hadn't needed Tommy's forgiveness, he had never blamed her. She had needed to forgive herself. She'd needed to understand that she'd been a child unfairly tasked with an adult promise. Her brother had moved on with his life. They weren't kids anymore. Their relationship had changed. They would spend time together, visit, talk, but she couldn't expect things to go back to the way they were.

That's what John had been trying to tell her all along. She had wanted to go back and relive the years, take up where they'd left off, when she should have realized their lives would never be the same.

Tommy had a new family. It didn't mean they weren't

a family as well, just that it had expanded. He was living his life. It was time for her to do the same. And she knew just where to start.

An hour later, standing before the door of the Elder ranch, Moira's courage faltered. She heard sounds from behind the house and circled around toward the corral. John stood in the center, his sleeves rolled over his forearms. He held a horse tethered by a long rope. The horse trotted around him while John flipped the extra length of cord in a wide arc.

He caught sight of her and did a double take. He clicked and the horse halted. Gathering the rope, he unhooked the lead before strolling over.

Moira's throat went dry. "I need your help."

"Miss Moira O'Mara. Asking for help. I never thought I'd see the day. You know, I was asking God for a sign, and I think He just might have sent it."

"I want to court someone."

He quirked an eyebrow. "And do I know the gentleman?"

"I believe you're intimately acquainted with him."

"I see. And what sort of help do you need?"

"First off, I don't know where to begin."

John planted his elbow on the top rail of the fence separating them. "You should tell him how handsome he is."

"He's quite the handsomest man I've ever seen."

"And you should compliment his intelligence. Men like to know a woman appreciates them for more than their good looks."

"He's quite the smartest man I've ever met."

John hitched his other elbow on the fence and rested his chin on his fisted hands. "And humble, too, no doubt."

"He's extremely modest."

"I'm starting to like this fellow."

"I've fallen in love with him."

John reached over the fence and cupped her cheeks with his work-roughened hands. "I suppose you ought to start there. With your feelings."

"I love you."

"I love you, too."

"I know, you already told me."

"I should have asked you to marry me properly, on one knee and everything. With a ring and some flowers or something. I was too nervous. You want me to try again?"

"Nope. It was perfect the first time." She smiled. "Thank you for letting me sort out things with Tommy."

"If you need time with him, I'll wait."

"No. I've been lingering around the edges of life, not wanting to get hurt. Not wanting to lose people. Now that we're together proper, I don't want to waste a single minute."

He slid his hand into her hair and angled his head. Their lips met in a sweet kiss and Moira sighed. "I should warn you. I have some conditions."

"Tell me."

"We're having dinner with my brother tonight."

"I can meet that demand."

Moira kissed him again. "And I want Hazel to live with us."

"Agreed."

He pressed his forehead against hers. "And I have one condition of my own."

"What's that?"

"I want a short courtship."

Moira clambered over the tall fence and launched herself into his arms. "Agreed."

Epilogue

One year later

Moira leaned against the stall door and sighed. John joined her and wrapped his arm around her waist, then rested his hand on the slight bump of her expanding stomach.

Five puppies whimpered and snuffed beside their mother in a nest of hay. They were squirming, fluffy bundles of brown-and-white fur, a mix of their sheepdog mother and collie father.

He shook his head. "Hazel, you're going to name every one of them, aren't you?"

"I've already decided on names," Hazel declared. "That's Violet, Rose, Daisy, Marigold and Lily."

"I should have guessed," John said.

Champion sniffed around the edges and lay down with a whimper. The mother belonged to their neighbors, the McCoys, but the sheepdog had taken up residence at the homestead shortly after Champion had arrived. The two families had tried to discourage the relationship, but love had won out.

John pointed at Champion. "Don't look so proud of yourself."

Moira elbowed him in the side. "You're one to talk. I believe a certain father-to-be recently bought the general store out of cigars."

The tips of his ears reddened. "Point taken."

Moira pecked him on the cheek. "I love you."

"Mmm-hmm."

"Is that all you're going to say?"

"Kiss me proper and I'll try again."

Moira tilted back her head.

"Ah, no," Tony spoke from the large double doors leading outside. "Are you two kissing again? Give it a rest. We've got a visitor."

John groaned and glanced over his shoulder. "Who is it?"

"You better come see for yourself."

Moira exchanged a glance with John and shrugged. "I guess we better see for ourselves. Hazel, will you keep an eye on the puppies for us?"

Hazel nodded without looking up. Since the puppies had been born two weeks ago, she'd barely strayed from the barn.

John kept a protective arm around Moira's shoulder as they emerged into the sunlight.

Her eyes widened. "Darcy?"

"Yep." Tony smirked. "It's her all right."

"Tony," Moira pitched her voice in a warning. "Be nice."

"Yeah. I miss you, too," Darcy grumbled.

She appeared years older than when Moira had last seen her, though only twelve months had passed. Her hair was caught in a loose knot at the base of her neck, with several loose strands falling over her shoulders. Her faded blue calico dress was rumpled and bags showed beneath her eyes.

"Preston is dead," Darcy said, her expression bleak.

Moira pulled away from John and embraced Darcy. "I'm so sorry."

She hadn't thought much of Preston, yet she mourned his passing for Darcy's sake.

"He got in a fight outside Chicago. Never recovered."

"Why don't you come inside?" Moira motioned toward the house. "You can sit for a while and have some lemonade."

A sound caught her attention, and for the first time she noticed a basket sitting at Darcy's feet.

Darcy knelt and lifted a bundle into her arms. "This is Preston Jr."

Tony made a strangled sound in her throat. "You had a baby with that moro—"

"Tony!" Moira shushed her. "Let's carry the rest of Darcy's things inside. I believe we all have some catching up to do."

Moira struggled against her shock and dismay. Darcy appeared too exhausted to answer the myriad questions flitting through her head.

Tony gathered the basket and a satchel and hooked her arm. "Follow me." She paused and stared at the face peeking from beneath the folds of the blanket. "He's pretty cute. I guess."

"Here." Moira reached out her arms. "Why don't you let me carry little Preston."

Darcy instantly relinquished the bundle. "I'm so tired. I don't think I've slept in the three months since he was born."

She yawned and pressed a fist against her mouth.

"Let's not stand here yapping then," Tony said, though

her voice had softened considerably since she'd spotted the baby. "Come on inside."

Moira stood in the fading sunlight and stared at the tiny, perfect infant in her arms. He was impossibly small and light, his eyes closed. He yawned, and his fingers splayed, then fisted once more.

In a few more months, she'd have one of her own. Sometimes she felt so much love for the new life growing inside her, her heart ached from it.

"Oh, my," Moira crooned. "Isn't he precious?"

John leaned in. "I should have seen this coming, but I didn't."

Her stomach plummeted. "You're not angry, are you?"

"Of course not. But you know what this means, don't you? Darcy still has a lot of growing up to do. If we take her in, chances are, we'll end up raising this baby just as much as her."

"Would you mind that very much?"

"It's you I'm worried about." He rested his hand on her rounded belly.

Moira blinked back tears. She never tired of looking at him. She'd memorized the tiny flecks of gold around his irises. The small creases that appeared at the corners of his mouth when he smiled. Beneath the warmth of his love, she'd learned to love herself. And that realization had opened her heart to a pure joy like she'd never experienced before.

She sighed. "You once said heroes don't always appear the way we expect."

"You know I can't deny you anything when you look at me that way. As though I'm your hero."

"You are."

A blush crept up his neck at her compliment. "We shouldn't make any hasty decisions."

"Darcy has no place else to go," Moira said simply.

"And we've got enough love, it seems a shame not to share it."

"If you're certain."

"All babies are a blessing."

John adjusted his hat to the back of his head. "It's going to be crowded when your brother and his family come to visit next week."

"I know."

"And Robert will be here the following month to purchase a few horses for his ranch."

"We'll make do."

"You know you can't save everyone." He pressed his forehead against hers, the dozing baby between them, the brim of his hat shading them from the last rays of the evening sun. "But I love you for trying."

"I do have one question."

"What's that?"

"Are you going to tell Hazel that some of the puppies are boys?"

John chuckled. "Just as long as she doesn't name the new baby."

"But she's already made a list."

"Now I'm terrified."

"She thinks Lancelot is a good name."

"No."

"Chester."

"Definitely not."

"Aphrodite."

"*Absolutely* not."

Moira trailed him back to the house, calling out increasingly ridiculous names along the way. When he paused on the porch, she smiled. "Thank you for knowing me better than anyone, and for loving me anyway."

He wasn't perfect, he had his faults, but then again, so did she. Together they made a good match.

"I love you, too, my fiery redheaded wife." He scratched his chin. "And I'm kind of warming up to the name Lancelot."

"No!" Moira shrieked.

They stepped into the house, still laughing, while behind them the setting sun cast golden shadows over the prairie.

* * * * *

Dear Reader,

I heard from many readers who enjoyed *Winning the Widow's Heart* and were eager for more stories about the Elder brothers, so it's my pleasure to bring you John and Moira. While John Elder is trying to escape his suffocating family, Moira O'Mara is desperate to reunite with her estranged brother.

As an author, I'm fascinated by families. Not only the families we are born into, but also the bonds we create with our friends and colleagues. Family dynamics shift over time, and I enjoy exploring how relationships change and grow through adversity.

While writing *The Cattleman Meets His Match,* I kept the words *Who are you?* scrawled on the dry-erase board above my desk. Both John and Moira are struggling to redefine their identities as their families evolve. It's an experience I believe most of us can relate to on some level.

I love to hear from readers! You can email me at sherri@sherrishackelford.com or visit my website, www.sherrishackelford.com. A special thanks to each of you who takes the time from your busy schedule to write a kind note and let me know you appreciate my stories.

Wishing you many blessings,

Sherri Shackelford

Questions for Discussion

1. John Elder feels overshadowed by his six older brothers. Do you think a person's placement in the sibling lineup can have an effect on their personality?

2. Moira is having trouble picturing her brother as an adult. She still thinks of him as her baby brother. Why do you think it's so difficult for her to admit that he has matured?

3. Moira doesn't think of herself as a leader, but she earns the admiration of John and the other girls. Name some of the qualities that make Moira a good leader.

4. "For which of you, intending to build a tower, sitteth not down first, and counteth the cost, whether he have sufficient to finish it?" (Luke 14:28) I chose this verse as inspiration for the story because both John and Moira are on a mission, but neither of them truly realizes the cost associated with achieving their goal. What are some of the unexpected consequences of the journey they undertake?

5. Both Moira and John fight their growing attraction. Have you ever held back a part of yourself because of something that happened in the past? What was the outcome?

6. John feels like a failure because he ended the cattle drive early. Moira feels like a failure because she couldn't convince Darcy to stay. What did each of them have to learn to be at peace?

7. When Moira and her brother are finally reunited, Moira must accept that the future she envisioned for them will never be. Have you ever clung to an ideal and found the reality was far different from your imagination?

8. Though John loves Moira, he realizes she must make peace with her past before they can have a future. He makes the decision to trust in God's timing. What does the Bible say about patience?

REQUEST YOUR FREE BOOKS!

2 FREE INSPIRATIONAL NOVELS
PLUS 2
FREE
MYSTERY GIFTS

Love Inspired
HISTORICAL
INSPIRATIONAL HISTORICAL ROMANCE

YES! Please send me 2 FREE Love Inspired® Historical novels and my 2 FREE mystery gifts (gifts are worth about $10). After receiving them, if I don't wish to receive any more books, I can return the shipping statement marked "cancel." If I don't cancel, I will receive 4 brand-new novels every month and be billed just $4.74 per book in the U.S. or $5.24 per book in Canada. That's a saving of at least 21% off the cover price. It's quite a bargain! Shipping and handling is just 50¢ per book in the U.S. and 75¢ per book in Canada.* I understand that accepting the 2 free books and gifts places me under no obligation to buy anything. I can always return a shipment and cancel at any time. Even if I never buy another book, the two free books and gifts are mine to keep forever.

102/302 IDN F5CN

Name	(PLEASE PRINT)
Address	Apt. #
City	State/Prov. Zip/Postal Code

Signature (if under 18, a parent or guardian must sign)

Mail to the Harlequin® Reader Service:
IN U.S.A.: P.O. Box 1867, Buffalo, NY 14240-1867
IN CANADA: P.O. Box 609, Fort Erie, Ontario L2A 5X3

Want to try two free books from another series?
Call 1-800-873-8635 or visit www.ReaderService.com.

* Terms and prices subject to change without notice. Prices do not include applicable taxes. Sales tax applicable in N.Y. Canadian residents will be charged applicable taxes. Offer not valid in Quebec. This offer is limited to one order per household. Not valid for current subscribers to Love Inspired Historical books. All orders subject to credit approval. Credit or debit balances in a customer's account(s) may be offset by any other outstanding balance owed by or to the customer. Please allow 4 to 6 weeks for delivery. Offer available while quantities last.

Your Privacy—The Harlequin® Reader Service is committed to protecting your privacy. Our Privacy Policy is available online at www.ReaderService.com or upon request from the Harlequin Reader Service.

We make a portion of our mailing list available to reputable third parties that offer products we believe may interest you. If you prefer that we not exchange your name with third parties, or if you wish to clarify or modify your communication preferences, please visit us at www.ReaderService.com/consumerchoice or write to us at Harlequin Reader Service Preference Service, P.O. Box 9062, Buffalo, NY 14269. Include your complete name and address.

LIH13R

"They're so cute," Brody said.

"Who can't like kittens?" Hannah scooped up another one and held it close, rubbing her nose over the tiny head.

"I meant your kids are cute."

Hannah looked up at him, the kitten still cuddled against her face, appearing surprisingly childlike. Her features were relaxed and she didn't seem as tense as when he'd met her the first time. Her smile dived into his heart. "Well, you're talking to the wrong person about them. I think my kids are adorable, even when they've got chocolate pudding smeared all over their mouths."

He felt a gentle contentment easing into his soul and he wanted to touch her again. To connect with her.

Chrissy patted the kitten and then pushed it away, lurching to her feet.

"Chrissy. Gentle," Hannah admonished her.

"The kitten is fine," Brody said, rescuing the kitten as Chrissy tottered a moment, trying to get her balance on the bunched-up blanket. "Here you go," he said to the mother cat, laying her baby beside her.

Hannah also put her kitten back. She took a moment to stroke Loco's head as if assuring her, then picked up her son and swung him into her arms. "Thanks for taking Corey ou on the horse. I know I sounded…irrational, but my reaction was the result of a combination of factors. Ever since the twins were born, I've felt overly protective of them."

"I'm guessing much of that has to do with David's death."

"Partly. Losing David made me realize how fragile life is and, like I told your mother, it also made me feel more vulnerable."

"I wouldn't have done anything to hurt Corey." Brody felt he needed to assure her of that. "You can trust me."

Hannah looked over at him and then gave him a careful smile. "I know that."

Her quiet affirmation created an answering warmth and a faint hope.

Once again he held her gaze. Once again he wanted to touch her. To make a connection beyond the eye contact they seemed to be indulging in over the past few days.

Will Hannah Douglas find love again with handsome
rancher and firefighter Brody Harcourt?
Find out in
HER MONTANA TWINS
by Carolyne Aarsen,
available September 2014 from Love Inspired® Books.

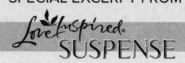
Biologist Dr. Tessa Cleary shielded her eyes against the
late summer sun. She surveyed her surroundings and
filled her lungs with the sweet scent of fresh mountain
air. Tall conifers dominated the forest, but she detected
many deciduous trees as well, which surrounded the
sparkling shores of the reservoir lake.

A hidden paradise. One to be enjoyed by those willing
to venture to the middle of the Pacific Northwest.

The lake should be filled with boats and swimmers,
laughing children, fishing poles and water skis.

But all was still.

Silent.

The seemingly benign water filled with something
toxic harming both the wildlife and humans.

Her office had received a distressing call yesterday that
dead trout had washed ashore and recreational swimmers
were presenting with respiratory distress after swimming
in the lake.

As a field biologist for the U.S. Forestry Service Fish
and Aquatics Unit, her job was to determine what exactly
that "something" was as quickly as possible and stop it.

"Here she is!" a booming voice full of anticipation
rang out.

A mixed group of civilians and uniformed personnel gathered on the wide, wooden porch of the ranger station.

All eyes were trained on her. All except one man's.

Tall, with dark hair, he stood in profile talking to the sheriff. Too many people blocked him from full view for her to see an agency logo on his forest-green uniform.

Tessa turned her attention to Ranger Harris. "Do you have any idea where the contamination is originating?"

He shook his head. "We haven't come across the source. At least not on our side of the lake. I'm not sure what's happening across the border." George ran a hand through his graying hair as his gaze strayed to the lake. "Whatever this is, it isn't coming from our side."

"Let's not go casting aspersions on our friends to the north until we know more. Okay, George?"

The deep baritone voice came from Tessa's right. She turned to find herself confronted by a set of midnight-blue eyes. Curiosity lurked in the deep depths of the attractive man towering over her.

Answering curiosity rose within her. Who was he? And why was he here?

For more, pick up DANGER AT THE BORDER.
Available September 2014
wherever Love Inspired books are sold.

His Most Suitable Bride

by

RENEE RYAN

No one in Denver knows how close Callie Mitchell once came
to ruin. Dowdy dresses and severe hairstyles hide evidence of
the pretty, trusting girl she used to be. Now her matchmaking
employer wants Callie to find a wife for the one man who sees
through her careful facade.

For his business's sake, Reese Bennett Jr. plans on making a
sensible marriage. Preferably one without the unpredictable
emotions that spring to life around Callie. Yet no matter how
many candidates she presents to Reese, none compare with the
vibrant, intelligent woman who is right under his nose—and
quickly invading his heart.

Offering an oasis of hope, faith and love
on the rugged Colorado frontier

Available September 2014
wherever Love Inspired books and ebooks are sold.